The Avenging of Nevah Wright

The Avenging of Nevah Wright

Mildred Davis
and
Katherine Roome

To order additional copies of this book or other books by the authors, contact:

HARK LLC

www.murderinmaine.com

Acknowledgements

We would like to extend our most grateful thanks to the late Dr. John Taggart for the medical information in the book, except that we assume all responsibility for any errors we made in transferring his information into fictional form. Our most grateful thanks also to Alan Winnick for his expertise on scuba diving, to Denise Film, Jim Russo, and Richard Aylesworth for their patient assistance in helping us to finalize the manuscript. Finally, we thank George Van Hook for permission to have his painting grace our cover, to Bob Warren for allowing us to use his lyrics, and to Darcy May for her map of our purely fictional Ledge Island.

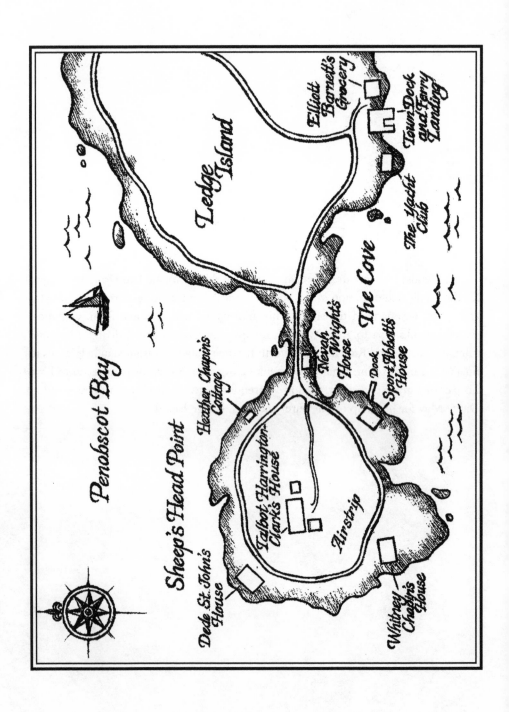

Prologue

A hot, sunny summer day in July. A man and his son driving up Route 95 in a faded blue Dodge minivan on their way to Maine; "vacationland" as the state line sign proclaims it. Populated by forty-one people per square mile through nine cold months of the year, and what feels like about forty-one thousand along certain parts of the coastline from Memorial Day through Labor Day.

The two of them had left New Jersey the previous morning and stayed in a motel outside of Boston. Now they were crossing the bridge from New Hampshire, heading for the fabled rocky shores of America's beautiful most eastern coast. The interstate asphalt glittered in the bright sunny morning light.

"So what do you think of Maine so far?" the father joked.

The boy, an immature fifteen-year-old who had not yet descended into terminal teenage boredom, did not hear the irony in the question.

"It's really cool. It's really different. Like, we don't have all these wild flowers along the highway in New Jersey."

At that point, they hadn't caught even a glimpse of the ocean. The boy had never been this far from his home. His mother was going to have her third baby in two months and her seven-year-old had been sick on and off with ear infections for weeks. The boy's grandmother was coming for a week to help out at home. Dan Schwartz, who had never since he'd been married taken a vacation without his wife, had suddenly proposed that he and his son should go to Maine for a week. Have a father-son bonding experience.

They'd eaten at an expensive steak place the night before. It was also the first time the two of them had had a fancy restaurant dinner by themselves. His father had let Steve have a Coke, two desserts and hadn't even mentioned a glass of milk. Then they'd watched TV in the hotel until midnight. It had felt wildly decadent.

Dan exited I-95 at a gas station. He didn't really have a plan, so desperate had he been to escape his fractious wife and her mother. Now, for the first time since they had left, he felt anxious about it. He took out a map and studied it while his son sat quietly in a state of silent suspense, as if awaiting a fateful pronouncement.

"Hey Stevie," his father said, "if we go another hundred miles or so, we can take a ferry out to this Ledge Island here. Whatd'ya say pal? Sound like fun?"

Steve had never been on a ferry. He'd never been on a boat bigger than a rowboat and he'd never stayed by the ocean. It seemed like madcap folly to suddenly decide to take a boat to an unknown island. Maybe his whole life would be changed by this. He'd no longer be the scrawny, nerdy kid who could multiply any two numbers in his head without even thinking. Come fall, he would return to school tan, taller, and the natural effect of this would be that he would stop saying stupid nerdy things and become strong and silent. After all, he would have had adventures, been away, seen things.

The ocean began to show itself as bits of silver through the trees along the highway. They left the interstate and kept heading north on Route 1, the king of scenic routes and summertime traffic congestion in the northeast. They spent half an hour trying to get through Wiscasset, which unabashedly declared itself on a large sign as being the "Prettiest Little Town in Maine." They arrived at Rockland around one in the afternoon. Steve had a fleeting impression of a narrow Main Street, sidewalks filed with tourists strolling slowly while licking ice cream cones, and then they were at the ferry landing. The ferry would be leaving for the island in just twenty minutes. It seemed like fate. They just had time to buy hot dogs at a stand.

Once on the ferry, they stood by the rail and Steve stared at the blue metal warehouses that housed the Rockland cannery. Then they passed the jetty and he gaped at a picture-story lighthouse at the end of the jetty. It was like suddenly coming upon Hansel and Gretel's house. He hadn't truly believed that there still were lighthouses perched on rock jetties. And then they were in the ocean, heading out towards the green hazy lumps that his father told him were islands. The impossibly bright sun made the water splinter into an infinite number of winking diamonds.

Steve was a little disappointed as they approached the island his father had so serendipitously chosen for their adventure. The boy had been so overwhelmed by the enormity of the ocean, by its promise of limitless adventure, that suddenly things became disappointingly tame as the ferry slowed. They moved smoothly past white and yellow farmhouses set in open meadows that ran down to the sea and then, as they approached the town, large Victorian homes with grey, worn siding and enormous porches perched at the edge of the shore. As Steve's interest flagged, his father's grew. He whistled and muttered, "It takes big bucks Stevie, very big bucks and about a hundred years, to own a house that big and crummy-looking."

As they approached the ferry landing, the boy's excitement welled up again. He felt as if he were in one of those books where the kid walks through a door into a magic land. The buildings around the ferry dock were ridiculously ramshackle and picturesque. It was hard to tell if this was life imitating art or the other way around. Either this miniature town was the inspiration for thousands of Hallmark cards or someone had very deliberately created a stage set based on one of those cards. Years later, he would discover that the answer fell somewhere in the middle.

They walked of the ferry, following the ten or so cars. There were about twenty people there to meet the ferry passengers. They were different ages but most of them seemed to be wearing khaki shorts or pants and pastel-colored shirts. Steve suddenly felt self-conscious in his jeans and black T-shirt. There was a great deal of hugging going on and it made him miss his mom and even his whiny sister. He and his father walked up the street towards the center of the town. It wasn't even really a town. Just a miniature grocery store, a post office, and a couple of gift shops scattered around the ferry landing. Apart from the clothes, there was something odd about the picture and it took him a minute to realize what it was. Parked haphazardly in the ferry station parking lot, with apparent total disregard for the faded lines painted on the pavement, were about fifteen cars. Two of them were beat up pickup trucks, and three of them were ancient battered sedans. But five others were expensive Volvo models, three were new Mercedes and the other two were BMWs. Steve didn't know about Victorian houses but he knew his cars. It took Steve just a second to calculate that he was looking at about one million dollars worth of automobiles in this tiny, cramped parking lot. Then why didn't they bother to paint the houses and falling-down barns? And why wasn't someone ticketing these cars for parking that way? None of it made any sense to his middle-class suburban belief system.

There was a small ice cream shop. His father bought him a cone and told him to wait there while he looked around town to see what was up. Maybe they could rent bikes or maybe there was a B&B where they could stay. Steve nodded and began licking the chocolate chip ice cream, still trying to understand what he was seeing exactly.

After a few minutes of waiting, Steve walked past the shops and a small copse of trees just outside of the village center, to a path that led down some steps through more bushes and trees to the water. There was a small red barn at the water's edge surrounded by floating docks and a small hand-lettered sign, as battered and grey as the houses, announcing this to be the Yacht Club. Steve didn't see anything that remotely resembled a yacht. Just some small sailboats and rowboats tied to the floating docks that surrounded the barn.

Five kids were taking turns climbing up the side of a piling out on the end of the dock. The piling was about ten feet above the water and they were diving off the top of it. A couple of them looked pretty young, maybe around eight, and Steve was impressed. In fact, he wasn't sure he would have been that eager to make the leap. Their hair was all the exact same shade of blonde and they were all identically tanned. They were laughing and engaging in horseplay, pushing each other off the dock while waiting for their turn to climb the piling. One boy even gave the piling a shove that sent another boy flying off the top before he was ready to dive so that he did what looked like a very painful belly flop. They would never have allowed this kind of horseplay at the Y pool where Steve swam. He didn't see any adults around at all. Where were the lifeguards? The normal rules didn't seem to apply here.

Then he noticed an older girl with darker hair sitting on the dock about ten feet off. She was a bit heavier than the other two girls. She was looking down at the water. He recognized that posture, that gaze. She was afraid to climb up the piling to make the dive and she was hoping the others wouldn't notice.

Steve's father's voice startled Steve. Steve looked down and noticed that the ice cream was running down the back of his hand.

"No luck, son. No hotels, motels, or tents to be had. Not even a restaurant. Guess they don't want a lot of visitors around here. And not only that. This ferry leaves for the Mainland in ten minutes and if we don't catch it, we're stuck here for the night."

Steve was suddenly anxious. Not only were they being driven away from here but they had no place to stay on the Mainland. What would become of them? The adventure had suddenly turned slightly scary. He looked up at his dad.

"We better hurry, huh? I don't want to miss the boat, as it were," this last phrase being one of Steve's precocious affectations that regularly won him the scorn of his schoolmates.

"Yeah, guess not," said his dad, putting his arm around Steve's shoulders. "We'll find a great fish place for dinner, ok?"

As they ran back to the ferry, Steve noticed that the process had been reversed. Now people were hugging those who were leaving. The people on the boat who had been so happy, eagerly scanning the dock for their friends and relatives, had apparently come to rest somewhere on the island and were preparing for cocktails and dinner. Those now leaving on the ferry looked somber and thoughtful, as if contemplating long hot drives, laundry and dreary dark offices on the other end of those drives. The ferry slowly, inexorably, moved away from the dock. The sun had settled into a Hallmark sunset now, casting the island and its buildings in sharp relief. The kids were still diving off of the piling, the dark-haired girl still sitting there on the dock as they were reduced first, to doll size and then to little dark toothpicks against a red and gold sky.

Steve looked up at his father.

"Weird place, dad. There don't seem to be any rules around here."

It would be another fourteen years before, lying beside one of those six people in bed, he would finally understand the rules.

PART I

One

Five Years Later

It was a night in late August on an island in Maine. Over the course of an hour, one by one, five teenagers converged in a meadow at the edge of the ocean. All five of them were dressed in black wetsuits. The scene suggested a Ku Klux Klan meeting as it would appear in a photographic negative.

First came a young girl, tall and fair, maybe around thirteen and then a boy, also tall and fair and a few years older. They arrived at almost the same time, both of them carrying scuba diving gear. They sat down close to each other on the grass and whispered for a while before another girl arrived, about the same age as the first. The boy and the girl moved apart slightly. A few minutes later two more teenage boys arrived together. They all had scuba diving equipment.

"Hey, Sport," said one of the boys to the girl who had arrived first, "What'd you tell your parents about where you were going?"

"You kidding? They think I'm asleep. I should have told my father. He would have thought this was a real gutsy thing to do. Character building."

"Yeah, but what about your mother?"

"Talk about guts, she'd probably gut me with a knife. She doesn't even know I still have my scuba gear. I bought it back from the thrift shop." Guiltily, she glanced back behind her to a house whose lights showed dimly through the trees.

"What about you Tal, do they know you're out?" asked the same boy. The boy called Tal just shook his head.

"Am I the only one who told my parents that I was going into town with you guys to pick up some pizza?" asked the first boy, his voice rising with laughter.

The girl called Sport replied.

"Whitney, you idiot, it wouldn't have made a lot of sense for Dede or me to say that. Our parents would sooner allow us to take ecstasy than drive around with you at night."

Whitney and the girls laughed. Talbot put his finger to his lips.

"Shut up, you guys."

The third boy said nothing but stood holding his air tank in his arms as if he were afraid that it might disappear on him.

"Ok," said Talbot, "Let's go. Keep quiet and don't let your gear bang around."

The five of them started across the meadow to the top of a bluff overlooking a cove. They were now just a little way below the back of Sport's house. At the bottom of the steep bluff was a dock. The three boys put their air tanks on their backs now, and two of them, Talbot and Whitney, were carrying air tanks for the girls. Each of the five wore a buoyancy vest and carried weights, fins and a flashlight, although the lights were turned off in deference to the secrecy of the occasion and a full moon overhead.

It was difficult getting down the steep hill and occasionally one or the other of them would grab at a rope that had been strung through the sparse spruce trees on the incline.

They walked out on a long wooden dock, a hundred feet in length, resting on huge granite pilings. The walkway was thirty feet above the water at low tide. Then they started down a steep steel ramp leading to the floating docks, moving very slowly so as not to bang the equipment against the ramp's metal railings. When they got down to the floating docks at the bottom of the ramp, they put the equipment down.

"Ok," said Talbot, "check through your gear, make sure everything's there. Whitney, help Nevah."

"Yes Sir!" said Whitney, goose-stepping for a few strides. "You know, Talbot, you're a born leader. You're gonna be president some day."

"That'll be lucky for you, Whit," Talbot replied, "Maybe I'll give you a pardon to get out of jail if you're nice."

"What am I going to be, Whitney?" asked the taller girl.

"You Sport, that's a stupid question, isn't it? You're gonna' be the first lady, but you knew that."

Laughing, she gave him a shove from behind.

"So what about Nevah and me?" asked Dede, pointing to the third boy who had said nothing since they had met in the meadow.

"Oh, well Dede, you're going to be a great artist. You'll live in Paris and have ten children to absorb your mothering instincts. And Nevah, oh, I don't know, he'll marry Sarah and be an engineer or something like that." His voice trailed off as he examined his equipment, no longer interested in the conceit.

Sport put her arm companionably around Nevah's shoulders. "I'd absolutely love to have you as my brother-in-law, Nevah. I'll tell Sarah as soon as she arrives next week."

Nevah didn't answer. In fact, he didn't seem to have heard.

"Really Whit, what are you going to be, before you go to jail, that is?" the girl called Dede persisted.

"Me? You mean when I grow up?"

"Yeah, if that should ever happen."

"Oh, well, I'll be an enormously successful, happily married man, just like my father wasn't."

"Ok, Nevah," said Talbot, "There's nothing to it."

All business now, he helped adjust the buoyancy vest around the silent boy's body. "To inflate, you push this button. To deflate, this one."

Nevah examined the indicated buttons and tried to veil his nervousness. Then he looked up and surveyed the peaceful scene as if searching for help. Neither the dinghies and outboards tied up to the dock, nor the smooth sea or dark sky offered any solace.

"If water gets into your mask," continued Talbot, "Put your head back like this, press the upper rim of your mask and snort."

As instructed, Nevah sat down on the edge of the dock and put on his flippers as Talbot buckled the tank on his back, attached the hose to the buoyancy compensator and placed the regulator in his mouth. Then he flashed his light on the gauge. "See this? It shows how much air you have. My dad had the tanks filled yesterday. Two thousand, two hundred and fifty P.S.I. It gets below five hundred, come on up."

Nevah took a few experimental breaths.

"Easy. Not so fast."

Nevah slowed down.

"When we go in, hold your nose and snort. It clears your ears."

Talbot demonstrated.

"And remember. Never hold your breath, ok?"

"Hey, Tal," Whitney said, "wanna' give him a physics lesson? Explain how water pressure increases about half a pound per square inch for every foot of depth? Maybe you can draw a diagram. Explain how at thirty-three feet below sea level it's twenty-nine point – "

"Shut up, Whitney. It's his first time."

" – four p.s.i. Hey, how about Archimedes' principle? Explain that since he displaces an average of three cubic feet of water – "

"Hey, Whit, knock it off," Sport snapped. "Don't forget, we've all had two summers of lessons."

"Nevah hasn't, Nevah will," Whitney joked.

"Old, tired joke, Whit. Can it," Sport said in a bored tone.

"You're losin' your sense of humor, Sport," Whitney replied. "Anyone ever tell you how good you look in basic skin-tight black?"

Sport ignored him.

"You, Nevah, on the other hand?" Whitney paused theatrically. "Not so great."

The boy named Nevah smiled distractedly, trying to seem amused and relaxed, although he was neither. He sat, snorkel and mask in place, tank strapped on, regulator in his mouth, on the edge of the dock and looked down at the black water of the inlet. Further out, he could see the silhouettes of the larger boats dipping and rising on their moorings. Although he was as big as the other two boys, he seemed years younger as he sat there, obviously trying to memorize the instructions.

"Who's his buddy?" asked Dede.

"I am," said Talbot. "You three stick together. Ok, let's go."

Nevah continued to stare into the water as if contemplating a plunge into a region beyond return.

"Hey, Nevah, you don't have to do it if you don't wanna." Concerned, Talbot shot his flashlight beam on the other's face.

Nevah shied away from the light. "I'm ok."

"Next we go into the decompression tables," Whitney intoned sonorously. "Listen up, Nevah. Should you decide to go down a hundred and ninety feet, which would be a neat trick in this cove, you can only remain at the bottom – "

Talbot gave him a shove. "Keep your shirt on."

"You mean tank," Dede corrected him.

" – for five minutes," Whitney continued, backing away from Talbot's reach, "that is, if you don't want to go through decompression. But on the other hand, if you should settle for sixty minutes at sixty feet – "

"What an ass you are," Sport told him.

"Let's go," Talbot said. "Don't forget. Press the sides of your nose and snort when you go down."

"Why're you filling my B.C.?" Nevah asked.

"We're going to hang out on the surface for a minute. Ready?"

"Moving right along," Whitney continued, "let's discuss Boyle's law. According to Boyle, as opposed to Hoyle, the volume of gas varies inversely – " His words were lost in a burst of bubbles as Sport pushed him into the water. In a moment he bobbed to the surface, choking but still laughing.

Nevah took a deep breath, glanced at the sky and dropped into the water. Immediately, he came up gasping, his mask half off and his regulator flapping on his shoulder.

"What a turkey you are, Talbot," Whitney scoffed. "The one thing you needed to tell him, to hold on to his mask, you forgot."

Talbot slid into the water beside Nevah. "Sorry." He adjusted Nevah's mask and regulator as if Nevah were a small child.

Sport felt embarrassed for Nevah. Although she had only just turned fourteen and Nevah was nearly three years older, she was sensitive to his insecurity and felt oddly protective of him. Even at this age, she recognized that she and the other three had the easy confidence of having grown up under affluent circumstances with supportive parents and plenty of nearly obsequious hired help around their houses. Nevah was the only child of Edith and Johnny Wright. The Wrights lived year round on the island and were, in fact, the caretakers for the other four children's summer homes. Nevah had a lot of pride and was plucky. He had spent all of his summers with the other four children swimming, sailing, kayaking, hiking and driving fast in small motorboats. The four families who owned houses on the Point had made it a point to include Nevah in all of their children's activities and to pay for any activities that the Wrights could not afford. Because Nevah was smart, athletic, and game, he had been able to keep up with the other four, notwithstanding the many more lessons their parents could afford to provide at other times of the year. But he never complained or even mentioned their advantages. It was possible that he truly did not care about, or much notice, the differences in their economic status.

Sport and Dede opened the valves of their tanks, checked their air, put on their B.C.s and weight belts, adjusted tanks, and helped each other to strap on their tanks. Then, holding the tank straps with one hand and masks with the other, they stepped off the dock at the same time.

As they bobbed on the surface, Talbot gave them last minute instructions.

"Nevah, you stick with me. You other three stay together. Don't leave this side of the cove. And check your air." He glanced up the hill and saw no sign of their noise having awakened anyone in the house at the top of the hill. The moonlight had paved a sparkling path across the cove, and aside from cicadas and a few frogs, it was quiet. The water looked as if it had been steam-rolled flat. A perfect night for a dive.

As they released the air from their B.C.s, Talbot flashed his light on Nevah's face. The mask distorted it, broadening his nose and distending his lips. Talbot formed a questioning "O" with his thumb and forefinger and Nevah did the same to show he was alright.

Beyond the low tide line, ghostly vegetation oscillated with the action of the sea. Mussels and periwinkles, starfish, crabs and barnacles decorated the rocks below the surface. A mackerel slithered past, its tail palpitating in the miniature forest. There were none of the bright colors of the Caribbean but the cove had its own charms at this late-summer time of night.

Tugging on Nevah's arm, Talbot pointed to a scuttling lobster and Nevah nodded as he flutter-kicked behind his guide. He was careful not to lose sight of his buddy as the pilings of the dock disappeared behind them. Repeatedly, he checked his air gauge and saw he was down to two thousand p.s.i. He made an effort to slow his breathing.

They caught up with the other three in time to see Whitney fooling around with the gauge on Sport's tank. She turned swiftly and aimed a kick at his crotch, which missed. Talbot's did not. Whitney doubled over in mock pain and the two girls appeared to be laughing.

The horseplay began to loosen Nevah's tension. He caught sight of a Pollock and made a grab for it, but since Talbot's lecture hadn't reached the part about objects appearing a third larger and a quarter closer under water, the Pollock was in no danger. Next his attention was diverted by another lobster, which disappeared under a ledge, and anxious to exhibit his casualness, he went in after it. The ledge was narrower than it had appeared, and after a moment Nevah became aware of something. He couldn't turn around. His teeth aching from gripping the regulator so tightly, he abandoned the chase and twisted frantically to loosen himself. Whirling and struggling in the tight space, he opened his mouth to scream and lost the regulator. His chest felt as if gripped by a monstrous claw.

Nevah's mind exploded in panic. He forgot everything except the desperate need to breathe. Among the things he forgot was the instruction to abandon the tank and the weights in an emergency.

Talbot, digging around in the seaweed and sand, captured four crabs which he dropped into the net bag he carried on his wrist along with the flashlight. Then he looked around for Nevah to show him his catch. And couldn't see him. After gyrating in circles, he followed another hard and fast rule he had neglected to impart to Nevah. When you lose sight of your buddy, head for the surface.

The black water, the silhouetted trees and starlit sky were all as serene as when they had descended. The ocean shimmered and undulated like silvery cloth in the moonlight.

Flinging the crabs away, he was about to descend again when another head bobbed up and he shouted with relief. "Nevah!"

But it was Sport. "I saw your light. Are we going back?"

"I can't find Nevah. I forgot to tell him to come right up if we lost sight of each other."

"He's ok. Did you see what that idiot Whitney did?"

"Sport, wait up here in case he surfaces. Don't let him go back down." "I'm sure he's – "

But Talbot was gone. Catching sight of a light, he flutter-kicked towards it, but it turned out to be Dede. He removed his regulator and mouthed the word "Nevah."

Dede shook her head and kicked in the direction of another light which turned out to be Whitney's. Whitney shook his head and mouthed "Sport?" Talbot pointed upwards.

The three began rotating, flashing their lights. Then Talbot shot to the surface again. "Have you seen him?" he shouted at Sport.

"You haven't found him?" Her voice, beginning to sound shrill with fright, shattered the quiet night.

Without answering, Talbot released his air and sank out of sight. The four remained within sight of one another as they gyrated frantically. Their eyes distended with apprehension and their movement became more and more erratic as precious moments passed. They forgot to check their air until Talbot took a breath and received nothing. Gesturing with his light at his gauge, he kicked upwards and the other three followed. All of them clung to the dock, gasping.

"What are you doing?" Sport shrieked. "Where is he? You didn't find him?"

"Maybe he's playing a trick on us," Whitney said faintly.

"You think he could've climbed up on the shore somewhere?" Talbot asked.

"Jesus Christ," Sport said in a whisper.

Sport checked her air. Then, adjusting her mask and regulator, she sank back below the surface of the water. At the same time Talbot unhooked Dede's tank, B.C. and weights. "Dede! Run! Get my Dad. No, get the ambulance. Shit, anybody!"

Barefooted, Dede raced up the ramp, along the dock, up the steep slope, and was lost among the trees. The two boys stripped off all of their equipment except for masks and flashlights and dove back into the water. Air bubbles floated towards the surface.

Suddenly Whitney went berserk. Snaking his light back and forth, he pointed to the ledge where Nevah had disappeared. The back strap of a rubber fin enclosing the round heel of a human foot stuck out from the crevice. Frantically, Whitney and Talbot began tugging with no regard for any physical injuries they might be causing. Sport held the light to help them. The foot didn't budge. Not at all.

Their lungs agonized, both boys shot to the surface, inhaled frenetically and jackknifed down again. Sport was still down by the ledge, holding the light on the foot, her eyes wide in shock. Shoving Sport aside, Talbot snaked under the trapped figure, and using his light to guide him, undid the buckles of the tank. Immediately the inert figure shifted loose and, between them, Talbot and Whitney brought Nevah to the surface.

Scrambling up first, Whitney hauled as Talbot and Sport pushed from below. When Nevah was on the dock, Talbot lowered his head over the side to shake the water out of him. No sign of life.

Whitney dropped to his knees and, fingers laced, elbows rigid, he pressed hard on Nevah's sternum. "One one thousand, two one thousand, three one thousand, four one thousand, five one thousand – "

At the fifth one thousand, Talbot pinched Nevah's nostrils shut, covered his mouth with his own, and gave him a lungful of air. Sobbing, Sport watched.

"One one thousand, two one thousand, three one thousand, four one thousand, five, *breathe*, goddamn you." Whitney's hoarse voice blended with the night sounds of the frogs and cicadas. There was no pulse on Nevah's neck, no lifting of his chest, no flutter of his eyelids.

"Change!" The two boys switched positions, Talbot compressing, Whitney trying to give Nevah the kiss of life. Talbot pried open Nevah's eyes. Sport screamed without knowing she had. The pupils were large and fixed.

From far off on top of the hill came the wail of a siren, the screeching of tires, car doors slamming, voices shouting, and finally, shoes thumping on the ramp.

The teenagers on the dock didn't look up. "One one thousand, two one thousand, three one thousand, four one thousand, five one thousand, *breathe*, damn you."

Two

From the *Ledge Island News*

It is with deep regret that we inform you that Edward ("Nevah") Wright, 16, was drowned in a scuba diving accident on August 26th. He and his friends, summer residents Talbot Harrington-Clark, 17, Whitney Chapin, 16, Anne ("Sport") Abbott, 13 and Dede St. John, 13, were exploring the cove on the south side of Sheep Head's Point when Edward became wedged in a cave and died, despite heroic efforts on the part of his friends to revive him.

Edward was the son of year-round residents, Edith and Johnny Wright. Edward is also survived by his grandmother, Hope Lantagne, of Augusta, Maine. Edward was a sophomore at Ledge Island High School and was the captain of the Ledge Island basketball team as well as his class president.

The Wrights have requested that instead of flowers, donations be made to the Ledge Island high school scholarship fund.

Three

George Harrington-Clark, Talbot's great-grandfather, bought the over-one-hundred-acre peninsula known as Sheep's Head Point on the west end of Ledge Island in 1940. It came with a decrepit farmhouse at its central and highest point of land. Over the years, the Harrington-Clarks renovated and expanded the house, and eventually transformed the top of the hill into a complex of small white buildings that could have been taken for a high-end neighborhood in Sturbridge Village, Massachusetts except that every building looked out over Penobscot Bay from at least one side. George's son inherited the property in 1948 and quickly sold smaller, ten-or-twenty-acre parcels of land to the Chapins, the St. Johns, and the Abbotts, all of whom were friends back in Connecticut, and all of whom eventually built their own houses.

Dede St. John's grandparents were the first to build. In 1949, they constructed what was then a very modern house with plenty of glass on the north edge of the Point. The architecture was supposed to suggest Frank Lloyd Wright and blend into the landscape but in fact, the house had offended almost everyone's sensibilities, including both summer and year-round residents.

The Chapins, Whitney's grandparents, followed in 1950 but wisely disguised their new house on the western end of the Point as a large weathered barn.

In 1952, Sport Abbott's grandparents built a modern but unobtrusive cedar-shingled house among the spruce trees on a bluff at the southeast side of the Point, overlooking the community dock and the protected cove where the four families kept their boats moored.

When Whitney's parents got divorced two years before Nevah's accident, Whitney's mother Heather built the fifth summer place, a small, picturesque cottage on the north side of the peninsula.

Many of the summer people descended from families that had summered on the island for several more generations, beginning when the island was first discovered by Bostonian investment bankers in the 1880s. These "old" families engaged in a subtle but persistent struggle to maintain a certain atmosphere of nineteenth-century English society by holding teas, awarding enormous three-foot silver trophies to each other at the end of each summer for victories accomplished in ancient, tiny sailboats, and vigorously engaging in writing and artistic endeavors to emphasize their freedom from ordinary drudgery.

The families on the Point were not really old money in the purest sense of the island's social hierarchy but still, when self-esteem in other areas ran low for whatever reason, at least they did have it over all the people who had arrived during the latter part of the twentieth century.

Edith and John Wright lived on the neck that connected the Point to the rest of the island, about a quarter mile east of Heather Chapin's cottage but on the south side of the neck, overlooking the cove and the moored boats. This made it easy for the Wrights to keep an eye, although from a half mile away, on the small fleet of small and large sailboats and motorboats in the cove.

Careful was the word for how the four sets of parents had treated Edith and Johnny even before Nevah's death. They had always remembered to send birthday cards to Edith and Johnny and presents to Nevah on his birthday. The kids had come up with the nickname "Nevah" for Edward but their parents had always been careful to call the boy Edward or Eddie.

Nevah always hung out with Talbot, Sport, Whitney and Dede when they came up for the summer and holidays. He was always included in their sailing trips, their picnics, and their time at the beach. The yacht club had reduced fees for islanders and Nevah took sailing lessons with the four and had been one of the better sailors in the quick little 420's the kids raced through July and August. Of course, there was always the awkward moment at the end of the summer when the four children from Connecticut and New York would be discussing returning to private schools, or when their friends came to visit and asked what school Nevah attended, but all in all, it had been as equitable as the adults could have made it.

The year before Nevah died, when he was in ninth grade and Sport was in seventh, the five teens, together with Talbot's parents, Marilyn and Spencer Harrington-Clark, Sport's parents, Anne and Henry Abbott, Whitney's divorced mother, Heather, and Dede's widowed father, Roger, took a sail on the Harrington-Clarks' boat – a fifty-foot Hinckley that was only referred to by its name "Yonder" and never as a "yacht" – to picnic on one of the many islands in Penobscot Bay. Picnics were only conducted on uninhabited islands. It was also considered impolite to choose an island that already had a picnic party in residence. However, it was rarely difficult to find an empty island in between the rocky shores of the bigger islands. The shores were simply too rocky and the water too cold to attract crowds.

Edith packed them a lunch of club sandwiches for the teens, and cold cuts, cheeses and fruit for the adults. They anchored the sailboat a hundred feet off the shore of one of several islands that was aptly named Scrub, and ferried themselves to the beach in "Hither", the dinghy that was always towed behind Yonder like a small dutiful child on these outings.

After lunch, while the teens lay on the rocky beach and talked, the adults sat on beach chairs further up on the shore, dressed in sweaters and sweatshirts against the cool sea breeze. As often happened, the discussion slowly came around to their children. In the past, these discussions had been very competitive and had subtly centered on whose child had won which athletic event, or was getting the best grades, or had the most friends. But that day, as a conversation about the children's college prospects wound down to desultory remarks about Dartmouth versus Princeton, Anne brought up Nevah.

"What about Eddie and his future?"

When Henry Abbott was thirty years old, he had given Nevah's father, the then twenty-year-old Johnny Wright, money to attend the University of Maine for two years during which Johnny studied engineering. Spencer Harrington-Clark had paid for Johnny to take flying lessons after his freshman year so that he could ferry the Harrington-Clarks from Connecticut to Ledge Island when weather permitted. The families had expected Johnny, as Henry expressed it, "to show some gumption" and get loans to pay for the other two years but instead, whether for lack of money or love of Edith, Johnny had simply come back to the island and never left again. This ended up suiting the families just as well since their investment paid off handsomely over the years in terms of Johnny's flying skills as well as his competence in plumbing, electrical work, carpentry and gardening.

Anne, Sport's mother, was the only actual "Mainer" among the parents on the Point. Anne had only been ten years old and living in central Maine at the time that Johnny came back to the Island to marry Edith. Anne had first come to the island to waitress at the solitary island restaurant the summer after her freshman year at the University of Maine in Orono. When she came back after her sophomore year, she met the forty-year-old Henry while waiting on tables and married Henry a year later, right after his divorce from Thora, his first wife.

"We owe it to Edith and Johnny," Anne continued as, with the care that she took with any task, she began to pack the left-over food and plastic picnic dishes back into the antique picnic basket. "Johnny never got to finish college because you were too cheap to help him, Henry. So now it's our chance to make up for that through Eddie."

"Anne, darling," Henry said in an affectedly bored tone, "I'd have to say that your noblesse oblige is showing."

"It's not that at all," she snapped back, "It's just the decent thing to do."

"Yes," said Henry, "It worked out so splendidly with Eddie's father."

Marilyn Harrington-Clark, ever the peacemaker, said in a mild voice, "That sounds like a *wonderful* idea, Anne and Henry. It wouldn't be that prohibitive if each family agreed to pay the difference between tuition and what Eddie can get in scholarships so that he doesn't have to take out any loans. Eddie excels in school, I believe."

Anne smiled warmly at Marilyn. They all knew that Henry was a bit awed by Marilyn: her classic if now middle-aged good looks, the wealth that she had brought to the already wealthy Harrington-Clark family, the apparent ease with which she and Spencer seemed to move companionably through life. Given that Marilyn and Spencer had been married for over twenty-five years, this last struck Henry as particularly impressive. Now that Marilyn had flung down this genteel gauntlet, Anne knew that Henry would have to go along.

"What do you say, Spencer dear?" Marilyn coaxed her husband.

Spencer leaned over in his chair to kiss his wife on the cheek. "Whatever you say dear, as always."

"Well, that's fine for all of you," Heather interjected sourly, "but my ex, sweet old Danny boy, keeps me on quite a tight leash and I can't possibly afford that."

Anne quickly answered Heather. "Oh Heather, we wouldn't expect you to contribute. Spencer will speak to Danny. I'm sure he'll contribute."

"Maybe," answered Heather bitterly, "if only so he can show his new sweetie pie how generous he is."

"Now, now," soothed Marilyn, turning to Dede's father, "How about you, Roger?"

Apparently Roger was not, as most of them had supposed, asleep. But he merely shrugged his shoulders and uttered a mumbled sound of assent. Since his wife had died two years ago, he had stopped coming to the island as often and Dede now stayed with Sport during August while he traveled on business overseas.

"We'll take that as a yes, Roger," Marilyn said as she stood up and swiped the sand off the back of her khaki shorts.

"There, that's settled. Who will talk to Johnny about this?" she went on briskly as she picked up the picnic blanket and folded it. She had the air of someone who had very satisfactorily concluded yet one more eleemosynary committee meeting.

Now that Henry had been cornered, the idea of giving Johnny the news seemed to appeal to him because he was the first to speak up.

"Oh, I will. Maybe I'll get the steam shower fixed in return. Seems like an expensive way to get a little plumbing done but I suppose I should be grateful for any bit of time that Johnny condescends to give me."

Marilyn ignored this remark, picked up the picnic basket and headed down towards the dinghy. Anne followed closely behind, perhaps to hide her satisfaction with this result.

Never one to postpone a diversion, Henry called Johnny as soon as they got home and invited him over to the house. Johnny, never one to lose dignity by asking why, arrived about forty-five minutes later to make it clear that he was not at Henry's beck and call.

Johnny walked into the house without knocking. Henry, who had been dozing, was a bit startled. Unhappily so since he did not like, quite literally, to be caught napping. He sat up quickly and waved expansively towards the living room.

"Have a seat, Johnny. What'll you drink?"

If Johnny had been surprised by the first invitation he had ever had to sit in Henry's living room, he hid it well. "Scotch on the rocks" was all he said and stepped down into the living room to take a seat on the sofa. Henry left the room to get the drinks while Johnny stretched his long legs out in front of him. He was a handsome man with thick greying hair. His even features and weathered face added to the general satisfaction the summer families felt about having such an able and conscientious, even if slightly sullen, caretaker. Henry returned with the drinks, handed one to Johnny, and sat down across from him.

"Well, Johnny, how are things going?"

"Well enough," Johnny said, clearly suspicious.

"Well, you know, we've been thinking about your son Eddie," Henry began, "He's a great kid. I know he gets good grades and he's on the football team, isn't he?"

"Basketball," Johnny corrected him, "Not enough kids in the school for football."

"Right. Now, you know he'll be graduating from high school before you know it. I can tell you from my experience with Sarah. She's just about to go off to college this fall. The hours that go into raising a kid may seem to go by slowly, but by God, the years slip by quickly. And so we've been thinking. Not just me but all of us on the Point, that maybe you could use some help with Eddie's tuition when the time comes."

Henry smiled benevolently. Johnny sat glumly silent.

"So, here's the thing. We'd like to promise you that we'll cover his tuition," Henry said, then paused slightly, and added, "at the University of Maine." This last hadn't been discussed among the families but it had apparently just occurred to Henry that Johnny might be expecting them to ante up a private college tuition.

Henry sat back in his chair and again smiled at Johnny, obviously waiting for something. But for what? For Johnny to tug at his forelock and look down sheepishly? Or launch into paeans of praise? Henry frowned, realizing even as he sat there, that it had been foolish to expect Johnny to show anything but resentment and possibly even anger.

Johnny slapped his palms on his legs and stood up.

"Well, Edith will be very happy to hear of it. And Eddie. He'll be pleased. Anything else?"

Henry stared at Johnny, uncharacteristically at a loss for words.

"No, no, that was all. Oh, except I was wondering if you might have a few minutes to take a look at that steam shower."

Johnny pulled on his ball cap and started towards the door.

"Not at the moment. I'll look in later in the week."

"Sure," Henry said. After Johnny had left, Henry stood there a moment gazing at the door until Anne came into the room. Henry had told her that he didn't want her there in case it embarrassed Johnny.

"So that's done then?"

"The son-of-a-bitch didn't even thank me. But then again, what'd I expect? He didn't thank me twenty-five years ago either."

Anne sighed and disappeared back into the den.

Four

"What art can wash her guilt away?"

In the four years that followed Nevah's death, there was no art and no time limit for Sport Abbott.

Every teen has a secret that can't be told, a secret that explains why their friends are unreliable, their parents are impossible, their looks are agonizingly wrong. Sport's secret was that she, through carelessness, had killed Nevah Wright. Other people had test dreams, Sport had murder dreams. She had been a relatively happy person before Nevah's death. After that night, it was as if there was another person living inside her: the person who had killed Nevah. She couldn't talk about it and yet it was the most important thing there was to know about her, at least in her own mind. In high school, she befriended a girl named Lucia who had killed her best friend Phoebe in a car accident. Lucia was dull and uninteresting. The friendship between Lucia and Phoebe had been based on a shared fascination with Leonardo DeCaprio. But Sport could not leave Lucia alone for the whole of her sophomore year in high school. When she was with Lucia, she would steer every conversation to the car accident until even Lucia tired of discussing the details: how horrible it was to see Phoebe's parents on the street, how relentless Lucia's nightmares were, how she felt panicked every time she heard a police siren. Notwithstanding that Sport was popular, and leagues above Lucia in social stature, Lucia finally told Sport that she didn't want to discuss it anymore. Since Sport never mentioned Nevah's accident to anyone, this left Sport and Lucia without a common interest and the friendship, if that was what it had been, was quickly reduced to brief hellos in the hallway.

Hey Abbott, Sport would frequently say to herself, it was an accident, for

Christ's sake. We never meant any harm. Nevah wanted to scuba dive. We were giving him a present.

But we should have kept a better eye on him. We were so God damned stupid, so cocky and careless. He was sixteen, gypped out of a lifetime. All our fault. Hey, Abbott, kids die all the time. Littler kids than sixteen. Some of them beaten by their own parents, for God's sake. We never meant any harm. Great excuse. When I'm standing in front of St. Peter on Judgment Day, I'll tell him I never meant any harm. Yeah, he'll say, and ask me if I know what particular material they use to pave the road to hell.

Talbot's life went just slightly off the rails after the accident. It didn't seem that way from the outside but that was what happened.

Talbot's father, Spencer Harrington-Clark, had been a lawyer with the Day, Berry law firm in Hartford, Connecticut before being elected to the Connecticut House of Representatives where he served for three terms before retiring.

The script had been written for Talbot since he was ten when it became apparent that like his father, he had the looks, brains and ability to excel. He was to go to a good prep school, a good college, join a big law firm and then, in the fullness of time, become a United States senator because, after all, the American dream required that he surpass his father in achievement.

At the time of the accident, Talbot had been president of his class at Choate Rosemary. Five years after the accident, he had graduated from Williams College and was enrolled in Stanford Law School, but it was becoming clear to him that he would never go into politics. It wasn't that he thought the accident would disqualify him for public office. After all, it hadn't been Chappaquiddick. They were a bunch of kids on an adventure that went very wrong. But he knew the price of politics on any grand scale would mean a lifetime of having his past examined, of people mentioning the accident, of associating him with the accident and even if he had not been at fault, it was something that he could not bear to defend and explain for the rest of his life.

Talbot Harrington-Clark's guilt detoured away from Nevah and came to rest on Edith and Johnny Wright, the two most devastated by the tragedy. Edith, who had always been cheerful, biddable and hard-working, gradually dwindled and shrank into a nearly skeletal version of her former self while her mind simultaneously dwindled and shrank into an early senility. She continued to clean the houses of the families of those responsible for her only child's death; she exhibited no animosity to anyone; her usual expression was of vague absent-mindedness. Johnny Wright, who had never been outgoing or sociable, retreated even further into his own dry pod. It was as if a sign, *"Enter at your own Peril"* had been engraved onto his life following the accident.

Talbot was obsessed with Edith and Johnny, not because he feared retribution, but because as the most responsible and empathetic of the four teens, he could imagine the Wrights' misery. It was Talbot who prompted the four families who lived on Sheep's Head Point to raise the Wrights' salary, Talbot who suggested renting a cottage in Florida for the Wrights to occupy for a few weeks each winter, and Talbot who showed the greatest consideration for their wants. The Wrights accepted the additional salary but refused the cottage.

"What good would it do Edith?" was Johnny's only response when Talbot's father made the offer to Johnny.

"What good does it do him or anybody else to keep wallowing in our guilt?" was Whitney Chapin's philosophy. Whitney, although not heartless, had made it the work of his late teenage years to erase that summer night from his memory. And for long periods he succeeded. But not entirely. In the middle of infrequent sleepless nights he wondered if he, Whitney, were the most to blame. For being so scornful of Talbot's precautions, so habitually careless.

Whitney lived with Heather, his divorced mother, in Connecticut and used the ample allowance he got from his father, Danny, to help him forget. Scaring himself helped a lot. He never scuba dived after that night but he took up motorcycles and went sky diving a few times. He went to the University of Richmond and did his best to get drunk and have sex most weekend nights. It wasn't that difficult really. He was good-looking, reasonably well-to-do, and happiest at parties. So for long periods, months sometimes, he would forget about the accident.

And what scar was left by the accident on the mind of Dede St. John? Perhaps the most introspective of the four, she was obsessively convinced that they would somehow pay for their collective sin. Not at the hands of the Wrights, but at the intervention of God or fate.

Dede got into the Parsons School of Design in New York City and immediately settled into a form of life which Sport referred to as "Bohemian Lite". She lived in a bad part of Tribecca during college, but her large and sunny apartment had two bedrooms, one of which she used for a studio. She was indifferent to clothes and dressed in thrift store attire but kept her SUV parked in an expensive garage for when she wanted to get out of town quickly. Her boyfriends during her freshman year looked like a United Nations committee on third world economics. In quick succession she dated an Ethiopian, a Saudi, and an Australian aborigine. On the other hand, the summer after her freshman year, when she came back to Maine without her boyfriends, she shamelessly flirted with Whitney, jumping on him when he was trying to read, making a point of sitting with her arm around his neck at parties and even going to bed with him on a few very drunk and apparently inconsequential occasions. It was certainly safe. Whitney liked Dede but was much too ambitious to marry her. She could afford to live an artist's life on her trust income but would not inherit great wealth. She was blond and pretty but not gorgeous. She was intelligent but not particularly intellectual. Whitney, the most outwardly ambitious of the four, was looking for bigger fish. On the previous New Year's Eve in New York City, Dede had shown up at a party with one of her ethnic exotics while Whitney came with a lanky Princeton heiress on his arm and neither of them had been particularly offended.

And through it all, by unwritten and unspoken consent, the four maintained a tacit pact that endured for four years never to mention Nevah's name when they were together, never to bring up that night.

Five

The next "accident" occurred almost four years to the day after Nevah's death. It was also the day after Sport lost her virginity to Talbot.

Actually, it was a surprise to everyone, including Sport, that she hadn't lost it earlier. Talbot had grown up in New York City while Sport's parents lived in Connecticut. But they had spent almost all of their summers together, including this one, the summer after Sport finished her freshman year at the University of Chicago, which was also the summer before Talbot started law school.

In fact, it had become an increasing source of discomfort to Sport that she still *was* a virgin after her freshman year at college. Dede had had a variety of affairs by then and Whitney had been regaling them for several years now with tales of his various conquests. Talbot hadn't said anything but his quiet assurance and slight smile when Dede and Whitney started discussing their sex lives clearly conveyed to the other three that he too had been initiated into the awesome mysteries of teen sex.

Making it even more embarrassing was the general assumption among several of the adults on the Point, that Talbot and Sport would have a series of summer romances that would, most likely, end in marriage. It almost seemed to Talbot sometimes that there was an unstated conspiracy among the Abbots to let Talbot and Sport sail together in sailing camp, to go biking and even camping together. To Talbot, it seemed as close to an arranged marriage as could happen in America in this day and in their social class. Sport was, had always been, in love with Talbot. And as for Talbot, well, he wasn't more in love with anyone else and it would save him a world of energy and time to simply let his destiny unfold as it had apparently been designed by Sport's parents, their schools, their social circle, and perhaps even his parents as well.

Nevah's death subtly changed Talbot's thoughts not only about his future but also about Sport. It tempered his sense of adventure along with his ambition. Before the accident, he would tease Sport, in a manner that pained her, about how he was trying to escape her and what appeared to be his fate. He stopped making that joke after Nevah died and now, when he thought no one was looking, he could be seen gazing at Sport thoughtfully.

The night Sport lost her virginity was, as it were, anti-climatic. All of the parents who were still on the Point at that late date in August had gone to a chamber music concert in the village to hear a quartet comprised of two islanders and two summer people. The four of them, Sport, Talbot, Dede and Whitney, had made hamburgers down at one of the Point's several beaches over an illegal fire and afterwards, after Dede and Whitney suddenly disappeared, Talbot and Sport lay on a blanket and looked at the stars. The stars always seemed almost overly bright in Maine, as if the wattage had been turned up at that latitude. They had a blanket over them, as much to deter mosquitoes as to keep warm. After a few minutes Talbot, who had only kissed Sport and occasionally caressed her breasts, simply rolled onto his side and began unbuttoning her shirt. He gently but firmly removed all her clothes as if he were a parent undressing a sleepy child while she lay there mesmerized but also somewhat relieved about getting past this hurdle. Talk about a type A personality, she thought ruefully. Then he removed his own clothes and after slowly moving his hands all over her body and between her legs, he gently moved on top of her and began to rock back and forth inside her.

The actual act wasn't an overly sensual affair, particularly given the rocky beach beneath the thin blanket they had spread for the picnic and the mosquitoes who managed to get under the top blanket whenever there was a gap. Nor was it as traumatic or painful as Sport's friends had led her to believe it would be. She even had enough self-possession at the time to wonder if the horror stories about childbirth were equally overblown. In fact, afterwards, she couldn't imagine what all the fuss was about. There was a little blood on the bottom blanket that she would have to wash out with hot water when they got back to the house and it had pinched a bit, but really, it was ridiculous to think how this minor physical initiation had played such a pivotal role in centuries of literature, theatre, philosophy and religion. Maybe it had seemed like a bigger deal before there was TV and other more graphic forms of entertainment, she reflected. It didn't even occur to her to worry about getting pregnant since her period had just finished.

If it wasn't sensual, it certainly was romantic. The sight of Talbot's calm, but intense expression and his broad shoulders and chest pressing down on her own chest, had moved her much more than the sex. He was warm and smelled like summer and if the pleasure she took in moving her arms across his back was not inspired by passion, it was certainly suffused with love and a deep gratification that at last, she held Talbot naked in her arms.

Afterwards, they walked up to Sport's house holding hands and Talbot kissed her on the lips before she went inside, just as he had been doing all summer, and walked away. Neither of them had said a word since they had first lay back on the blanket to watch the stars.

*   *   *

Once a year, whichever of the "children" were around in late August made a picnic for the adults on the beach on the western most end of the Point. This year, the picnic had been scheduled for the day after Sport's trauma-free rite of passage.

After lunch, the parents sat on the beach in folding chairs and watched, as they had been doing for over two decades, while their children stood knee deep in the mild surf, splashing each other with the cold water.

Sport was being careful to ensure that she was always equidistant between Whitney and Talbot but Dede had no such compunctions. She leapt at Talbot and Whitney, over and over, trying to pull them down into the cold water. Then she climbed onto Talbot's shoulders and challenged Sport and Whitney to a chicken fight. Sport was reluctant but Whitney insisted so that Sport had no choice if she was to play at being her usual competitive, active self.

Dede and Sport wrestled vigorously from atop Talbot's and Whitney's shoulders for a while. But Sport had the uncomfortable feeling that her mother was watching her a bit too closely. Maybe she suspected something. The thought made her so uncomfortable that she feigned a chill and went to lie on her towel on the beach beside her mother. But her mother just continued watching the horseplay with either a bored or distracted expression on her face.

Johnny came back with the truck around two and the children packed up the lunch, tables and chairs. Then their parents started walking slowly up back to their houses, stopping to turn back and look at the ocean, presumably to enjoy the view. The younger group came running past them and Whitney yelled back over his shoulder that they were going to get their wetsuits and try out Sport's new wind-surfer.

As the young people, attired in wetsuits, converged about thirty minutes later on the dock, Sport glanced back up the steep incline towards her house. She was hoping that her mother wasn't watching. Anne Abbott had always been protective of Sport but since the accident she had become, at least from Sport's point of view, absolutely neurotic. Anne had, of course, cut short the scuba diving lessons after Nevah's accident. And it came as no surprise to Sport when Anne flatly prohibited

Sport from taking flying lessons with Talbot. But then she had forbidden Sport from jumping her five-year-old Thoroughbred, and Sport had become bored with riding and sold the horse before she went to college. And the previous winter Anne had forced Sport to cancel plans to go back-country skiing in Utah. It had gotten to the point where Sport had deliberately provoked an argument between her parents by making a joke about changing her nickname from "Sport" – a tag Henry had given her when as a child she had insisted on trying every available athletic activity – to "Couch Potato." Sure enough, Henry had made a crack about Anne not being able to appreciate the thrill of sport since she had never had an opportunity to engage in sports as a child. At that, Anne had left the room in a silent rage.

When Henry bought the windsurfer for Sport, he assured Anne that it was entirely safe, safer than waterskiing even. Nevertheless, Sport planned to be well out of view from the house before she started weaving in and out of the rocks that jutted out of the water at low tide.

Talbot tried it first. He approached it in his usual studied way, sailing on a broad reach towards the Wrights' house on the far side of their cove. Once he was out of sight of the Abbott house, there were no houses on the shore between the dock and the Wright house: just the rocky shore and the spruce trees and fields coming down to the water. Halfway across the cove, Talbot was a tiny twig against a sunset sky. When he got to the other side, knowing that he'd be unable to turn the board without falling in, he jumped off, swiveled the board around and sailed back on the opposite tack. He did this three or four times while the other three sat on the dock, dangling their feet in the water and talking.

Dede described a series of paintings she was creating of her naked lovers' bodies.

"I kind of enjoy objectifying them," she said, "I mean, they're always thinking about my body, so I thought it would be fun to have them experience someone staring at their naked bodies for long periods."

"That is *so* romantic," Sport said with heavy irony.

"Well, what's so romantic about men panting after my body all the time?"

"You're right," said Whitney, "Absolutely nothing."

Dede shoved Whitney's shoulder and went on.

"The thing is, they're all so proud of their bodies. I don't get it. One of them has, like, this little budding paunch and he does nothing to hide it. There I am, always sucking it in, and he slouches around as if he were pregnant and trying to make it show. And this other guy, he has these little stringy legs. You'd think he'd wear long pants. But no, he wore shorts straight through November. What's going on in their heads? What is it about the male mind that prevents them being the least bit objective about their own bodies?"

Whitney, whose wetsuit was pulled down around his waist, looked at his stomach. "Well, would you deny that this is a thing of beauty? I mean really, Dede, even your aesthetic sense must be fully satisfied by the sight of the undulating muscles just beneath this tanned skin."

Dede looked over indifferently and then turned to Sport, "See what I mean?"

Whitney stood up, picked up Dede under the arms, and dropped her into the frigid water. Dede, whose wetsuit was zipped open down to her waist at the back, shrieked, swam quickly to the ladder and climbed out. They wrestled for a little while until Sport stood up and suddenly lunging forward, pushed them both into the water.

At this moment, Talbot came up on the board and jumped off the side, letting the sail drop into the water.

"Ok Sport, show us how it's done."

"Yeah," said Whitney, pulling himself up onto the dock and shoving Sport into the water. "Make us all look bad."

Sport, secretly pleased at this opportunity to show off in front of Talbot, swam gracefully over to the board and pulled herself up onto it. She stood and waited for a few seconds, getting her balance, and then easily pulled the heavy sail out of the water and immediately took off across the cove.

Dede sat back down on the dock between the two boys and sighed, "Everything's so easy for that girl. I'd like to see her struggle just once."

"Don't be hard on her. She's got her problems like everyone else," Talbot said, his eyes watching her quickly recede into the distance.

"Like what?" Dede asked, sincerely curious.

Talbot shrugged. Discussions about emotions were not his home turf and in any event, the thing that Sport probably felt most insecure about was his feelings towards her. He actually felt a little pressure about the upcoming weeks. Certainly neither of them had committed to monogamy yet. And where could they go where either their parents, or the Wrights, or their friends wouldn't find them? Maybe out by the town beach? It was a problem. It was so much easier to get laid in college than here. And then there was that very subtle pressure from Sport. He felt her need for control, her need to know her future, bearing down on him like an oncoming bus. Yes, he could easily imagine them married to each other, but he didn't want to commit just yet. Sport had always been right there in front of him. He'd enjoyed sleeping with other girls the last few years. True, they didn't know him the way Sport did, but not being known was a relief sometimes. For instance, it was a relief to go to bed with some-one who didn't know that he had gotten the scar on his butt when, as a five-year-old, he had sat on broken glass down at the dock. In fact, just as an experiment, he had told one girl that he got the scar parachuting and she had been impressed. This freedom had allowed him to try on other personas. It was, he sometimes rationalized, a way to confirm that Sport was the one.

Dede spoke again, startling him out of his thoughts with one of her eerily perceptive comments, "You mean a problem like getting you to propose so she can cross it off her 'to do' list?"

"Yeah," he answered quickly, "and how she's going to get rid of you two so that maybe we can have a little sex now and then."

Dede shrieked with laughter and turned to Whitney, "Did you hear that? The big stud. God, I'm so very, very hurt. Whitney, they're already plotting how to get away from us. Come on," she said, draping her arms around Whitney's shoulders, "Let's have a mad love affair that will drive Sport and Talbot absolutely crazy with envy. They're almost like an old married couple already. But you and me, Whit, there's still some passion left in us . . . . 'What is wedlock forced, but a hell, an age of discord and continual strife? Whereas the contrary bringeth bliss . . . .'"

"Whoa," Whitney answered, "Listen to you, the big intellectual. What the hell they teaching you in that art college anyway? They letting you read poetry? I thought you were supposed to be creating art, throwing paint around and using a welding torch to make sculpture."

They talked a while longer before Sport came back, neatly turning the windsurfer just as it approached the dock. She jumped off the board onto the dock, still holding a line attached to the boom.

"You hot bitch!" Whitney said, glancing up at her. Sport tried to be offhanded but could not suppress her deep satisfaction at the compliment. She looked over at Talbot and was disappointed to see that he was looking not at her, but out towards the sunset.

"Okey, dokey," said Dede, standing up, "here goes nothing."

She jumped into the water. Whitney jumped in after her and held the board steady while she climbed onto the board and reached forward to grab the boom.

Slowly, the board began to move. Dede whooped with glee and then turned to look back at them with a hint of panic in her expression, "How the hell do I turn this thing around to get back?"

Sport and Whitney laughed. Talbot called out to her, "Step around the front and change directions. There's nothing to it, Dede."

There's nothing to it.

Sport grabbed Talbot's arm.

He turned his attention from Dede to Sport. "What's the matter?"

"God, Tal, remember the last time we heard those words?"

"What? What words? What're you talking about?"

"There's nothing to it."

Gingerly, Dede was inching along the board, trying to get to the front. The next minute she was in the water.

"I don't know what you're talking about," Talbot said to Sport.

"Those were the words you said to Nevah when you were teaching him to scuba."

A line appeared between Talbot's eyebrows. He disengaged his arm from Sport's grasp and turned to watch as Dede caught hold of the downed sail and, throwing her body across the board, climbed back up. Carefully, she headed towards the shore.

Thoughtful now, without looking at Sport, Talbot said, "We'll never get over it, will we, Sport?"

Over the next few minutes, the sun went down below the horizon and the sky turned from silver and blue to rose and gold. As persistent as a hungry dog gnawing on a bone, Dede kept falling in, climbing back up, hauling up the sail, and taking off again. As long as she headed in one direction, she managed to maintain her balance. But whenever she had to change direction, she fell over backwards into the water.

The other three watched. Whitney called out sarcastic advice every time Dede capsized. Talbot and Sport sat immersed in thought. Peace descended on the cove. A matron duck and her progeny went by the dock on a staid outing while plovers and ruddy turnstones kept to the safety of the shore. Now the three on the dock sat silently as the light began to fade.

Out on the eastern side of the cove now, nearer the Wrights' house than the Abbotts', Dede felt as if she had the world to herself. Except for the Wrights' house, the houses of the compound were hidden by spruce and oaks. It was mildly and pleasantly scary being out this far. It was slightly concerning that she still hadn't figured out how to turn the board and she was getting tired of climbing back on. But one of the others could come out with the Whaler and retrieve her if she got stuck on the far side of the cove.

Dede was so absorbed she didn't at first hear the sound of the approaching motor. When she did become aware that the cove had lost its exclusivity, she tried to peer over her shoulder to see what was coming up behind her. A noisy and decrepit-looking outboard was coming from the direction of town towards the compound's dock. She had a sudden insight into how the panorama might be viewed by an outsider: four spoiled progeny of the rich amusing themselves on their remote playground with their expensive toys.

Talbot stood up as the boat suddenly veered off course and headed north in Dede's direction. He stood shielding his eyes, suddenly intent on the scene in front of them.

"What the fuck . . . ?"

At that point the peaceful scene went berserk. As if the motor had exploded, as if the distant yellow-slickered figure at the wheel had had a seizure, the boat almost jerked towards Dede.

Dede couldn't move fast enough as disaster bore down on her. Although generally quick-witted, she held on to the windsurfer's boom instead of letting go and diving deep into the water to avoid the boat. With the boat only a few feet away, she finally let go and tried to dive off, but quick as she was, she wasn't quick enough.

From the dock, Sport, Talbot and Whitney heard the agonized scream and saw the outboard speed away, this time to the south and away from the island. Whitney tripped Talbot as the two of them scrambled into the Whaler. Sport stood on the dock, unaware that she was screaming for her mother. Talbot and Whitney reached Dede in time to see her head bobbing above the water and the water churning with blood.

Six

From the *Ledge Island News*

Dede St. John, 18, a summer resident, was seriously injured last week in a hit-and-run boating accident. According to witnesses Anne (Sport) Abbott, Talbot Harrington-Clark and Whitney Chapin, who were standing on the dock in Ledge Island Cove at the time of the accident watching Dede windsurf, an outboard described as a twenty-five-foot Mako or other similar make of boat apparently struck Dede. Police are seeking the driver of the outboard. Anyone with any knowledge of the incident is asked to get in touch with Deputy Asa Coombs.

Dede is the daughter of Roger St. John who lives with his second wife, Doria in Florence, Italy. Dede's mother, Abagail (formerly Abagail Pyne) died of leukemia seven years ago. According to a report from Penobscot Bay Hospital, Dede is in stable condition but will be confined to a wheelchair for the indefinite future.

Seven

Five Years Later

The trip to Ledge Island still hadn't lost its appeal for Sport Abbott. Although her parents preferred flying to the Rockland airport, for Sport getting there was at least a third of the fun. Her spirits edged up a notch with each passing landmark: Hartford, 495 to the Lowell Connector, I-95 to Portsmouth, signs that informed her "You can make it in Amesburg", license plates that instructed her to "Live free or die."

As she drove, she sang a song from an old CD that her sister Sarah had left in Sport's room. Sport had found it last night and had been listening to it for the past hour.

"It's a dark road
But it'd be a darker road
If I had no one
To come home to."

When she reached the New Hampshire state liquor store, she stopped in accordance with her parents' instructions to stock up. Henry, in particular, was obsessed with saving small amounts on hard liquor although he was extravagant with his wine purchases. Crossing the bridge into Kittery, she felt the very texture of the air changing. To her, it was like the difference between a stagnant pond and a mountain stream.

"What if I drove into the driveway
And there was no sign of life
No smoke rising from the chimney
And in the windows, no light."

After a while came the Bath Iron Works, a favorite of Talbot's who had nearly driven off the Bath bridge a number of times trying to see what the Navy was building in the yard. After that came Wiscasset. Even a week after Labor Day, Wiscasset was still a terrible traffic problem. It was there in Wiscasset that a narrow two-lane bridge came into direct conflict with the tourists' insatiable appetite for an imaginary Maine. A Maine without mosquitos, without damp, foggy rainy days, a Maine where one ate only lobsters for dinner and the water always sparkled . . . then the Boothbay Region where they sometimes stopped to visit friends, and then Damariscotta, where they had spent two nights on a sailboat a couple of summers ago, weathering an unexpected storm.

"Unlock the front door
Step into the dark
No smell of something cooking
No silly dog to bark."

Her thoughts were mixed as she drove. On the one hand, she was excited about going to the Island. On the other hand, it hadn't been a great summer so far. She had finished her Masters in social work at NYU. That was bad enough as far as her father was concerned; he had wanted her to go to law school. But then she had announced that she wanted to take a year off to start what might end up being her doctoral thesis on the biological and evolutionary roots of ethics. When she had told her father last June, he was enraged.

"What the hell is that about? I just spent tens of thousands of dollars giving you a private undergraduate education and then, after I fork over two more years of graduate school tuition, you decide to start a doctoral thesis? Talk about ethics and biology! Where's the morality in that? Don't you think you owe it to your biological father to earn a living after twenty-three years? Listen kiddo, you're on your own financially from here on out. A doctorate in social work!"

As penance, she had stayed in New York City that summer tutoring the sons and daughters of parents neurotically concerned about their children's SAT scores, earning enough money to get her through a year on the island.

Should she be worried about her financial future or not? She couldn't tell. At home, she had always felt privileged. Her father was an estate and tax partner at the

LeBoef Lamb law firm. As he had explained to her when she was seven years old, he wrote instructions for how to give away people's stuff when they died. It had sounded to her as if he had the power to make wishes come true, at least for the inheritors. She had promptly gone into her room, taken out a piece of paper and pencil, and written out detailed instructions for her sister Sarah to get her pink blanky and clothes but not her Barbies, for her mother to get her books, but not her secret box, and for her father to have her money in the piggy bank. The Barbies and secret box were to go to her friend Talbot, "if Talbot still likes me then."

Unbeknownst to her at the time, being an estate and tax partner was probably the least prestigious and remunerative partnership in the firm. He and his family had many wealthy friends which made it a natural choice. With a ready list of potential clients he knew he could make partner quickly. But it wasn't what he had meant to be. By temperament and inclination he would have made a much better litigator. He enjoyed a good competitive fight the way other people enjoyed music or literature. Almost everything Henry did became a competition. He had no interest in sailing unless he was racing, no interest in tennis unless he was in a match, and no interest in his children except to the extent that they were excelling at one endeavor or another.

But he had been successful as a lawyer and they had lived well in Wilton, Connecticut and spent summers at their inherited house on Ledge Island. Sport felt privileged because her mother had never had an office job while Sport was growing up, because they went on ski vacations in Utah, and because her father paid not only her tuition at the University of Chicago but also gave her pocket money. She didn't care about clothes so that was never a problem and when her father asked her what kind of car she wanted for college, she asked for a Honda Civic and got it.

It was different when she got to the Island because she immediately became almost poor among their summer set. Talbot's family flew to the Island in a twin engine Beechcraft while her family either flew commercial or drove. The Harrington-Clarks sailed a fifty-foot Hinckley while her family sailed a twenty-five-foot O'Day. Her mother talked about dances at their local country club. Talbot's mother talked about society balls in New York City. It was sort of like being on a Cinderella merrygo-round: too much money, too little, too much, too little.

She wondered if she loved Talbot because he was rich or because of the way his straight blond hair fell across his forehead. Was it because of his ability at age fourteen to be completely casual about walking into the best restaurants in NYC, or because of his nearly invisible belly button and his complete lack of petty malice? She couldn't tell. It was all just part of the package she'd decide, and then go back to wondering if she would have fallen in love if Talbot's family lived a middle-class life in Watertown, Connecticut.

The five years since Dede's accident had been ones in which Sport's already ambiguous relationship with Talbot had remained in suspension, neither progressing nor faltering. She had been at college in Chicago and then graduate school in New York City while Talbot had spent three years at Stanford Law School. After law school and the bar exam, he started grinding out seventy-hour work weeks at the Paul Weiss law firm in L.A. They were both ambitious and neither was brilliant enough to excel without working. Their lives had been consumed with school and work, and they saw each other for only a week at Christmas, a few scattered, frantic weekends during which they inevitably ended up spending their days in either an academic or law firm library. And then, three months ago, he had been transferred to Hong Kong to work in the firm's office there. Sport had been bitterly disappointed. Talbot had seemed resigned, perhaps because he could not suppress his excitement about living in Asia for two or three years. She hadn't seen him since he had left. At first she had wondered whether he might ask her to marry him so that they could live in Hong Kong together but it hadn't happened. Sometimes Sport wondered if this wasn't the result of her own stubborn resolve to at least pretend to be independent. Maybe Talbot thought that she really cared about doing her doctorate and having a career as a social worker above all else. Well, yeah, she thought ruefully, she wanted to finish the doctorate but she wanted to get married even more. This was what feminism got you. Yes, you wanted to be independent, strong, ambitious but fuck it all, at the same time, a few million years of evolution screamed out that hooking onto a strong caveman to produce and protect your young was a hell of a lot more to the point.

She sighed from time to time as she drove and considered all of this. Maybe if she got her thesis underway, she could somehow tell Talbot at Christmas time how easy it would be to finish it in Hong Kong. Assuming he wanted her in Hong Kong. What if he didn't? She didn't know if he was being faithful to her. Their eventual marriage seemed inevitable but still he hadn't proposed. He seemed to be waiting, she wasn't sure what for. Certainly Dede's accident had thrown and scared them all but it had been five years since then. They had all settled back into their lives, hadn't they? Even Dede seemed to have found her footing, Sport thought, and then winced at the pun. Dede was still in a wheelchair.

As a teen, while still unsure if Talbot's affection for her would survive puberty, she had had a series of dreams about being an old woman who had never married, and not being quite sure how this happened, wondering where Talbot had gone. Now the dreams were coming back. Maybe she'd be one of those women who waited for the right guy, right up until the last egg dribbled slowly down through her fallopian tubes.

Her spirits rose once she got to Rockland. She had missed the last ferry of the day, but she didn't mind. After signing in at an oceanfront B&B, she wandered along Main Street, past the cluttered sporting goods store, the hairdresser, the tiny old pharmacy on the corner that survived, notwithstanding the huge Rite-Aid that had reared up behind it, the historical society, the museum, and the second-hand bookstore. The place had changed dramatically during her life from being a half deserted nineteenth-century fish cannery town into a crowded, almost frenetic Nantucket wanna-be. Even at this time of year in September, the shops and restaurants were crowded. She found a book about the intersection of religion and morality in the bookstore and then walked down to a restaurant by the shore. She ordered a glass of white wine and mussels before remembering that she would be literally knee deep in mussels once she reached the island.

Sitting on the upper deck of the ferry the next morning, she watched the Mainland, shaped like giant fingers reaching out into the ocean, slowly recede. Seagulls swooped for mackerels. They plowed by one of the Camden schooners with all her sails spread. In fact, there was no wind and the schooner was actually being pushed by a discrete motorized dory from behind. Sport pitied the tourists their brief four-hour glimpse of Penobscot Bay. She herself had never spent a stretch longer than eight weeks on the island. The coming year lay before her like a limitless treasure trove. She was almost glad for an instant that Talbot was over-employed on the other side of the World. It was sort of like keeping him in the deep freeze while she had this one last fling unless, of course, he fell in love there . . . . She cut off that line of thought and concentrated on how the wake behind the ferry spun silver ruffles on the water.

The Ledge Island harbor was choked with lobster boats, sloops, ketches, small outboards, one catamaran and two huge yachts. A monster sign attached to the boatyard warned incoming vessels of a hidden water pipe. As the ferry slid slowly into the dock, one of the ferrymen lowered the ramp. Sport waited in her car for her turn to drive up the ramp as trucks, loaded with building materials, plumbing supplies and food, rumbled off. She parked next to the ridiculously cute library – a weathered cape house in perfect condition restored by the summer residents. She walked past the more genuinely weathered grey and white clapboard buildings along the edge of the harbor to Barnett Elliott's market. The low-ceiling, dark-raftered room was fragrant with a hodgepodge aroma of fresh produce and breads. Wooden boards echoed under her jogging shoes. Barnett knew well how the summer people loved to hear those boards creaking. Sometimes she imagined Elliott digging out the space just below the floor in order to give the boards that antique springy feel. That floor was worth more than marble floors to Barnett's trade.

"Well theah', Sport, I hear tell you're plannin' on stoppin' with us all yeah." Barnett, uncrating celery, greeted her casually as if he'd seen her the day before instead of July 4th weekend two months ago.

"How are you, Mr. Elliott? Yes, this time I'm staying all winter."

"Not wu'th the trouble."

Sport shrugged. "Well," she said self-consciously aware of her effort not to sound like a spoiled rich kid, "I earned the money this summer to stay here a year and do some writing."

She immediately imagined Barnett suppressing the observation that if your parents loaned you the house and paid for the utilities, it didn't take a hell of a lot more to buy groceries at his store over the winter. Why did she have to feel guilty half the time she was on the Island? Certainly she had her own share of problems.

"Some folks as had the money, might prefer a trip t' Europe."

Sport laughed and didn't say, I had that my junior year abroad.

She began wandering up and down the narrow, crowded and not too clean aisles. Since Barnett apparently either disdained or cleverly avoided amenities like carts or even baskets, she placed her purchases – apples, bananas, lettuce, bread, dried beans, cereals, canned soups – on a free counter and walked into the refrigerated area for milk, butter, eggs and chicken.

"How you farin', Sport?" asked an elderly woman.

"Fair t' middlin'," Sport said before she could stop herself. She hadn't meant to ape the island speech that the older people still used, but it tended to pop out her first few days on the Island, a form of Tourette's syndrome she had to work to bring under control. Hurriedly she added, "I hope Mr. Kinnicutt is feeling better." Also stupid. Last she had heard, he had cancer.

"He wasn't feelin' good all summah."

"I'm sorry to hear it."

"The new doctah' don't hold out much hope."

Again, Sport was stuck for the appropriate response.

"I'm very sorry to hear that," she said, hearing how lame it sounded.

They parted after a few more awkwardly polite exchanges and Sport climbed the worn-out stairs to the upper floor in order to scavenger for a supply of soap, napkins and toilet paper. Kelsey Coombs, the deputy sheriff's wife, was buying penny candy for her three young children.

"Hi, Sport. Glad you're back."

"Hi, Kelsey, how's crime?"

"Aside from all the Budweiser cans and Marlboro cigarette packs all over the roads, things are quiet. Will Anne and Henry be coming up soon?" Kelsey was from "away" and had no Maine speech patterns.

"They'll come up for Columbus Day weekend."

"How about the rest of your gang?"

Sport counted on her fingers. "Dede is remaining in the City at the moment. Some of her paintings are being exhibited at a gallery. Whitney got a job – God knows how – with an investment firm. And Talbot's law firm has him cornered in Hong Kong for at least another year."

"You get lonely, you're welcome to stop any time. We can have a nice cup of tea. I'm not as good at baking as some, but I can fix a mess of donuts." Laughing, she added, "And I do mean mess."

It took a long time for Sport to pay for her small stock of groceries since there was no scanner at the checkout and two people ahead of her. After paying, Sport loaded the groceries in the Honda and went to consult the bulletin board on the outer wall of the market.

Kitten. Desperately needs home. Contact Cooper. 4155

The July 4th committee is seeking men who are full of vim and vigor and are willing to help make our traditional get-together even better next year. Contact Frank. 2008

Lost at the dump. Nine gallon air tank. Call Mary. 4916

Coffee Wednesday. Legion hall, nine to eleven. To help defray expenses to repair the walk behind the memorial foundation. If you are unable to attend, but still want to make a donation, send it to Shirley, Box 323.

Making a mental note to mail a donation to Shirley, Sport returned to her car and drove out of town. Many of the village houses she passed, although small and in need of repair, were fronted with gardens crammed with cone flowers, mums, asters and other late summer flowers that competed for space with children's bicycles, wood piles, rusted skeletal cars and wire-mesh lobster pots. As the village houses thinned out, the scenery alternated between opaque woods and glimpses of sparkling ocean. Hand-painted signs announced cottage industries such as knitwear, produce in season and engine repair. At the crest of a rise she turned off the engine and got out of the car so she could look back across meadows and hills to the harbor. From a distance, the village lost its warts and was transformed into an eighteenth-century watercolor. Her reverie was cut short by a passing Chevrolet and she lifted her hand in greeting – an island custom whether or not one knew the driver.

At the town grange, where meetings and sales were held, she left the main road and took the left fork toward Sheep's Head Point. By now she was driving a little too fast for these roads in her eagerness to get to the house.

She passed the town dump, barred with a chain and staked with a sign, "Dumping on Tuesday and Saturday only." It reminded her of the night that the five of them – Talbot, Dede, Whitney, Nevah and herself – had strung balloons and crepe paper across the entrance, removed the dump sign and replaced it, for the benefit of the newly arrived renters, with: JULY FOURTH PICNIC 4 P.M.

Nearing the narrow neck that lead to the western point of the island, at the point where you could see the ocean on both sides of the road, she saw the small cape house where Nevah Wright had once lived coming up on the left. It was where his parents, Edith and Johnny, still lived. Although inhabited, the house had an air of abandonment. Shabby and small, it was in need of paint and repairs. The front yard was littered with debris and wood. The windows were streaked, and what had been a white picket fence was now grey and missing large sections. It reminded Sport of some of the old-timers' teeth.

Although Sport had been to the house many times since the night nine years ago when five teenagers had gone scuba diving, the house had never lost its association for her of blinding lights, screaming sirens, cries of inconsolable heartbreak, a babble of accusing voices, the grim questions of Deputy Coombs.

Always do the thing you hate most to do first, her father had often told her. He called it "eating the frog." Well, this was a frog if ever there was one.

Her stomach muscles tightening, she parked the car on the side of the road, walked up to the front of the house and knocked on the door.

The woman in the doorway had never been pretty, but now, nine years after the accident, her head seemed overly large for her bony frame and her face had slowly dissolved from cheerfully competent into a blank mask. Her straggly grey hair looked uncombed and was held back by an incongruously bright red hair band. Sport was relieved to see that at least her dungarees and bright yellow tee shirt seemed clean. She was a brightly colored shell with the tenant gone.

She smiled vaguely at Sport, searching for a name to fit the physical presence in front of her.

Finally she had it. "Sport. Come in and set awhile."

Sport felt a wave of shame and embarrassment wash over her so that she could barely speak. "Hello, Edith. How've you been?"

Edith's face kept lighting and dimming like clouds on a gusty day, sliding across a blue sky. For one moment, so tenuous it was nearly invisible, an expression akin to revulsion seemed to cross her features. Sport wasn't certain if she imagined it or it was real. In any case, it was immediately replaced with what seemed to be genuine warmth.

"Tol'able well. I overdid and I'm kinda' wore out."

"Edith, please don't bother to clean our house while I'm there. I'm alone at the moment and I can easily – "

"I already did, best I could. Johnny turned on the watah' like Anne said."

It was odd how meticulous Edith was about the houses on the Point even as her own house fell into disrepair and ruin around her.

On a wooden rack beside the door were bent nails, each hung with keys, names taped beneath them. Handing Sport the Abbott keys, Edith said, "I heah' tell you'll be spendin' all wintah."

"Yes, that's right." She couldn't think of anything further to say. The clouds on Edith's face shifted again. Cheerfully, she said, "Then I expect we'll be seein' lots o' you when Eddie gets back. He's up t' Augustah visitin' with my mothuh'. Her as I stayed with when Eddie was born."

The keys slipped from Sport's fingers and clattered to the linoleum floor.

"Eddie? He's not in Augusta," she said stupidly. Was Edith getting worse? Was she slipping from being merely forgetful into insanity? Sport bent down to retrieve the keys and, as if to punish herself for her sin, she smacked her head hard on the edge of the front hall table. Her face was blood-colored and a pulse throbbed in her throat.

"Edith, Nevah, I mean Eddie is not in Augusta," she blurted and was immediately ashamed of herself for speaking. What was the harm of granting Edith illusory peace?

But Edith only smiled indulgently. "You kids is allus makin' up jokes."

Did she really believe Nevah was in Augusta visiting with Edith's mother? Or did poor Edith know that her son was irretrievably lost and was patching the knowledge over with torn bits of faded memories? In any case, it was obvious that Sport's presence was disturbing her and that Edith was anxious for her visitor to be gone.

"Thanks for the keys, and for opening the house. See you soon."

"Stop by any time."

"And, oh Edith, maybe Johnny can help me bring up some wood to the house whenever he gets a chance."

"You know he'd help nobody sooner'n you, Sport."

Behind the wheel again, Sport sat for several minutes without moving, inhaling slow deep breaths, as if to replace the sad, musty air of Edith's house with fresh Maine air. She glanced back to see if she was being watched, but Edith had melted back into the dusty labyrinths of the kitchen and her own mind. Johnny was nowhere to be seen. Probably working on one of the other houses.

About a quarter mile beyond the Wright house, Sport passed the small and discrete sign that read "private" on a weathered piece of wood. It was here that the public road ended and the private road began that led to the compound on the Point. The first white cottage she passed on her right belonged to Whitney Chapin's divorced mother, Heather. It stood starkly, as replicated in countless Maine water-colors, in an open field with the sea just beyond. In fact, it had been built right after Heather's divorce from Whitney's father but it had been carefully sited and designed by an architect who doubled as a landscape painter.

A short distance past, on the opposite side of the road and at the highest part of the point, was the deceptively simple-appearing conglomerate of buildings belonging to Talbot Harrington-Clark's family: a long rambling ten-bedroom white farmhouse, low-lying whitewashed barns to house the antique car collection and the plane that could take off and land on the field to the left of the house, and six-foot-high-fenced corrals for the llamas and other mildly exotic animals. About a quarter mile further down the road, on the right, on the edge of a cliff looking northwest over the ocean was the house inherited by Dede St. John when her mother died of leukemia and her father went to live in Italy with his second wife. The large glass windows on that northwest side provided beautiful views of Blue Hill as well as an endless source of leaks and aggravation for Johnny Wright.

After that the road descended slightly into a spruce-lined, tunnel-like woods saturated with the composted glacial detritus of ancient volcanoes. It was what was known as a climax forest, emanating from the distant northlands, and laced with saprophytes, mycelia, oyster fungi, toadstools, mushrooms, morels, ferns, mosses and lichens. Beneath it all, revealed only when the bulldozers clawed away at new foundations, were the granite chips, sand and clay reaching back to the Neolithic era.

The tunnel of trees opened into another field that sloped gently down the western side of the Point towards the water. In the middle of the field was the Chapins' weathered-looking barn. It too had been white but had weathered to streaky grey. It was tall and impressive from the outside but impractical inside with vaulted barn ceilings that made it difficult to heat in the winter.

From there, the road led down through more spruce trees to the Abbott house. The Abbott house stood amongst the spruces at the top of a steep hill that wasn't quite a cliff, overlooking the dock and the cove. The long dock, originally built by Talbot's great-grandfather in the early 1940s, hung suspended between stone pillars. The wood planking had been replaced a number of times but it was still supported by the original gigantic chunks of granite stacked unevenly on top of each other as if they had been piled up by a clumsy child giant. Even the wealthiest of Island families would have found it to be prohibitively expensive to build a dock of this type any more. Aside from a rowboat and a couple of dinghies, the cove held only the Abbott Boston Whaler and mock lobster boat. All other vessels belonging to the compound families had been taken to the small marina on the island or, in the case of the Harrington-Clarks' yacht, to Stonington.

This grey-shingled house was also fairly modern but since it was hidden among the trees, it had not offended the part- and full-time residents of the Island as the glass-sheathed St. John house had done.

The Abbott house was neither large nor imposing, but each time she arrived, Sport was overcome by the ability of this particular patch of ledges, spruce and sea to spin her into euphoria. She could not arrive without being struck by the beauty of her surroundings as well as memories of friendships that transcended kinships, a pampered childhood and adolescence, picnics on deserted islands, overnight sails to isolated harbors, parties and dances, and of course, Talbot.

Standing on the railed deck at the back of the house, she looked down at the tangle of spruce trees and decaying tree trunks that covered the steep drop to the dock and rocky beach. Unlike the land belonging to the Harrington-Clarks – cleared and carefully sculpted by Johnny Wright and his crew – the Abbott terrain had followed its own inclinations. The fibrillated light sieved through the oak leaves onto the pine needle floor of the forest. The ocean was only partially visible in tantalizing patches, which was the way Sport preferred her views. Too open a vista lacked the enigmatic beckoning appeal of one which could not be easily encompassed. All her life Sport had been drawn to the less accessible and more challenging, whether it was rock climbing, scuba diving . . . her mind faltered and paused over Nevah's accident . . . or Talbot she concluded ruefully.

A pine grosbeak, undulating its rosy wings, chee-cheed at Sport and landed on the railing. It triggered a memory of the sign that a fourteen-year-old Whitney had once painted in huge red lettering on a bed sheet and hung over the railing so that the message was invisible to those inside the house, but reasonably visible to passing vessels: ABBOTT WHOREHOUSE.

Inside, the dwelling was not a typical Maine cottage. It was open and airy. A lower-level living room spiked from the entrance hall to the left. Off the right from the entrance hall was a lower-level den. Kitchen, dining area, laundry and bathroom meandered in unlikely directions. A gracious and gently spiraling staircase led to a balcony opening onto five bedrooms and three baths. From there a trapdoor led to an attic. An olive and apricot Aztec rug dominated the two-story wall of the living room. From the lower-level living room, another short staircase led down to an all-purpose game room. There was no basement, only an attached shed, reached from the outdoors on the back side of the house.

It took Sport less than a half hour to unpack her clothes and to put away the groceries. She set up her computer and research materials in the downstairs bedroom.

Then she headed for the path which ran north along the top of the coastal bluff towards the neck of land that led to the Point. On either side were patches of witch hazel and sumac, junipers, cedars, balsams and hemlock. A haze diffused the sunlight, turning the water the color of pewter. Whitecaps ran before the offshore breeze, and between tree trunks, she caught sight of a ketch, close-hauled on a port tack, leaving a tusk of wake.

Suddenly she came upon the miniature herb garden that Sarah, her older half-sister – same father, different mothers – had planted years before and nurtured ever since. The small clearing evoked a childhood memory that did not resonate as happily as the others. Asked by her father, Henry Abbott, "Why in hell would you want to have all that penny royal and tansy and God-knows-what-else here in the middle of nowhere?" Sarah had replied, "Because I have to have *something* that belongs to no one but me."

Sarah. God, she had a lot of freight to carry around. A father she had had to share with his new family. A mother, Thora, enraged by the loss of her husband to a younger woman, and a Mainer at that. A kid sister to whom she was constantly compared unfavorably.

Sport spotted a few small, end-of-season raspberries and tasted them. Contemporary American life offered such gigantic helpings of all manners of food that it was oddly satisfying to experience a taste so delicious and yet so fleeting. She kept walking until she reached the point where she could see the eagle nest on a rock outcropping that jutted out over the water. No one appeared to be in residence.

A clonk on the path behind her yanked Sport out of her reveries.

About ten yards away, nearly hidden by alders, was a deer. It had dark-ringed eyes and short but spiky early fall antlers. As Sport whirled to face the animal the deer, unlike any normal deer that would have literally turned tail and dashed off, started walking straight towards her with his antlers lowered.

Sport sprinted for the nearest spruce tree. The abrupt movement spurred the animal and it made a dash for her. She caught hold of a knobby branch and scrambled up the ladder-like bars. She was experienced when it came to spruces.

Looking down from a height of about twelve feet, she watched as the deer's head swung back and forth, and the animal rubbed its antlers almost angrily against the bark. Then it lifted its forelegs and rested them against the trunk in order to get a better view of her. As scared as Sport had been a moment before, the idea of a dangerous deer suddenly struck Sport as silly, as a sort of mammalian oxymoron.

"I don't believe you," Sport scolded. She eased her weight to a more comfortable spot on her perch. Evidently the patient sort, the deer retreated several paces and waited. Clearly it had no other pressing engagements. Neither did Sport. However, it occurred to her that a disadvantage of the hermit life was that when the hermit went missing, no one came looking.

The minutes passed and Sport kept shifting positions as each one became increasingly uncomfortable. One of her moves caused a limb to creak dangerously, and hastily, she transferred to a stouter one. As she waited out the siege (surely it would get bored soon, wouldn't it?), she remembered the time Sarah had entangled a kite in a spruce tree and she, Sport, had climbed to retrieve it. How their father had gone on endlessly about Sarah's fear of heights.

"Is this some new kind of bird-watching?"

At first, Sport thought the deer had spoken. Nothing was impossible with this creature. But examining its saturnine features, she shook herself free of the hallucination and looked about. She spotted a man approaching through the trees. He was slim, dark-haired, and a little over medium height. As he came closer she guessed he was about thirty years old.

"Boy, am I glad to see you!" she called out.

The newcomer shifted his gaze from her to the deer, which now resembled a National Geographic model, peacefully posing for its portrait.

"Shoo," the man said, "Scat." He picked up a fallen branch and waved it.

The deer thought a moment and then, contemptuously, turned and disappeared into the woods.

"Now why didn't I think of that?" Embarrassed, Sport quickly descended from her perch, scratching her bare arms and ankles against the branches and trunk.

"You're Sport Abbott."

Sport brushed her hands on her jeans and took a closer look at her rescuer. "As they say in English novels, Sir, you have the advantage of me."

"Some of us make more lasting impressions than others. We met at a party last July 4." He held out his hand. "Steve Schwartz."

Accepting his hand, Sport asked, "Whose?"

"What? Oh, you mean whose party. Dudley Goff's."

Accepting his hand, Sport said, "Oh right," although she had no recollection of him from that weekend's lobster party on the beach. "Lucky you happened along."

"I didn't happen along. Barnett Elliott mentioned that you had arrived so I dropped by to say hello."

"Good thing too or I might have spent the night up there."

"Were you born with deer phobia or did you have a traumatic experience?"

"Hey, that was no picture-book Bambi. That must be a new arrival at the Harrington-Clark zoo."

"A private zoo?"

"Yes, for outwardly mild-looking but actually hardened-criminal animals." Without thinking about it much, she said, "I was out walking. Want to come along?"

"Sure," he said and started following her. Sport wasn't sure if the invitation was the reaction to a mere hour of solitude or just semi-automatic hospitality. She was actually a bit relieved to note how quickly she had left behind her New York City wariness of strangers.

They continued walking north along the path which led gradually downhill until they reached the beach. Sport removed her sneakers and waded in up to her ankles. "Do you come here often?"

"Apart from a couple of visits when I was a kid, no. I'm renting a house in the village."

"For how long?"

"A year."

"Just like me. I'm trying to write a doctoral thesis. What's your excuse?"

His orthodontically straightened teeth gleamed whitely. "I allowed a new-born baby to die. Intentionally."

She turned back to glance at him. Several beats went by. After a pause she said, "Are you a doctor?"

"I thought you said you remembered me."

"What was wrong with the baby?"

"You name it. For one thing its brain was damaged."

"Were you disbarred? Dismedicated?"

"No, in the end I was vindicated. But in between I was disinvited. From the medical group I had just joined. So I decided to take a year off and hang up a shingle on an island."

"And when the year is over?"

He lifted his shoulders and dropped them. "How about when *your* year is over?"

"Well, assuming, as is likely, that the authoritative final word on the biological roots of ethics is not a hotcake seller, I'll probably look for a job. One that doesn't require special training. You know, mother, wife, President."

They walked on for a few minutes.

"So," she continued her gentle inquisition, "How did you settle on this particular island out of all the other places in the World that could use a doctor, even a suspect one," and for the third time that day, immediately regretted her last words. She didn't know this man. He seemed to have some sense of irony but it was hardly appropriate for her to make a joke out what had clearly been a life-changing trauma for him.

It had taken Sport until graduate school, where she had shared an apartment with a brilliant but deeply serious Indian woman, to realize that her glib sarcasm was a luxury, a way of showing off the subtleties of English that an expensive education could buy without much regard for how her remarks affected others. The Indian woman had been baffled by Sport's sarcasm. She had no time and no use for such a circuitous means of communicating. She had to get an education and return to the slums of Bombay as soon as possible.

Steve shrugged. "Well, as I said, I came here a couple of times as a kid."

"Who did you stay with?"

"Stay with?"

"Yeah, I mean, there are no hotels or inns, so where did you stay?"

"I came here with my dad and we didn't know anyone so we didn't stay here. We just came over for a couple of hours to look around."

"Ah, day-trippers."

"Yeah, that was us. Maybe that was what appealed to me about this job. It was the only way I could figure out how to spend a few nights in this really quite beautiful place."

"Wow, that was the long way around if hanging out here for a few nights was your goal."

The path had sloped downwards and now they were standing on one of the small pebbly beaches that dotted the eastern side of the Point. The sky was hazing over into oyster color, the ocean developing a chop and the shore birds beginning to screech more piercingly.

"You've known Edith Wright a long time, haven't you?" He asked abruptly.

Startled at the change of subject, Sport kicked at a rock and took a moment before answering. "Of course, why do you ask?"

"I've been treating her for a . . . uh . . . minor ailment. She talks as if her son were still alive. And I know he died years ago – "

"Nine, to be exact."

" – and I was wondering if this is a recent development or if she's always been . . . uh . . . ."

"I don't know for sure but it's certainly been getting worse the last couple of years. She's been behaving, well, unnaturally, ever since Nevah died."

"Nevah?"

"Eddie. Nevah was his nickname because – oh never mind."

She hesitated. "I suppose people told you."

"Told me what?"

"That I killed Nevah. I and Talbot and Whitney and Dede, we killed Nevah."

"Aren't you being melodramatic? I did hear something about an accident."

"We're just a couple of murderers, you and I," she said and smiled without mirth, once again immediately regretting her sarcasm. However, he didn't seem to have heard her.

Some distance off, outlined against the sky, was a black and white guillemot, considering its next dive into the bountiful fish market below. Other anglers, long billed curlews, plovers, grebes, and Bonaparte gulls dived and cracked their mussel dinners against the rocks. Gently, it began to rain, the first drops spilling down

Sport's cheeks like tears. She put on her sneakers and they veered away from the beach onto one of the trails leading inland. At the top of the rise where they met the road, Sport asked, "Where did you leave your car?"

"In front of your house. Only it isn't a car. It's a bike. Not the motorized kind."

"Then you'd better come in until the rain stops."

"I'd love to, but I can't. Afternoon visiting hours. I'll take a – " he smiled, " – rain check."

"Any time. Wait, I'll lend you something to wear."

They went into the front hall and she chose one of her father's slickers off a hook. While her back was turned, he looked into the rooms on either side of the foyer as if he were rushing through a museum, trying to absorb information as quickly as possible.

"Thanks. It'll be my excuse for coming back."

"You don't need one."

As she watched him cycle off, she wondered why she was being so cordial. Was even a few hours of isolation already making her overly susceptible to new friendships?

But then, weren't most friendships the result of proximity? People learned to like their neighbors if it didn't come naturally. People became friends with those who had offices next to theirs because you could tell when they didn't have other lunch plans; that made it easier to invite them with less risk of rejection. Parents of children in the same class became friends because they found themselves standing shoulder to shoulder at soccer games, parents' night and PTA meetings. As the old rock song said, if you couldn't be with the one you loved, love the one you're with. She mentally shook herself. This was someone she had met only thirty minutes ago. She turned and walked back into the house.

Eight

Whitney called her at the end of her second week. She had been alone much of that time, trying to write, realizing that she should do more research before she could begin, and trying to figure out how she could get the research done. She had no broadband access from the island and it would have taken hundreds of hours to do the research through a phone line.

So instead, she had just started writing, leaving large gaps labeled "research needed" throughout.

She was staring out at the spruce trees and a large maple on the north side of the house, noticing how much earlier the leaves began to change in Maine than in Connecticut, when the phone rang.

"Hey, Sport, how's the hermit life?"

"Solitary."

"I think that's a substantial part of the job description. Hey, I have a three day weekend. How about a visit from your old pal?"

Sport was startled by how excited she was at the prospect. Whitney had always seemed like a kid brother to her even though he was two years older than she and only a year younger than Talbot. In fact, he seemed like Talbot's kid brother also. Whitney was always the one who started the horseplay, who dared the others to try jumping off a cliff or to drive the boat at maximum speed. Talbot was always trying to distract Whitney from pursuing his more dangerous exploits. There flashed through her memory the image of Whitney and Talbot the night that Nevah died, how Talbot had been the careful – even if not careful enough – instructor while Whitney had heckled Talbot about his detailed instructions.

Whitney broke into her thoughts.

"You there, Sport? Are you calculating the chances of me trying to seduce you? Or the chances that if you did, Talbot would garrote me to death?"

"Neither actually. But both possibilities sound promising."

"Nice. Ok, so how about I roar up to your door tomorrow evening around seven on my brand new Biposto Ducati Monster."

"Sounds like something out of a Stephen King novel. But now I get it. You're all dressed up with a big new toy and nowhere to go."

"Yeah, there's a little bit of that, but I also miss you kid. We've barely seen each other since last summer."

"Isn't it depressing that now we're grown up, we hardly get any time together on the island? How come our parents seem to spend their entire summers here?"

"Because they're rich and we're not. At least Talbot's parents are rich. And my father."

"How's your mom?"

"Heather? Permanently embittered about my father dumping her and moving to Arizona. She can't believe that she was left for an older woman. And one that wasn't even that rich. It's completely humiliating. She has nothing to blame it on but her own rotten personality."

"How about his rotten personality?"

"Well, that too of course. Also, the Arizona part is like salt in the wound."

"Huh?"

"Well, she thinks of Arizona as sort of tacky. To her it's like an old person's place, full of condos and golfers. She can't believe that she got left for an older woman to live in a crummy state like Arizona. So anyway, ok if I come for a visit? I'll tiptoe around whenever you have to write."

"Of course," she said, surprised again by her eager anticipation.

*   *   *

Whitney arrived about nine on Friday night. Sport had anticipated an even later arrival and had prepared a chicken Caesar salad that could be kept at room temperature. She set the table with placemats and cloth napkins, and took a bottle of red wine from her father's carefully assembled stock. She glanced at it, knowing nothing about wine, hoping it wasn't one of the more valuable ones.

There was no element of surprise about Whitney's actual arrival. She could hear the deep low throb of the motorcycle while it was still a quarter mile away and by the time he turned it off in front of her door, she had to resist putting her hands over her ears, so loud was the noise after her days of solitude among the spruces.

She ran out to greet him and was again surprised by how welcome his hug was. Well, Talbot had been gone for a long time now.

She and Whitney had a good time at dinner, Whitney making fun of his colleagues at the investment bank, but then waxing enthusiastically about the work itself. Whitney liked everything about money: making it, counting it, and spending it. He was thinking of becoming a commodities trader. He was good on his feet, both physically and mentally, and he needed something to absorb his reservoirs of energy.

The next afternoon, after Sport had put in a few token hours at her desk, Whitney took her for a ride on the motorcycle. Sport loved it. The romance of spending this year in quiet isolation was fading around the edges. She liked the feel of Whitney's strong torso under her hands. She reveled in the wind that whipped her hair back – neither of them wore helmets – and even in the stares they got as they raced through town, although she was ashamed of this narcissism. Not Whitney. He was in his glory, his only regret being that he had not had the bike last summer when the summer people were around to gape and cluck their tongues over the noise his bike made.

Whitney made the dinner Saturday night, boiling some lobsters. He served them with baked potatoes and with what he informed Sport was an even more expensive wine of her father's than the one she had so graciously provided the night before.

After dinner, they made a fire as the nights were beginning to be chilly. They sat side by side on the sofa watching the fire. It would have been a classic picture of romance except that Sport's attraction to Whitney had begun to wear off over the course of the last few hours. His excessive excitement about the new bike and his careless attitude about her father's wine had prompted a series of unfavorable comparisons with Talbot. Talbot would never have spent money on so ostentatious a toy. Talbot would have asked about the wine before choosing one. Talbot would have asked her many more questions about her writing and her plans than Whitney ever would. In fact, Whitney's visit had begun to change her desire for Talbot into a gnawing need. She ached for not only Talbot's body but his calm, kind presence and quick-witted commentary on what went on around him. Talbot was the only person in the world who had no ability to disgust her in any way. Although Talbot could be maddeningly distant, he could not be clumsy or unattractive in her eyes while even Whitney, as attractive as he was, had thick blunt fingers that were, to Sport's mind, a bit repulsive.

Whitney put his arm around her shoulders. "So Sport. What d'ya say to a little roll in the hay? Tal would never know. It would relax us both."

She wasn't sure if he was being serious but she decided to treat it as a joke.

"You? You big stud? You must have dozens of girls in the City. I'm flattered you have either the energy or desire."

"Ah Sport, you know you've always been the love of my life."

"Yeah, that's why when I was thirteen and Talbot was away and I was desperate for someone to take me to Dede's square dance, you invited Talbot's sister instead. Even though she was six years older than you."

"Yeah, I was into the older-woman thing at the time." Whitney said. He lapsed into uncharacteristic silence for a minute.

"You figure you'll end up marrying Tal?"

"In all honesty, Whit, and if you ever tell anyone else this, especially Tal, I'll have to kill you, but it's up to Tal."

"He's mad for you, Sport, you know that."

"Do I? I hope so. He seems awfully far away right now."

"Hence my invitation to climb into the sack with you."

The phone rang then. For an instant, Sport half expected it to be Talbot sensing an urgent need to defend her monogamous loyalty from the other side of the world. But it was Anne Abbott. She sounded irritable. Henry must be giving her a bad time about something Sport thought.

"Annie, how are you doing?" Her mother never called Sport anything but Annie, hating the nickname that Henry had given his younger daughter when she was seven and already beginning to show unusual athletic ability.

"Fine. Whitney's here."

"Yes, his mother told me he had gone up there on this new motorcycle."

"See, Whitney?" Sport said in a slightly louder tone, ensuring that her mother could hear, "We're being chaperoned. Now I certainly can't go to bed with you."

"Annie Abbott, stop that." Her mother also hated her daughter to make careless crude remarks. Her life's work since she had given birth to Sport, apart from trying to please her husband, had been to sculpt her daughter into the epitome of elegance and refinement. It was, everyone agreed when the topic arose, the inevitable result of Anne's need to reinvent her own unhappy, and apparently impoverished, upbringing by vicariously living her daughter's affluent childhood. Overhearing Whitney's mother make this observation at a cocktail party when she was eighteen, Sport had concluded that every woman in America felt fully qualified to opine on the most intimate psychological details of others' lives. It was the twenty-first-century equivalent of hanging over your backyard fence to discuss another woman's cooking or housecleaning with a neighbor.

"So," Sport went on, "you were calling to check up on us?"

"Hardly. No, it's just that I hadn't spoken to you all week and wanted to catch up."

Whitney took this opportunity to let his hand slide slightly down the front of Sport's shoulder towards her breast. Sport swatted at his hand and stood up with the portable phone.

"Annie," her mother was saying, "I worry about you up there."

Sport sighed. Her mother worried about her safety incessantly. Sport had spent her life being pushed and pulled between her father's urging to take risks, to be gutsy, to be bold and her mother's constant concern for Sport's safety. Some girls argued with their mothers over makeup and boyfriends. Anne had always encouraged Sport's attraction to Talbot but had engaged in long arguments about whether or not Sport could take diving lessons or play ice hockey.

As a child, when Sport had gotten her first pony, her father had encouraged Sport's riding instructor to set up jumps that were much too high for both rider and horse. Sport had charged at the jumps over and over, falling off over the pony's head each time the pony quite reasonably decided that the risk of jumping wasn't worth it. Meanwhile, her mother would be standing beside Henry, pleading with him to stop risking her only daughter's life and threatening to sell the pony the next time Henry went on a business trip. Once, Sport had even seen her start to weep with worry when Sport fell off for a third time in one lesson and the pony nearly stepped on her. Of course, her mother was too inhibited to plead in a voice that might be overheard by any of the other children's mothers or bystanders. And after the riding, skiing or rock climbing lessons were over, Anne could never seem to resist taking pleasure in the compliments she received from the other parents about her daughter's athletic prowess and courage.

"What could you be worried about?" Sport asked now. "I never get in a car, I cook my own food. This seems like an unlikely target for terrorists, at least off season. Where could I be safer?"

"I don't know. Does Johnny check up on you from time to time?"

"Yeah. He was here yesterday. Scared the hell out of me when he knocked. I hadn't seen or heard another human for three days."

"Why was he there?"

"To check up on me. You just said you wanted him to check up on me."

"I didn't say I *wanted* him to. I just asked if he had."

"Well he did. So do you feel better?"

Instead of answering, Anne started describing a difficult probate that was making Henry's life – and obviously Anne's as well – a living hell. Sport couldn't tell whether her mother was more angry about the person who was challenging the will Henry had prepared or Henry's typically explosive reaction to stress. She spoke in whispers that suggested Henry's proximity. This made it difficult for Sport to follow the thread of the story although she listened patiently until Anne brought a rather sudden close to the conversation. Henry must have approached.

Glancing over her shoulder, Sport was gratified to see that Whitney had fallen asleep during the telephone call. As annoying as Whitney could be, she didn't want to hurt his feelings and besides, except for two brief and unfulfilling experiments in college, she had remained faithful to Talbot since he had taken her virginity five years ago.

Sport tiptoed upstairs. She awoke early enough the next morning to find Whitney still sprawled on the sofa, his arms thrown out at his sides and one leg dangling off the edge. She noticed that he was snoring gently. She didn't remember that from their childhood camping trips. She doubted that Whitney would grow old gracefully; that is, if he survived long enough to grow old at all.

Whitney had a big breakfast of eggs, toast and cereal but seemed restless and eager to leave after that. Sport politely gave him the excuse to go by pretending to be eager to get back to her work and he left before lunch.

He stopped for some food and a beer in New Hampshire and was in northern Connecticut by early evening.

He cruised along a secondary road in fifth gear, admiring the shocks which absorbed the rough road surface, the bucket seat that supported his rump like a cradle, and the way that the bike swooped through the curves in the road like an Olympic bobsled.

He passed no one: no joggers, no cars, but that wasn't unusual. His mother lived just at the outer edge of the commuter ring, where the houses were spaced far apart on five-acre lots. Heather had gotten her husband's house in the divorce and the expensive homes were occupied mostly by older couples. The husbands might still commute to the City but their children had grown up and left for college or work. Now, at least during the week when the mothers were at the club, playing bridge or volunteering at churches, it sometimes seemed as if the only inhabitants of the neighborhood were the Latin American landscapers and caretakers. They did a reverse commute in their trucks from places that Whitney could not quite imagine to these hilly wooded suburbs, three or four of them crowded together in the front seat sometimes. Their tools of the trade – rakes and shovels, lawn mowers and grass trimmers – would stick up behind in the truck bed like weaponry on a tank being driven into battle against weeds, overgrown plants and vegetative disorder. It was surprising how uniform their trucks and tools were. Almost as uniform as the dark-suited men who swarmed with their briefcases and newspapers onto the commuter trains each morning to travel in the opposite direction.

A fresh wind arose, stirring the asters and goldenrod along the side of the road, and he breathed deeply, inhaling the fragrance of freshly mowed fields and lawns. It wasn't until the sky suddenly darkened to purple-dappled grey that his exhilaration dampened and for some reason he thought of Nevah.

In particular, he remembered a rainy evening in Maine, a few weeks before

Nevah's accident. The five of them had been huddled around the fireplace in Sport's house. Their parents, except for Nevah's of course, had been at a clambake on the other side of the island.

Nevah had told them a "ghost" story. A true one, he'd sworn. He'd been sledding alone one winter day on the island when, along about dusk, he had headed home. Dragging his sled along on the fresh, unmarked snow, he had caught sight of a woman darkly outlined against the white background.

"She had on this dress, long, down to her ankles, and a funny hat that tied under her chin, and a furry thing covering her hands." He had approached the strange figure, features hidden by the bonnet, and had been about twenty yards short of her when she disappeared.

"Come on, Nevah," Sport had protested.

"I knew you wouldn't believe me."

"She was probably hiding behind a tree . . . ," Talbot had suggested.

"There were no trees near her. Besides . . . ." Here Nevah paused dramatically, but before he could deliver his punch line, Whitney did it for him. "There were no footsteps in the snow."

"I believe you, Nevah," Dede had said. "Besides, how would *you* know about that 'furry thing' on her hands? I mean how would you know about fur muffs?"

"He could've seen them in a million movies," Whitney scoffed.

"I saw a ghost once too," Dede had said. "Or, I mean I heard him. I was –"

"How do you know the ghost was a him if you didn't see it?" interrupted Whitney.

"I was all alone in the house. Maybe it was a she. I don't know. Anyway, you know that funny little staircase to the attic from my bedroom? I never liked it. I was lying in bed and all of a sudden I heard footsteps on the stairs."

They waited. Nothing. Finally Whitney had prompted, "Well?"

"Well what?"

"What happened?"

"Nothing. You don't think I got out of bed and investigated, for God's sake."

"What a fascinating story, Dede," Whitney said. "I see it as a two-hour feature movie. Gwyneth Paltrow as the young Dede St. John, waking up and hearing the ghost. Then going back to sleep. Maybe having, oh, Cheerios for breakfast in the morning. It will be a sort of short movie. Ten or fifteen minutes perhaps."

"Stop being an asshole, Whit. There is no way to that attic except through my bedroom and I didn't see anybody."

"Maybe it was a mouse or a squirrel," Talbot had said, still trying to find excuses to protect the story-tellers from their skeptical audience.

"They were human footsteps."

"How could a ghost have human footsteps?" Sport had asked.

Whitney had ended it. "What a stupid conversation."

Now, years afterwards, racing along the deserted, darkening road, Whitney recalled every detail of that evening: the five of them sprawled on the rug in Sport's living room, eating popcorn and drinking Mountain Dew; the curtainless windows blackly opaque against the night; short jumping orange flames in the fireplace.

Abruptly, Whitney shuddered. It wasn't the memory of the ghost story. Nor the chilly, oncoming dusk. It was the fact that two of the five who had been gathered that evening were no longer as they once had been.

He was heading up a steep hill when he heard the approaching motor. As the vehicle crested the rise, Whitney was momentarily blinded by headlights. For a second the car appeared to be suspended, like a frozen motion-picture frame.

Whitney veered as far to the right as he could. And then the inconceivable happened. The car shot across the road straight at him. Whitney, screaming, flew over the handlebars and landed on his head. The car roared off.

Eleven minutes later, a passing motorist was appalled by the sight of an overturned motorcycle and a body sprawled several yards away from it. She had read stories about pseudo-accidents and good Samaritans who stopped and were robbed and murdered. She could tell nothing about the inert figure except that it was male and dressed in chinos, sweater and sneakers. Two helmets were buckled to the back of the seat.

With her motor still running in case she had to make a quick getaway, the motorist dialed 911 on her cell phone and waited for the first sound of a siren.

Nine

Sport looked down at the two dozen mussels she had just emptied from her hod into the sink without registering the clatter they made as they fell.

"How did . . . where? When did it happen?"

Her mother's voice was flat and expressionless. "He was on his way back from Maine. On his motorcycle. He didn't see the car and I suppose the driver didn't see him."

"Who? What driver? Was he drunk?"

"Nobody knows anything about the driver. It was hit-and-run. Actually, the driver barely grazed him. It was the fall that did the damage. And even the fall wouldn't have been that bad except he wasn't wearing a helmet."

"Hit-and-run," Sport repeated mindlessly. What did it mean? She saw a teenaged boy lying on a dock and a frantic voice saying, "One one thousand, two one thousand, three one thousand." Then a small sturdy figure doubled over a windsurfer as a swerving motor boat toppled her into the water. And now a motorcycle driven off the side of the road into a ditch, the rider somersaulting through the air.

The images faded as if the slide projector had been turned off. Or as if it were waiting for the next frame.

And who would that be?

"Mom, I'll be on the next ferry."

"No!" Anne's voice was sharp. "It's a waste of time. Whitney's refusing to see anyone except his mother. I'm heading for the hospital right now. Not to see Whitney but to do something for Heather."

"Will he . . . are they sure . . . ?"

"Doctors aren't that blunt. They're vague at the moment. But the damage was extensive."

Outside the window Sport saw a squirrel running along the sill as if trying to get inside. The dew soaked grass was covered with filmy webs and the lawn looked as if it were covered with miniature trampolines. The Labrador Current curling down from the Arctic, and the Gulf Stream lapping away from the southern beaches, were clashing together to produce yet another grizzled Maine fog.

" . . . landed on the base of his skull and injured the occipital lobes of the brain which apparently causes visual blindness . . . ."

"What other kinds are there, mom?"

"What?"

"What kinds of blindness are there except for visual?"

Pause. Then Anne Abbott continued. "I'm not sure when we'll be up. What with Heather . . . ."

"It's ok, mom. You don't have to apologize for not coming up right away."

Her mother was silent. There was not even the proverbial humming on the wire.

"You know," said Sport musingly, without thinking. "I was riding the bike with him on Saturday. It was so much fun."

Her mother interrupted her.

"You were *what*?"

"Riding the bike with Whitney. Around here," she added as if to clarify that she hadn't been with him during the accident. She belatedly realized her mistake in telling this to her mother.

"How could you be so stupid, Annie? How could you be so irresponsibly stupid?"

"People ride motorcycles all the time. It's not like hang gliding."

She recalled the motorcycle ride, the way her hair had whipped madly about her head, and made a fervent wish that no one would tell her mother about their bareheaded drive through the center of town.

"Annie, this has got to stop. You are an adult now. You have to stop taking the sort of stupid risks that teenagers take."

"Dede and Whitney weren't taking unusual risks when they had their accidents."

"Don't be an idiot. Whitney wasn't even wearing a helmet."

Her mother lapsed into silence on the other end of the line.

"Thank you . . . I mean I'm glad you told me, mom."

They exchanged curt good-byes and then hung up.

As the fog swirled closer, the sea disappeared from view first, then the spruce-covered hill and finally even the deck railing. From far off came the muffled clanging of a bell buoy and the seemingly perpetual honking of the two fog horns, one to the south of the island and the other to the north. She knew that as the foggy days went on, she would no longer even notice the sound of the bell or the fog horns.

They would blend into her surroundings the way that traffic noise did when you lived in a city but right now, it grated on her nerves. The air was saturated with the scent of salt and seaweed. She had a fire going and the heat was turned up to seventy but still, the room felt damp and chilled.

Sport shut her eyes and waited, testing what Whitney's world would be like from now on. She inhaled deeply, still standing at the sink, and opened her eyes to watch her tears splashing into the sink. Finally, she began scraping the barnacles off the mussels with a small stone.

Her thoughts moved to Dede. Sport had been at college in Chicago after the accident. Dede hadn't wanted to see anyone the first year. Sport had barely seen her until the end of the summer after the accident when Dede made her first trip to Maine. Dede had arrived in a van driven by her father. The van had been customized to accommodate her wheelchair. Sport made a point of being there to greet her, waiting while the chair was unloaded, trying not to be distracted by the interesting aspects of how one lived with lifeless legs, how the chair was reassembled, how Dede was moved into it. Trying not to think about how Dede managed in the bathroom or whether she could have sex, or where the paralysis began.

She spent the entire first day with Dede, the two of them lying in lounge chairs on the lawn behind Dede's house overlooking the ocean. Dede had lain nearly prone. She explained how exhausting it still was to sit upright in the wheelchair for extended periods of time. Almost without thinking, Sport lowered the back of her own chair so that she came to rest at the same angle as Dede. In this attitude one saw more sky than ocean. It felt a little odd, as if one were watching a TV screen with an improper vertical adjustment.

They began by discussing Dede's artistic life.

About six months earlier, Dede had had someone make an easel that could be used from a prone position. She had started by painting collages, strange bits of people and flowers and automobile engines, as if she couldn't stand to think of her own life or that of anyone else's as a whole. Instead, everything she painted was in pieces and broken. After a few months, she had tired of watching the paintings pile up, unsold, in the corners of her apartment and started to paint portraits, using a mirror to see her model while she lay prone.

She was good at portraiture. She could produce a resemblance that was only just slightly better-looking than the original. And the portraits had begun to sell. She didn't make much money at it but if she could keep it going, that income added to a modest amount of trust income, would make her financially independent.

As lunchtime approached, Sport went into Dede's house and made a big salad and iced tea for them both. After lunch she wheeled Dede up a recently built ramp into the house and Dede went to the bathroom. Sport was grateful that she didn't need any help.

The afternoon wore on. They sipped white wine and maybe because of the wine and the warm sun, they began to talk about the harsher realities of Dede's life.

Dede described the crushing depression she had experienced during the first few months after the accident. She had been in almost constant pain as well as being incontinent. After a few months she had, through surgery and therapy, regained control over her bladder and bowels. Her doctors had arrived at a drug therapy to manage the pain.

"I don't want to sound like a Pollyanna about this but really, I'm luckier than most paraplegics. Actually, the most PC way to refer to me is as someone *with* paraparesis, not a paraplegic. I can move my arms, I even have a bit of sensation in my lower body." She paused and closed her eyes. "Aw shit, I'm a gimp any way you look at it."

She sounded so glum that Sport suddenly laughed out of nervous tension and for some reason, this made Dede laugh and open her eyes.

"You're right. It's kind of funny. You know, it can even be kind of cool in a way. One night last winter my father took me to the skating rink in Central Park. It was just about to close but I had this crazy desire to try the ice and my father let me do it. So there I was, sliding around on the ice in my chair. It was nuts but it was really fun. That was the first time I had laughed since the accident."

It was now five years since that afternoon with Dede. And now it would be Whitney's turn to start his life over again. Whitney had always been energy and motion incarnate. He had thrived on scaring himself with sports, driving and drinking. Well, it'd be a lot easier to scare himself now. She choked, trying to suppress a sob. If she began crying, it would be hard to stop. She was trying to hold off until she got in bed. What if he could never see again? Could someone learn Braille in their twenties? She recalled how his strong body had enfolded her in a hug only the day before. Oh God, she thought as despair washed over her, what had become of his handsome laughing face?

The sound of footsteps on the steps at the front door made her freeze into place, squeezed between the shock of Whitney's news and fear of the unknown. Dropping the mussel and stone into the sink, she went out into the hall.

"Who's there?"

Nothing. No sound. No figure in the glass panel beside the door.

She decided she had imagined it. A hallucination brought on by her mother's news. She thought back to Nevah's and Dede's ghost stories. What had been so scary about an image of a lady standing in the snow or the sound of footsteps on stairs? Where was the terror in that compared to the terror of being suddenly blind or unable to walk? She wondered if her fear were temporary or if she would, from now on, always be fearful, looking over her shoulder, jumping at any odd noise, feeling the adrenaline rush through her brain at every unusual sound or sight. A sob escaped her and she slowly collapsed onto the floor weeping.

Ten

While Johnny Wright sawed, Sport steadied the logs for him and then, once the logs were cut, stacked the freshly cut sections in neat piles inside the shed. Helping Johnny saw wood was not some new effort at appeasing guilt. She had often helped Johnny stack wood when Nevah was still alive. Nevah wasn't lazy but he didn't like helping his father. He preferred to do odd jobs for the summer people on the reasonable premise that it paid better – much better. Work on the island during three seasons of the year paid minimum wage, but a kid could earn twice that, and sometimes three times as much, weeding or mowing lawns in the summer. Sport recalled Nevah telling her how bizarrely fussy the summer people were about the quality of their yard work. They expected you to lower the blade on the mower at certain points in the lawn so that the height of the grass would be as exactly the same as was possible all across the lawn. When he weeded their gardens, they went nuts if he overlooked weeds among the squash plants or in their pathetically tiny patches of sweet corn. As if it mattered to the squash plants or sweet corn. These gardens were not planted for nutritional purposes. They were planted to create ambience. They were more like art than agriculture. There was a woman who had had him sweep out her basement every week and a man who had paid Nevah to artistically arrange and rearrange large pieces of driftwood in his back yard. There was even a woman who had paid Nevah to scrub the trunks of her birch trees with Comet to make them whiter and brighter. Nevah didn't mind. In fact, Nevah had never seemed particularly riled about anything, now that she thought back. Hell, he'd said, they were paying by the hour. If they wanted him to rip out every dandelion in their lawns with his teeth, no problem, he'd do it. He'd managed to buy a nearly new Ford truck on the proceeds of two summers of work.

Sport tried to pace herself as she worked with Johnny. She tended to work too fast, to expend her energy too quickly. She had started out this morning practically sprinting back and forth between the newly cut logs and the wood shed until she had to slow down. Maybe this *was* a way of appeasing guilt. Not a very good one, this lugging around firewood some of which would, after all, end up in her own fireplace. Not a great swap for a dead son.

With Johnny's attention focused on the chain saw, she was able to study his handsome profile and wonder, not for the first time, how he had managed to get himself tied up with someone like Edith. Even when she'd been young, Edith had never been pretty. And now, there was no trace of lost beauty on that haggard, plain face and sagging bony body.

Hey, Sport scolded herself, love wasn't based on physical attributes one hundred percent of the time, although it was astounding enough how often it was. Edith, before the tragedy, had always been a kind, capable, loving woman. In every practical area – cooking, baking, gardening, sewing, knitting, and so forth – Edith was far more capable than Sport.

Sport remembered watching Edith bake a pie one day, a few months before Nevah's death. She recalled how carefully Edith had laid out the ingredients on the counter before she started. The last ingredient she pulled out of what she called her "baking cabinet" had been Crisco. But the Crisco was in an unfamiliar container. When Sport asked about it, Edith had said that Smuckers had changed the formula for Crisco and that the new Crisco simply didn't make the same quality of flaky crust.

"So how do you find the old Crisco?" Sport asked, trying not to look out the window towards the cove where Whitney and Talbot were water-skiing. She had promised to help Edith bake this pie, a pie for Anne Abbott's birthday, weeks ago.

"Oh, I just take the ferry over to Rockland, then drive ovah' to this little country sto' where you can still git the old good Crisco."

Sport thought of her father, who billed his time at the office in six minute increments. He would lay out his clothes, razor, shaving cream, toothbrush, toothpaste, deodorant, and cuff links each night before he went to bed so that he could spring up at 6:00 a.m. and be out the door by 6:30 to drive to the train station. That took twelve minutes, including parking. He'd catch the 6:42 and spend every minute of the seventy-minute ride reading the *New York Times*, the *Wall Street Journal* and as much office mail as he could. Finally, he'd nearly race-walk from Grand Central to his midtown office to be at his office by 8:03. Why did one person select his deodorant, as her father did, on the basis of how fast it slid around his armpit, while another person thought nothing of spending an hour in the car to find the best grade of

Crisco for making pie crust? And then Sport thought about her own frenetic pace. Even as a kid, she had been frantic to complete the most homework, to do the most sports, to play two instruments, to do more of everything than any of her peers.

Ironically, it had been her father who would tell her to slow down. "Life isn't a race, Sport. Take it easy." That's what he said. But then if Sport decided to go see a movie, he'd be all over her.

"What are you doing, wasting your life that way? No one ever lay on his death-bed and regretted watching too few movies you know. 'You'll regret the things you don't do far more than you'll ever regret the things you did.' Do you know who said that?"

This was her cue to quickly name the author of whatever little aphorism he was quizzing her on. It helped to appease her father when he got into one of those moods.

Her thoughts drifted back to Johnny as she watched him cutting the ten-foot logs into three different lengths of logs: one length for the kitchen woodstoves that her family and Dede's had, another length for the bedroom fireplaces at Talbot's house, and then the third, largest length for their living room fireplaces. He was just as precise as Edith. He would lay one end of the log on a small sawhorse. Then, while she held the end that lay on the ground, he would take up his chain saw, and after carefully measuring out the correct length, saw a clean straight line through the wood. Her father and she were slapdash in the way they went about life. As hard as she worked, Sport made careless errors all the time in her homework, on her tests, when she was playing tennis. Haste makes waste, her father would say as he went peeling out of the driveway to the golf course, not infrequently incurring fender-benders on the way. Sometimes Sport wondered about all the things she and her father had failed to notice as they raced through life.

At this time of year, the trees had been denuded of their orange, yellow and red raiment and were now hoary ghosts holding their skeletal arms up to the sky. The last of the summer people, like the birds, had flown south and Sport was well along in her year alone, or at least alone with those others on the island who didn't have a choice about it.

She felt a mixture of fear and excitement about the coming winter. How would she do? Would she come up to the mark? Would she cut and run in November when the Island became a bleak, cold plain in the middle of an even bleaker and colder ocean, instead of a Shangri-La of sparkling water, blue skies and cool breezes? She liked to think of herself as hardy, resourceful but as measured against what? Yes, she was amazed by city friends who couldn't even drive, who had never shoveled a walk, jumped a dead battery, or fixed a broken toilet. But that didn't exactly make her an Eagle Scout. What if the water froze this winter? Would she take the next ferry to the nearest motel on the Mainland? She felt unduly virtuous about this wood business, as if by spending a few hours walking across Johnny's lawn with armfuls of small logs, she was preparing herself for life on the Maine frontier.

"Johnny, do you still hold it against us?"

If the question startled anyone, it startled Sport. Although the thought would often resonate in her mind at odd moments, she had never before given voice to it so baldly. As often happened, she wished she could suck the words back into her throat, leaving them unsaid.

Johnny continued sawing and, with a sense of relief, she decided that he hadn't heard her. The woods quivered with the roar of the chain saw, scaring off squirrels, chipmunks, deer and other wildlife. But wherever they went on the Point, they would still hear the saw. They too had limited options.

Johnny suddenly released the trigger on the saw and the sudden silence was startling. "Why did you kids call him Nevah?"

Johnny's question disturbed Sport almost as much as her own had. "Oh. You know. Kids like nicknames. Like Sport."

"It wasn't kids gave you the name Sport. It was your father. Besides, I don't recall nicknames for Whitney or Talbot."

"It was a dumb joke. With a last name like Wright it sounded funny."

Johnny's voice was expressionless. "It was fitting. He wasn't dumb, though give him two choices, like as not, he'd pick the wrong one." He went back to sawing, and as the logs dropped off onto the ground, Sport retrieved them.

"Do you still hold it against us, Johnny?" she repeated.

"Why should I?" was Johnny's unsatisfactory answer.

As often happened when nervous, Sport began to chatter on. "We never meant to harm him. You know that, don't you, Johnny? And it wasn't as if we were pushing him. He always looked, well, kind of wistful when we went scuba diving. And we thought it would make a dandy – " Sport winced at her use of the word "dandy" before continuing. " – if we gave him the equipment for a birthday present. And you should've seen the way Talbot gave him the most detailed instructions." No harm in putting in a good word for Talbot.

But *had* there been an impure motive behind the birthday present? Smug noblesse oblige on the part of the summer kids towards their less fortunate island friend?

"And we all stuck together." But had they stuck together more closely, Nevah wouldn't have wandered into the cave. "You see he miscalculated the size of his tank. That's how he got himself wedged in between the rocks. We did everything we could – "

"That's enough wood for now." Johnny straightened and looked up at a crow cawing overhead. He rubbed the small of his back with his free hand.

"I know I shouldn't bring it up after all this time, but of course I just can't forget."

The expression on Johnny's face – muscles tight, eyes looking away from her – finally brought her to a stop. He clearly did not intend to hand out cheap absolutions in return for blurted out confessions. Johnny had always had this effect on her. He was one of the few people who were completely immune to her efforts to charm. So of course, that made it all the important to her to keep trying, to get him to recognize her as an individual, even if not a likeable one, and not just as one of the rich kids on the Point.

"Yes, that's enough," he said with a clear tone of finality, "Thanks for the help."

He stood in the front yard as Sport started walking back to her house. When she looked back to wave, the light filtering through the bare branches of the maples and oaks made him seem oddly insubstantial, as if he had become a part of the woods.

Back inside the house, Sport changed from jeans, sweatshirt and an old army jacket of her father's into clean corduroys, turtleneck and sweater. Then, attaching the wire basket to the rear of her bicycle, she began pedaling to town. Nevah wafted out of her mind as she maneuvered the rutted road that led to the main road. The grass had rusted to a greyish brown and a northeast breeze ruffled the dead goldenrod.

She was out of breath when she cruised down the last hill facing the harbor and came to a stop outside the small white post office. Her post box held four Christmas catalogs – prompting her to wonder how marketers knew she would be here for Christmas – a telephone bill, the island newspaper, and a letter suggesting that she had already won six million dollars but would need to buy a magazine subscription to seal the deal. Last was a picture postcard from a boarding school friend with Bonnard's *After the Shower* on the front and neat rounded script on the back that was the hallmark of female prep school alum. She dropped the mail into her wire basket, went to the library, chose Gunter Grass' *The Tin Drum* because someone at a cocktail party last summer had seemed appalled that she had never read it, and headed to Barnett Elliott's store.

She was reaching for a can of V-8 juice when she became aware of a voice from the narrow, musty aisle just one over from her own.

"I hear tell the doctah's ovah' t' her house 'bout once a week. I got a hankerin' for clams t' night."

"I won't help you dig the clams but kin I join you for suppah'?"

Laughter.

"I wondah' what Talbot'll have t' say when he gets back from that place he's at in Asia."

Sport wasn't sure if it was fear of being discovered or curiosity which kept her immobile.

"Funny thing how Whitney lost the use of his eyes and Dede the use of her legs aftah' little Eddie's accident."

"I can't believe you're hintin' somebody's aftah' them. Those kids were scarce sixteen. They meant no harm."

"You kin come t' suppah', clams or no clams. There's Edith sent clear outta' her head. Losin' an only child 'specially aftah' waitin' so long. Some might think it's fittin' them as is responsible for it."

"I wouldn't want for anythin' t' happen t' Sport nor Talbot neithah'."

"They nevah' had hardships. Actin' so careless and payin' no attention t' consequences."

"I can't help sorrowin' for Dede and Whitney."

"I hope you won't be sorrowin' for the othah' two one o' these days."

"I can't see Edith nor Johnny – "

"I haven't a word o' accusation for anybody, but them two aren't outa' the woods yet."

"'Twould distress me considerable if somethin' happened t' Sport. How she recalls her mothah' at that age."

Sport began to walk silently towards the stairs to the upper reaches of the store, but just as she started up, two elderly women emerged from the aisle. They stopped in consternation as they faced the topic of their conversation. Not knowing what else to do, Sport smiled, greeted them and hurried upstairs.

Eleven

Steve Schwartz was clearly incredulous. "You think *what*?" He swallowed, rather hastily, a mussel and touched his lips with one of Anne Abbott's embroidered linen napkins.

"Hey, Doc, it's not that unbelievable. Someone could be out to get us. Talbot, Dede, Whitney and me."

"And your theory is that even the deer was part of the plot? How could the – uh – perpetrator count on you and the deer meeting?"

"We were bound to meet sooner or later."

"Suppose this extraordinary deer met with someone else?"

"You know anyone else who walks these woods at this time of year?"

"Did you ever ask Johnny Wright how that deer got loose?"

"He said that Edith spread hay that day and forgot to latch the gate."

"If you really feel at risk," Steve said, "then you shouldn't stay here all alone."

"It won't matter where I stay. True, Dede was run down here, but Whitney had his 'accident' in Connecticut. If I'm fated to meet my Samara or Waterloo or psychotic deer, it could happen anywhere."

"You don't seriously think Edith could get herself to Connecticut to attack Whitney?"

"No, but Johnny could. He knows how to fly."

She wasn't sure she believed this herself and she wouldn't have suggested it if she hadn't been lonely, if her work had been going better, or if she weren't so bored during the day. It was belatedly beginning to dawn on her that she might not be the hermit type and that this year might not live up to the alluring image of herself as a young scholar and writer, alone in the woods, writing brilliant prose about the biological roots of morality and ethics through a long Maine winter.

"You can't believe it was Johnny?"

"Who has a better motive?"

"But what would make him go off the deep end that way?"

Perhaps it was this last bit of Sport's train of thought that prompted her to respond in an academic manner.

"Well, actually, at the moment, I'm somewhat of an expert on that. Most people, whether or not they believe in God, behave in a manner that we call moral. There is a version of the Golden Rule in almost every culture. This type of cooperation and 'doing unto others' is a product of evolution. Without it, the species wouldn't have survived. Think about the Cold War. Maybe we didn't blow up the Russians, or vice versa, simply because at some level everyone in power had the genetic wisdom to realize that it would lead to mutually assured destruction."

"Then how do you end up with a Hitler?"

She shrugged. "Most humans behave pretty well most of the time because, at some partially subconscious level, we understand it's essential for survival. On the other hand, being the first man to shoot down the mastodon or the woman who gets to mate with – and be protected by – the most testosterone-laden male also helps ensure survival. Individual survival."

"And how does this explain Johnny?"

"Well, at some level, protecting his young – Nevah – is a very basic drive that might, in an illogical way, prompt him to go after his killers."

"Revenge is a result of the survival instinct?"

"It's not logical but the competitive instinct in us could make some of us feel, at least sometimes, as if revenge *is* essential to our survival."

"Not just plain old insanity?"

"Well, that's how we legally characterize the illogical part of it."

"Very interesting, Dr. Abbott."

"Not 'Doctor' yet. Now how the hell am I going to prove something like that?"

Steve shrugged. "Well, for starters, find out who ran over Dede and Whitney."

Sport smiled, but just slightly.

Silently they dipped toasted bread into the wine and garlic sauce in which the mussels had been cooked and tossed empty shells into a bowl. It was late November and this was the third time Sport had invited Steve over for dinner. It had taken a while for her to work up the nerve to call and ask him. It was mortifying to think that he might suspect her of flirting. This had made their first dinner even more awkward as she brought up Talbot's name in unnatural contexts in order to forestall any such suggestion. Steve had responded by asking her to dinner at a small pizzeria in town, the only restaurant that remained open during the winter. That had gone better. He had told her about growing up in the New Jersey suburbs; medical school in Rochester, New York; his dream, now crushed, of getting a job at Mt. Sinai in New York City. He certainly didn't plan to stay on the island indefinitely but had no idea what he would do next.

Steve interrupted her thoughts.

"Did you try to check up on Johnny's movements the day Whitney was hurt?"

"I have no idea where Johnny Wright might be at any time of the day or night."

"The ferry guy, Ross, he might remember the day Johnny was on the ferry. Since Johnny probably doesn't go over to the Mainland that often."

"What makes you think Johnny would take the ferry? He could take his own boat over to the Mainland. I would have noticed if he'd used the Harrington-Clark plane but he could have rented a plane from a pal over at Owl's Head . . . ."

"Wouldn't the guys at the airport remember something like that?"

"I doubt it. And besides, I'm no Nancy Drew."

"Who's Nancy Drew?"

Her eyes widened in mock amazement. "Next you'll be asking me who Amelia Hozenphefer is."

"Ok. Who's Amelia Hozenphefer?"

"I've no idea."

Laughing, he said, "Well then, for safety sake you'd better move in with me."

The smile disappeared from Sport's face. Thoughtlessly, or at least with no conscious premeditation she said, "Talbot will be coming home for some R&R soon. Then he has to go back to finish out his sentence there." When she realized how she'd linked Steve's joke to Talbot's return, she felt her face grow hot. Steve realized it too. Pretending he hadn't, he said, "I thought you told me you can't cook. The mussels were delicious."

"Wait'll you taste my blueberry sauce. Made it myself from island blueberries."

She rose to clear the mussel and salad dishes and returned with a bowl of blueberries in a crystal bowl, individual crystal dessert cups, and vanilla ice cream in a cardboard container.

"You take this living-off-the-island stuff pretty seriously, don't you?" he said.

"You bet. Nothing that I can't pick, fish, hunt or grow touches this here kitchen."

"Sure. You served bourbon from Kentucky, Gouda from Holland, crackers from England – pardon me – biscuits, ice cream – "

The ringing of the telephone cut him off.

Sport picked it up. "Hello? Yes, he is." She handed the telephone to Steve.

Wiping his mouth with his napkin, he dropped it on the table, rose and said to Sport, "Sorry, I left your number with the answering service." Then, into the receiver:

"Yes? . . . that's ok . . . when did it start? . . . Where? . . . You did? Thanks. I'll be there in a few minutes."

Hanging up, he said, "Speaking of Johnny Wright, I have to ask Johnny to fly us over in the Harrington-Clark plane – "

"You're going to the Mainland? You can't handle a birth?"

"Who said birth. I think it's appendicitis. Lucky I came in my car." He was out the door.

Sport was surprised by her disappointment. Disappointment? Because Steve had left?

After cleaning up the kitchen, she went upstairs and ran the water in the tub. Undressing, she lowered herself into the steaming fragrance.

The telephone rang again.

"Right on cue," she grumbled as she wrapped a towel around herself and ran to her bedroom.

"Ready to come home?" her older half-sister, Sarah, asked.

"Sarah Abbott, I presume? I thought you had forgotten me. What have you been up to since we last were in contact? Like yesterday."

"The usual. Bridge. Ladies' lunches. Garden club. Church bake sales." None of which Sarah did. She was a third-grade teacher in Connecticut.

"So are you fed up with this 'My Side of the Mountain' stuff?" Sarah asked.

"Hey, I'd forgotten about that book. That's the one where the kid from New York has to survive in the woods?"

"Yeah, it's a third-grade classic. I figure I've read it aloud more than fifteen times. So how are you whiling away the hours?"

"Wanna' hear my schedule? From seven to eight I jog. From eight to nine I breakfast and catch up with the world via radio. From nine to noon I write. After that I do my household chores. Unlike my mother, I'm not up to my ass in indentured serfs. There's vacuuming, dusting, scrubbing floors, laundry – "

"The reason I called – "

"Then there's hunting and gathering tasks, digging for clams and mussels, picking berries, skinning and butchering my kill. At three, I hop on my bicycle and pedal into town, six miles each way in case you've forgotten, and do my marketing – "

"How come you go to the market? I thought you live off the land. Although I was going to ask how you organically raise Wisk."

"You sound just like Steve."

"Steve?"

"And after putting essentials away, I check out the boats in the harbor. Harbah'. And gathah' wood for the fahr, talk on the telephone – "

"Promise you won't get mad at me, Sport, but – "

"Been sniffing coke, Sarah? Lifting merchandise from department stores? Conspiring with terrorists perhaps?"

"Worse. I've been coercing little children to go to computer class three times a week where they are forced to sit for an hour, all twenty-one of them, in rows of seven. Stuck there in front of computer terminals, learning how to touch-type. What a pitiful sight it is to see them squirming in their chairs, holding their wrists perfectly flat but still getting carpal tunnel syndrome. It ought to be illegal."

"Sarah, what was it that you said would make me angry?"

"Skip it. I'll tell you next week."

"Sarah."

"Actually you ought to get mad at your mother. It was Anne who talked me into calling you since she was afraid to do it herself. She's torn down the wall between the hallway and the maid's room – "

"Mom's got to learn to control that temper of hers."

" – because she wants to convert that space into one large study with a sunroom at the back."

"Ok, I'm not mad at you. It's not your fault."

"And since the whole house is in an uproar – "

"Oh no!" Sport burst out. "Now I see where this is going. Mom wrecked the house so that she and Henry can renege on their promise to leave me alone and you're all going to descend on me – "

"Descend on you! You think Anne's spending two hundred thousand dollars just because she misses you?"

"Yes. And now I suppose I'll have to stop work so that I can wait hand and foot on all of you. Arbitrate your spats – "

"If you'll shut up for a minute, I'll explain. All we're asking is, can we celebrate Christmas in Maine? You wouldn't want to celebrate Christmas alone, would you?"

"Oh, Christmas! Why didn't you say so? Even Shakespeare took off for Christmas. Maybe even Danielle Steel. Sure, come on up."

"My, that's generous of you."

"What about Thora?"

"What do you mean?"

"Well, where is your mom going to spend Christmas? I thought you usually spent it with her."

Sport didn't know Sarah's mother well. She came up to the island from time to time, mostly to ensure that everyone knew that after Henry left her, she had managed to marry a man who was actually much wealthier than Henry, although she had had to settle for someone twenty years older in order to do it. Her second husband had died a couple of years ago but she still showed up on the island during the summer, either renting a house or staying with friends. She kept herself busy by arranging elaborate parties – clambakes, picnics on nearby deserted islands, post-sailing race teas – from which she pointedly excluded Henry and Anne. Where Whitney's mother, Heather, was prone to tears and depression on those relatively infrequent times when Whitney's father showed up with his new wife, Thora seemed to revel in her encounters with Anne. She would make a point of rushing over to Anne, kissing her on both cheeks, holding Anne by the shoulders at arm's length while she examined Anne carefully before lavishly complimenting her on her makeup or hair or clothes.

"Mom is spending Christmas on Sea Island," Sarah said, "I think she has a beau there."

"No kidding?"

"Yeah. From the fact that she's paying for the rental I suspect he's not so rich. So he must be younger than Chuck." Chuck had been the second husband. Sport's thoughts wandered away from Christmas.

"How's Whitney?"

"He'll be coming up too with his mother. In fact, the whole gang will open their houses. Your mom invited Dede to stay in our house . . . ." Sarah stumbled a little on the word "our", never sure of her status with her father's second family. "Hey, I have another call, Sport. I'll talk to you tomorrow."

"I don't know if I can fit you into my busy schedule. Don't forget, I jog at seven – " Sarah had hung up. But before Sport could get back into her tub, the telephone rang again.

"Jesus." Wrapping the towel more tightly around herself, she snatched up the telephone and snarled, "I know. You forgot to tell me to wipe my – "

"I don't give a damn whether you wipe your arse or not. For all I care you can stuff-"

"Oh Dede! I thought you were Sarah. I hear – "

"Is that the way you talk to your sister? That patient martyr who's put up with all the crap you've been giving her since you were born?"

" – everybody's joining me for Christmas and you're staying with us."

"Yup. Little Orphan Annie, that's me. So what's new with you?"

"As I was just this minute telling Sarah . . . never mind. How's the painting coming along?"

In her apartment, Dede considered a half finished portrait of a friend of her mother's. It was a life-size portrait from the waist up. She had taken off about ten years and twenty pounds from the real thing. Her patron would love it, especially how Dede had swollen the emerald and diamond necklace. From these objects, Dede's eyes shifted to her pants-covered legs. Vivaldi's Concerto in A Minor played in the background. Dede actually found classical music boring but she thought that it might inspire her to paint better.

"Future generations," she replied, "will be grateful to the Almighty who, in His infinite wisdom, destroyed the use of Dede St. John's legs, thus forcing her to abandon her frivolous life and devote herself to creating masterpieces. Let us hope that Whitney too will discover a so-far hidden, deeply hidden, talent. Playing the bassoon, perhaps. How's the writing coming along?"

"I doubt that future generations will be grateful for my abandonment of the frivolous life. Awfully glad you'll be here Christmas."

"Tired of being a hermit, Sport?"

"Who're you calling a hermit? I chat with Barnett Elliott every day, and just yesterday I had tea with Mrs. Coombs. And I met the new doctor on the island – "

"Trust Sport to find a man. Even when living as a hermit in the Maine woods." There was a touch of bitterness she couldn't control in her voice. "Tell me more about this young doctor. Who, what and where?"

"How do you know he's young?"

"Just a hunch."

"His name is Steve. I met him in the woods. He rescued me from a deer."

"Rescued you from a *deer?*"

"I can't go into it right now, Dede. I'm standing here dripping wet – "

"Does Talbot know you're involved with another man?"

"Involved with another . . . Jesus. No, I haven't told Talbot yet, but you can be maid of honor at my marriage to Steve."

"Nah. I don't like dentists and doctors. They put their hands in the most unspeakable places. Believe me, I'm an expert on that point."

"Then it's lucky it's *me* he's marrying instead of you. Well, now that we've settled that . . . ."

They discussed other friends and relatives but after that the conversation began to dwindle. Dede and Sport had been very competitive as girlhood friends. Not only at things like sailing, tennis, croquet, ballet and golf – their lifestyles supplied a multitude of opportunities to compete – but also about whose family had more money, who had more pets, whose nails were longer, whose hair was more blond or longer, whose mother was prettier or skinnier or taller or younger. Almost anything was fodder for comparison. It was only when they had gone off to college, Sport to the University of Chicago and Dede to art school, that their lives had diverged sufficiently for them to disengage just a bit. Dede's friends were artists, while Sport's friends were in academia. And now, now that Dede's life had so spectacularly crashed and burned, now that the competition had simply vaporized, the almost sexual tension had gone out of the friendship. What was left on Sport's side was a sad desultory sense of sympathy. On Dede's side was left a bitterness, but one that was tinged with relief at having, at last, finished the race, however badly it had turned out.

Twelve

"Sport! It's me!"

"Talbot!" Sport shrieked. "You're back! Why didn't you . . . never mind. Where are you? When can – "

"I'm in my folks' apartment. I just this minute – "

"I'll catch the first ferry and drive down – "

"No. Stay there. I'll drive up in the morning. I want to see you there. I'll take the plane to Portland tomorrow and rent a car to the ferry. I can't wait to see you."

"Oh, Tal, me too. Why didn't you let me know?"

"I didn't know myself until about forty-eight hours ago. They have a burning need for me to read leases in a conference room in New York City for a couple of weeks but they're kindly giving me the weekend and Monday off to ensure that my jet lag doesn't wreak havoc with their malpractice insurance."

"So how has it been?"

"There were times I was all set to chuck it in and come home regardless of whether I had a job or not. Luckily – "

"How's Hong Kong?"

"Hong Kong? I'm not sure. I've been in a conference room ordering in bad Chinese food since I got there. You know, the Chinese food in New York City is a hell of a lot better than what you can get 'to go' from a Hong Kong restaurant."

"Oh Talbot, I've missed you so much."

"Yeah, I've missed you. How you keeping busy up there?"

"Oh you know me. I could keep busy in a cardboard box. I jog, I write, I clean, I sit around thinking about you – "

"Sure, I bet. How're your folks and Sarah?"

"Same as always. Henry's driving my mom crazy. Sarah thinks that teaching third-graders to type should be criminalized. Mom is tearing the house apart to make a new sun room – "

"Didn't she do that last year?" Talbot interrupted.

"No, that was a greenhouse off the kitchen. A sun room is something else or at least that's what I assume. Hey, everyone's coming up here for Christmas. You'll be here then, right? They have to let you come home for the holidays."

"I don't know. That's just, what, seven or so weeks away. But maybe I'll still be in the States, if I get stuck in that conference room long enough."

"Read slowly. Ask for more boxes of documents. Tell them you can't get enough of that sort of thing."

"Right. Listen, I've got to make a few more calls and get some sleep. I'll see you tomorrow, ok?"

"Ok Tal. Hey, I can't wait."

"Same here, Sport."

Sport was suffused with happiness when she hung up the phone. It was as if, in the middle of a long hard run, her feet had suddenly lifted off the ground and she had taken flight. She had been hoping that Talbot might come home for Christmas and now here he was, right in New York. Why not get into her car and just drive down right now to see him? No, he had said that he would come up. It would be much better to have him here with her on the island. They would be completely alone. In fact, she couldn't remember another time that they *had* been alone on the Point. And they were predicting that it would be warm this weekend. Maybe it would be warm enough for them to kayak around the Point.

Sport had a habit of scanning her life in her mind, sometimes two or three times a day. It was a neurotic habit she knew, but one she couldn't shake. She could remember being in second grade, thinking about an upcoming weekend that included a sleepover at a friend's. How perfect life was, she had thought at those moments. She lived in the safest country in the world, in the prettiest town in Connecticut, in what her parents assured her was the most beautiful house. Everything in the universe seemed to have been perfectly arranged for her benefit.

She felt that same childish satisfaction now. All of life's problems had disappeared. She would complete this dissertation, it would mark her for life as an intellectual, she'd marry Talbot and spend her life doing philanthropic work. People would love her, not only for her gifts, but for her personality which would mellow into a gentle benevolence once she was married and the complexities of what to do with the rest of her life were laid to rest. She would have three beautiful children.

She skipped over several decades.

She imagined herself at the age of 94, in full possession of all faculties except perhaps, for one small faulty artery that would enable her to die gently in her sleep after, let's see, ok, after a full day of sailing with her grandchildren, or great grandchildren across the cove that she was gazing at this very moment. Every aspect of her life seemed suddenly to have come to rest in a state of absolute perfection.

Having wrapped up that fantasy, she stood up from her desk. There was no point in trying to work. She declared a three-day holiday weekend for herself. She could get lobsters and oysters in town. And she would take the lobster boat to Rockland, right now, before it got dark and buy the rest of the ingredients for Oysters Rockefeller, a favorite of Talbot's. It was too late for fresh corn, but she'd make his other favorites: cornbread, artichokes, a big salad. She'd find a fancy dessert at a bake shop in town. She'd get out her mother's Royal Doulton china and set the table with the white damask tablecloth and, to make sure it didn't feel like two middle-aged people sitting down for dinner, that weird candelabra Dede had made that looked like a cross between a birthday cake and three and a half people having an orgy.

And what would she wear? She had put on an extra five pounds sitting at a desk and wandering absent-mindedly back and forth between her desk and the refrigerator over the past few weeks. She could still wear her black silk pants and a new black silk sweater she had bought since she last saw Talbot. He'd be here by lunch tomorrow. What would she give him for lunch? Maybe sex would be enough. Make them hungrier for that delicious dinner. She checked the weather forecast. Yes, still warm and sunny for tomorrow, as of course it had to be. While she dressed to go over to Rockland, she reviewed every part of her plan, taking greedy delight in every sensual detail. She was putting on her parka – even in this unusual warm spell it was plenty cold on the water – when the phone rang.

She grabbed it and said hello impatiently into the receiver. It was Steve.

"Sport. Bad news. I have to cancel tomorrow's dinner. Something's come up."

There was just a hint of a pause while Sport tried to remember what had been planned. Then she recalled Steve had, for the first time, invited her over to his house for dinner. He had offered to make his specialty: roast duck with orange sauce.

"Oh," she said, "that's ok."

She wasn't sure if he had caught her hesitation. She hoped not, but then, without thinking, she added. "Talbot has unexpectedly come home. He's coming up for the weekend."

Later, she would try to analyze why she had volunteered that. Was it sheer excitement or was it wounded pride because of his failure to come up with a good excuse for the cancellation? Maybe both, she later concluded.

Again, there was a hiccup in the flow of the conversation while Steve absorbed this but all he said was, "Well then, that's fine all around. I'll talk to you next week." And he hung up.

*　　*　　*

Talbot carried his canvas bags up the beige-carpeted stairs of the duplex, and in moments, his pristine room – still furnished with twin beds for sleepovers, shelves filled with classic children's literature, and teenage sports equipment – was littered with soiled clothing, two bulging brief cases, piles of paper and a number of wrapped gifts. Without stopping to change from his traveling clothes of jeans, sports coat and loafers, he took an address book from his briefcase and went downstairs again. Picking up a cordless telephone from a desk in his father's study, he stretched out on the ivory damask sofa in the living room. First he dialed his younger brother's number at Dartmouth. After a series of conversations with several co-eds, he learned that his brother was in the library "or someplace." The sitter at his sister and brother-in-law's Manhattan apartment told him they were out at a dinner party, and no, he couldn't talk to the children, they were asleep. His next call was to Whitney Chapin. It was Whitney's mother, Heather, who picked up the telephone.

"Talbot, darling! You're home! It's so good to hear your voice. Whitney will be so glad. Oh God, your parents aren't home you know. They had no idea. They're still in Greece, I think. They'll be devastated – "

"Whoa! Hold it, Heather. It's ok. Really. It isn't as if I'm Johnny-came-marching-home from the war. In any case, I'm heading for Maine tomorrow. I just wanted to say hello to Whit."

"He isn't here, Tal. He'll be so crushed he missed you."

"I'm batting zero at getting a hold of people."

"He and Dede went to a movie. I'll have him call you the minute – "

"A movie? Whit went to a movie?"

"He listens to the words and Dede tells him what's happening on the screen. She's beginning to uses crutches occasionally, you know. It's so marvelous to have you back. I want to hear all about Hong Kong."

"Hot, humid and no deals on anything except wool suits."

"Oh Talbot, it must be awful to return home after such a long time and not have anyone there to greet you. I feel like I should come down to the City and take you out to dinner."

"Thanks, Heather, but I'm bushed and I want to get an early start in the morning. Besides, I had dinner on the plane. Such as it was."

While he spoke, Talbot's eyes were circling the room, getting reacquainted with the familiar artifacts: the shimmering Tekke Turcoman carpet, a Bodhisattva of the

T'ang dynasty, an eighteenth-century English cabinet in which reposed (along with unread Ovid, Virgil and Horace), Bristol glass, Lowestoft porcelains, Sheffield silver, and other expensive souvenirs, a carved Robert Adam side table, a Chippendale mirror, Duncan Phyfe and Hepplewhite chairs, a Lipchitz bronze, a small Matisse above the fireplace.

"Talbot." The change in Heather's voice snapped his attention back from his contemplation of the room.

"Yes, Heather?"

"I just wanted to . . . never mind. Forget it."

"Cut that out. What were you going to say?"

"You're going to think I'm being . . . . it's just . . . take care of yourself, Talbot."

"Hey, I'm back home."

"Yes. Well. You know what I mean. I tell Sport the same thing."

"Tell Sport what, Heather?"

"You know damn well what I mean."

He was silent a moment. Of course he knew. Teetering between scoffing and assuring her he would be careful, he chose the latter.

After he hung up, Talbot leaned back, looking at nothing. *Take care of yourself.* How do you take care of a boat coming out of nowhere? A car crashing into your motorcycle?

You hide under the bed and never leave the house.

He was grateful his parents were away. He wasn't sure he could summon the requisite enthusiasm for his job that they would expect. He knew he had to stick it out for a couple of more years at least. The first born son of Spencer Harrington-Clark wasn't allowed to be a quitter. He rubbed his neck on the back of the couch and dialed the Abbott house in Connecticut.

Henry Abbott picked up the telephone. "Talbot! You're home! Speak to Sport yet?"

"No, Henry, I called you first."

"Don't get snippy with me. She might have been out. I hear she's dating the local doctor up there." In the background Talbot could hear Anne telling Henry not to be a pain in the neck.

"Old Dr. Jespersen?" Talbot asked politely.

"Not on your life. There's a new young doctor. Very dashing, I hear."

"Then it's good I'm back."

"How was Hong Kong?"

"Terrific. I'm working on a real interesting deal that brought me back here for a few weeks. I can't tell you a whole lot about it at this point but it's been great. The people at the firm have been terrific."

Undeterred, Henry wanted to know how the American dollar was affecting Hong Kong banks, how the shipping business was developing, what was up in Hong Kong politics.

"Henry," he could hear Anne calling, "the boy's been up in the air for twenty-four hours."

"He's been up in the air a lot longer than that," Henry couldn't resist saying, but just then Talbot heard the beep announcing another call and he used that as excuse to get Henry off the line.

"I called to tell you," the voice on the other end said, "to get your feet off the table."

Talbot's feet crashed to the carpet. "Mom! I thought you were in Greece!"

"They do have telephones here, darling."

"How'd you know I was home?"

"I called the firm and they told me. How are you darling? It's so good . . . . damn, your father is grabbing the phone."

"Hello, Talbot, how's Hong Kong?"

"Great, great. How's Greece?"

Spencer did not need any details beyond knowing that his son was well and cheerful sounding. "Glad you asked. I'm all feta'd up with Greece." He cackled. Talbot decided to play straight man. "I don't get it."

"You don't get it? You've been away too long. In Greece . . . ."

They talked for a few minutes more before Talbot asked to speak to his mother.

"Hey. What's wrong with me?"

"She won't tell me Greek jokes."

"Talbot, honey, I'm back on the phone," his mother said. "Guess what your father is getting you for Christmas?"

"I can't."

"Come on. Try."

"There's nothing I need except for a lot of sleep."

She laughed. "Ok, we'll surprise you."

"Listen, Mom, I'm going up to Maine for a couple of days to see Sport. When are you coming home?"

"We'll be home Tuesday."

"Ok, see you then."

Exhausted, Talbot went back upstairs, cleared the debris off his bed and took off his outer clothes. Lying down on the bed, he found he was too keyed up to sleep and he turned on the news. During the time it took him to fall asleep, he learned about the rape and murder of a six-year-old, the president's fishing trip, the latest hostage crisis and a tenement fire in which six children were burned alive. He fell asleep during the weather report.

When he woke the following morning it was to the suggestion that he buy a drug with a catchy name. After a few groggy seconds listening to the possible effects – nausea, vomiting, diarrhea, headache, and possible death – he recalled where he was and switched off the TV with the remote. He yawned, stretched and went to the bathroom. After his shower, he pulled on corduroys, turtleneck sweater, wool socks and running shoes – much as Sport would be dressed in another hour – and went to the living room window to look down on Fifth Avenue and Central Park. From this height, the city looked pure and crystalline in the grey autumn sunlight. New York looked almost quaint and old-fashioned after the miles of new skyscrapers in Hong Kong. It suddenly struck him that New York was really a nineteenth-century city.

He packed a clean set of clothes and a few toiletries. He would have whatever else he needed in the Maine house.

He assured the daytime doorman that Hong Kong was great, especially the food, and then headed towards his favorite coffee shop on Madison. He passed men and women heading for work, their clothes starched and their hair still wet from the shower. It was too early for kids or shoppers. He saw a drunk lying on the steps of a church and reflected that there seemed to be more beggars on the streets of New York than in Hong Kong. It was about the only cultural observation he'd had time to make since arriving in Asia. He dropped a dollar in the empty coffee cup that was lying beside the drunk.

He bought a newspaper and read while having orange juice, cappuccino and a brioche. Fourteen people had been blown apart in an Israeli bus, several thousand were dying of starvation in a country he had barely heard of, and Mattel was looking forward to a great Christmas for toys.

Back on the street, he stepped off the curb to hail a cab. At the same moment, he remembered that he had left Sport's gift, jade and gold earrings, on his bedside table. If he hadn't turned back without warning, the driver of the innocuous rented Honda, which had been double-parked across the street, would probably have only smashed a rib or a leg.

Thirteen

Sport had been waiting at the ferry. It had been a beautiful early November afternoon, the wind whipping small whitecaps on the water, the air so clear that it felt as if she were wearing a new contacts prescription.

There were only a few people at the ferry dock this time of year waiting with old cars and trucks to drive a son or a spouse home from the ferry dock. Sport felt sorry for them, locked in their dreary daytime routines while she waited for Talbot.

As the ferry came into view, her heart began to pound. She reminded herself not to create a scene, not to jump into Talbot's arms. That was for August ferry arrivals when the summer people lined up in their brightly colored clothes to greet their families and friends.

As the ferry came to a gentle stop, she suddenly saw her parents and Sarah at the rail. Damn. She wanted to be alone with Talbot. Did they think that a surprise visit would be a treat right when Talbot was arriving? She started to look away, to search for Talbot, but then she saw their faces and her stomach lurched towards her throat.

"What the hell . . . ," she murmured and then broke off. There was no room for doubt. Instead of embracing her, they stopped short. They gazed at her as if at someone whose entire life was about to be channeled in an entirely different direction. Her father's face was drawn, her mother was staring at her, and Sarah was crying, her shoulders shaking.

"What happened? Why are . . . where's Talbot? Why isn't Talbot here?"

It was Sarah who stepped forward first. Almost fearfully she approached Sport. "Sport, sweetie, let's go back to the house . . . ."

"It's Talbot, right? He's been in an accident. He's in the hospital. Let's go straight back to New York. How bad is it? Why don't you say something?"

The three of them seemed incapable of answering. Struck dumb, they stared at her. Years later, Sport recalled that the sun had chosen that instant to come out from behind a cloud, almost blinding her. Also branded into her memory was the distant pounding of a lobster boat out in the bay, the sight of a gull wheeling slowly in the sky.

But that was much later.

At that instant, Sport Abbott lost all semblance to the cool, controlled image she always tried to project. Screaming uncontrollably, she ran past her family and Jake Halstead, the ferryman, onto the ferry. "I don't believe it! It's a mistake! Take me back this minute! I have to see him! I have to see him!"

While Jake held her back from boarding the ferry, Sarah made the call on her cell phone. It took Steve Schwartz twelve minutes to make it to the ferry, and only a few seconds more to inject Sport with thiopental.

The next night, they gathered at the Harrington-Clarks' house on the Point.

Marilyn Harrington-Clark, Talbot's mother, was still dressed in a bathrobe. Although Sport had been in and out of the Harrington-Clark house every summer of her life, frequently unannounced, she had never before seen Talbot's mother in a bathrobe. It was the thing that finally made Sport realize that she'd never see Talbot again. She rushed over to Marilyn, put her arms around her neck, and despite having girded herself to remain calm and under control, burst into uncontrolled sobbing. Marilyn patted her on the back, her eyes blank and said nothing. When Sport was finally able to open her own eyes, she was looking over Marilyn's shoulder into the eyes of Talbot's father. Spencer was staring at his wife and Sport almost as if they were an abhorrent sight and maybe they were, this picture of barely controlled and uncontrolled abject misery. Spencer had always been fond of Sport. He had called her Annie Bananie until she was twelve. He had always been far more patient with small children than Henry. It had been Spencer who taught Sport to swim. He had also taught her to ride a bike, patiently bringing her and the bike back to the top of a little rise in the lawn, over and over again, gently letting her bike go as it started down the sloping lawn. In fact, since Spencer had retired early, he had been more of a father to her during her summers on the Island than Henry who had to stay at work in New York City and came up for only a few weekends in July and two weeks in August.

But now, when Sport let go of Marilyn and approached Spencer, he looked at her as if he almost didn't recognize her. His face was sunken in and he seemed incapable of blinking. Sport hugged him but it was like hugging a statue. She had imagined hers and Talbot's wedding a thousand times, including the way that the two families would all hug one another after the ceremony. Now, it occurred to her that she might never hug Talbot's father again.

Henry had reacted to this tragedy as he reacted to all bad news: with angry depression. He wouldn't talk to anyone and stood in a corner of the living room, his arms crossed, looking out towards the ocean. Anne, like her daughter, reacted to stress by keeping physically active. She carried food back and forth between the living room and the kitchen, helped clear dishes, answered the phone with curt, quiet efficiency and when she could find nothing else to do, disappeared outside for long walks.

Whitney and his mother Heather had arrived next with Whitney's older sister Sabina. Whitney's eyes were uncovered because, aside from a tendency to flicker spasmodically, they appeared normal. Sport noticed when she went up to hug him how much muscle he had lost. He had always been the hyperactive one, the kid who on rainy days would use his mother's bed as a trampoline no matter how many times he was told this was verboten. He was no longer the brawny, boisterous boy of their childhood but suddenly, a somber man of indefinite age. He sat slumped on the sofa, his head jerking back and forth as he tried to look at each speaker. It looked as if he had been told that he should do this in order to appear more involved in discussions. He had a white lab guide dog who seemed even more blind than Whitney and kept leading Whitney into coffee tables and chairs. Whitney tried to make a joke about the blind leading the blind but no one laughed and he kept repeating it since he was never sure who was, or was not, around to listen to him. Heather, the most emotional of the parents even under ordinary circumstances, spent a good part of the day making ugly guttural sounds in her throat as she tried to silence her nearly hysterical sobs.

Sarah and her mother, Thora, came. Thora arrived in a Citation 500 jet. She wore dark glasses all day although it was cloudy outside and was, so far as anyone could tell, completely expressionless. She hugged everyone, including Anne, and then spent her time smoking in the sunroom or talking in ostentatiously hushed tones on her cell phone.

Although neither Whitney's nor Dede's father came, Dede had come with the Harrington-Clarks. Sport had the impression, when she surfaced from her grief long enough to notice her surroundings, that Dede felt awkward being there with no parents and so needy for help herself. She kept asking if she could help with the food or making phone calls although no one seemed to even hear her offers.

Edith and Johnny Wright were there. Edith was wearing a tent-like faded blue dress and what looked like bedroom slippers. She shuffled back and forth with Anne between the living room and the kitchen. Once Sport heard her ask Johnny when Talbot would be arriving. Johnny frowned at her and made a "sshh-ing" sound with his lips but didn't answer.

The Harrington-Clark plane flew back and forth from Rockland all the next morning. Sport held her hands over her ears and closed her eyes each time she heard it approaching or revving up to depart. It was not that the sound was loud. It was just that she had spent a lifetime associating that sound with exciting happy arrivals. Now, she didn't think that she would ever be able to hear that sound again without feeling this intolerable sadness.

A crowd gathered outside the house at about three that afternoon. Sport had the impression of people from all parts of her life – Connecticut, college, graduate school, and the island – hugging her and murmuring how sorry they were. After the first few people, she could no longer bother to come up with a personal greeting for each person and simply stood still, barely noticing who came and went.

As predicted, the weather had remained balmy and sunny for early November with a five-to-ten-mile-per-hour breeze coming out of the southwest. A perfect bitter-end-of-the-season sailing or kayaking day. They walked down to the dock in a long procession on a circuitous path that avoided the steep hill at the back of the Abbott house. Johnny helped Dede with her wheel chair and Whitney held onto Heather's arm while the guide dog went down the path, seemingly oblivious to the overhanging branches that would have whacked Whitney in the face had Heather not been helping. An Episcopalian minister came up each summer to tend to the summer residents but at this time of year only the Baptist minister was on the island. He stood at the end of the dock, facing the crowd with his back to the water. Since he didn't know Talbot very well, it was a brief and generic service to cover the situation of youth cut down in its prime. When the service was done, Talbot's mother stepped forward out of the crowd. Sport noticed for the first time that she was carrying a small wooden box. Marilyn's hands were shaking and everyone's eyes were suddenly fixed on her hands and the box. Sport felt her stomach turn over. It was impossible to believe that her tall, blond Talbot with his broad shoulders could have been reduced to a mound of ashes in that box.

Sport suddenly had a memory of a night the previous summer when she and Talbot had walked down to the dock and then, spontaneously, made love on the dock, in fact very near to the spot where she now stood. She remembered how, at one point, she had started giggling and explained to Talbot that she felt like the peanut butter and jelly between the hard boards of the dock beneath her and Talbot's hard muscled body on top. She felt a sob begin to convulse her and was able to keep it down only with the utmost exertion of force.

They sang "Lord of the Dance", a favorite hymn of Talbot's, in a haunting minor key to the accompaniment of Sarah's guitar.

And then Marilyn, who had spent every summer of her life on the water sailing and kayaking, who regularly won the highly competitive dinghy races in August, opened the box and, instead of turning her back to the breeze, flung the ashes directly into the wind so that ashes flew back into the faces of the families standing on the end of the dock. There was a sound as if of small pebbles falling on the wooden surface of the dock. Bits of bone Sport thought, just before all other thoughts were blown out of her mind by the sound of Marilyn's high pitched sobs. Sport had never known what the word "keening" might mean until that moment. Heather's jagged crying started up again, like an ugly counterpoint bass to Marilyn's sobs. Without knowing what she was doing, Sport covered her ears and didn't even notice that her own mother had collapsed onto the dock until she saw Johnny lifting her up and holding her while she swayed unsteadily between him and her husband.

*   *   *

Sitting on the edge of the bluff a few weeks later, overlooking the same dock and watching the early December sun scatter diamonds on the tips of the waves, Sport contemplated the remaining span of her life. She supposed it was a good sign that she could even think about her future. The antidepressants must be kicking in. She hadn't worked on her dissertation since Talbot's death. It seemed perfectly pointless. Her family had tried to induce her to return home. What for? She reminded them that Whitney had been attacked on a lonely Connecticut road; Talbot on a crowded city street. In the end, the best they could do was to ask Deputy Coombs, Johnny and Steve to check up on her regularly.

She had loved Talbot and not for his money. But because of the money, none of her thousands of daydreams had ever included the necessity of getting a job, of finding a husband, or even thinking about where to live. The thought of relying on her father for financial help was abhorrent. She recalled the grating satisfaction he took from Sarah's gratitude when he gave her money for vacations or a loan for a car.

It was like Sleeping Beauty in reverse. She had woken out of a wonderful dream into a nightmare reality. No, she chided herself, it was a tragedy but not a nightmare. She was young, healthy, well educated. She'd find a job after Christmas. But she could think of nothing that she wanted to work at and nowhere she wanted to live except on the island. Somehow she felt that her last connection to Talbot would be broken if she left. And then, as Whitney had done on his last motorcycle ride while skimming up and down the Connecticut hills, she was reminded of Nevah's ghost story.

And she would have given anything to see Talbot's ghost emerge from the sea, looking as she had so often seen him in the past, tanned, dripping wet and laughing, as he lay down beside her. And ghost or not, she would have welcomed him into her arms.

Fourteen

She woke up to a world that had been cleansed and purified: alabaster fields, branches laced with icicles, every blemish concealed by a cosmetic sheathing. For a moment she was filled with the exhilaration that always accompanied the first snow. But then she remembered. There was nothing she could think of to look forward to, nothing but a drab dreary future stretching out ahead of her.

She dressed in a turtleneck, wool sweater, corduroys and heavy socks and went downstairs. The snow had nearly reached the windowsills of the living room, and was still falling. Beneath the birdfeeder, on the otherwise smooth surface of the snow, were the claw marks of sparrows and chickadees.

Checking her supplies, she saw that she had violated the first rule of rural living. She hadn't stocked up for emergencies. She was nearly out of milk and completely out of eggs, cheese, juice, fruit and vegetables. What she did have was a quarter loaf of bread and shelf provisions: peanut butter, jelly, crackers, baking powder, molasses, gelatin, condiments, a can of tomato sauce and three tins of smoked oysters.

She softened the bread with water, shredded it and opened the door in order to feed the birds since the birdfeeder was almost empty. Snow cascaded into the hallway.

"Idiot!" she yelled. The sound was jarring in the hushed stillness. The sound sent all the birds into hiding. She scattered the pieces of bread and went for the broom. When she had shoved as much snow as she could back outside, she was able to push the door shut. She began scooping the rest of the snow up with a dust pan and dumped it into the sink. Then she mopped the floor.

She breakfasted on peanut butter and crackers while she sat at her desk in the study. For a while she did nothing. Finally, she turned on her computer. She started at the last page she had been working on. She was in the midst of analyzing the famous "shock experiments" of the 1960s. The experiment involved a set of "teachers" asking questions of a group of adult "students." The teachers, who were the unwitting subjects of the experiment, were instructed to shock any students who gave wrong answers. There was a range of shocks from light to severe. The shocks weren't real and the students were shills but the teachers believed the shocks were real. Disturbingly, one hundred percent of the "teachers" chose to shock their students; sixty-five percent at the most severe level. The point being, of course, that everyone has the capacity to be completely immoral sometimes under certain circumstances.

This was only about five pages further than where she'd been at the time of Talbot's death. She couldn't really recall what she had been doing the rest of the time over the last four weeks. She sighed, looked up from the computer, and stared unseeing at a sparkling white world. When the telephone rang, she jumped up in relief.

"Sport, I just heard on the radio that Maine is having a blizzard."

"Sarah, what are you doing at home in the middle of a school day?"

"Have you been away so long you've forgotten that private schools shut down at twelve forty-five on Fridays?"

"Oh right. It slipped my mind that the overly-indulged little buggers need an early start to get to the ski slopes or their Caribbean beach houses." Since her emergence from abject depression, Sport had adopted flippancy as a first line of defense against complete collapse. She refused to appear despondent in front of anyone, and in particularly, in front of Sarah. Sarah's empathy could pulverize anyone's defenses.

"Sport, are you snowbound?"

Sport glanced out the window. "Ayuh."

"How awful."

"Why?"

"Why! Isn't it awful? I mean, it could be fun, I suppose, if you had company to go skating or sledding with. But there you are, all alone on an island in the middle of the ocean – "

"Yeah, how about that?" Marginally cheered by Sarah's romantic view of her plight, Sport watched the birds, now recovered from their trauma, feuding over her largess.

"And if I know you," Sarah continued, "you haven't stocked up on food."

"As long as the smoked oysters hold out, I won't starve."

"Smoked oysters?"

"My mother's idea of basic nourishment. Well, I suppose it includes at least a couple of food groups if you count the minerals that come off the insides of the can. How's the world of academia? Such as it is in the third grade?" She was instantly dismayed at her own thoughtless putdown of Sarah's job, but Sarah was too preoccupied to notice. "Sport, there's something weird going on."

"It took you all these years to notice?"

"What I mean is that something weird must have happened to the universe about eight or nine years ago. Half the kids in my class are hyperkinetic. The headmaster wants to put them all on drugs – "

"Tut, tut."

" – but some of us don't think it's ethical to turn them into semi-zombies, no matter how difficult they are. You're the ethicist, what do you think?"

"Well, if it were up to *me* – "

"Sport, what do you think happened in the universe eight or nine years ago?"

One of things that happened in the universe eight or nine years ago was that Nevah Wright had gone scuba diving. Aloud, Sport said, "Was there a nuclear explosion somewhere? Did Bin Laden slip something into our water?"

"I think it might have something to do with how we're scaring the shit out of these little kids all the time. We just spent a week on 'stranger danger.' I had a kid who wouldn't go home with his aunt because she couldn't remember his birthday. And another kid fell asleep in the middle of class and woke up screaming for the police."

"I thought everything could be blamed on MTV."

"Well, I was discussing this with our science teacher and – "

"Male?"

"What?"

"Married?"

"You're always worried about my single state. Just like my m-mom." Sarah sometimes stumbled over words associated with the fact that their mutual father had deserted Sarah's mother in favor of the one who had become Sport's. "Never mind. *Do* you have enough food?"

"I told you, as long as long as the tins of – "

"Is it still snowing?"

Sport checked. "Ayuh."

"What will you do if the power goes off?"

"I'll wander into the 'compassionate wilderness' to die. Why do so many books talk about the compassionate wilderness? What makes wilderness compassionate?"

"I think the loneliness is beginning to affect your mind."

"At least I'll be warm if the power goes off. Johnny chopped wood for me."

Pause. Then a tentative, "How *are* the Wrights?"

"Talk about weird. You should hear Edith."

"I think *you're* weird. Spending a year alone up there, especially after . . . ." Her voice trailed off.

"And how about you? Spending your life with hyperkinetic kids. But I love you anyway."

Mistake. Sarah, like dried food to which water had been added, turned mushy.

"Oh Sport, I love you too. And I don't want anything to happen to you."

"How can anything happen to me when I'm surrounded by all this compassionate wilderness?"

"*You* could get into trouble anywhere."

There it was again. The indirect, almost subconscious reference to the series of "accidents".

"So Sarah, you'll be here for Christmas, right?"

"I'm not sure."

A wave of disappointment washed over Sport. "What do you mean? Everybody's coming up."

"I can join you if my mother goes with her new boyfriend to Sea Island for the holidays. Otherwise I'll be at her house pretending we're having a holly jolly holiday together at home."

"Is he cute?"

"Who?"

"The boyfriend."

"How would I know? I haven't met him. In fact, mom hasn't admitted to having him. She's still referring to him as her gender neutral 'friend'."

"I'm surprised she doesn't want to bring the boyfriend up here to prove to my mom that she still has the right stuff."

"Don't do anything foolish, Sport," Sarah said.

"Like what?"

"Being you, you'll think of something."

After she had hung up, Sport put on a parka, ski hat, mittens and boots, and pushed her way out of the door. Struggling with each step, she finally made her way around to the shed door beneath the deck overlooking the bluff and the water. The cold air swept the clutter out of her head and the soft falling flakes caressed her lips and eyelids like kisses. She scooped up a handful of snow, hardened it between her mittened palms and, looking for a likely victim, aimed at an unoffending squirrel on the deck railing. The snow disintegrated harmlessly in midair.

By kicking and using her hands, she managed to get the shed door open far enough to squeeze through. She took a shovel off a hook, cleared the snow off the wood pile under the deck, and began clearing a path from the shed to the front door.

A song had come back into her head and as she worked, she sang out loud.

"What if I drove into the driveway
And there was no sign of life
No smoke rising from the chimney
And in the windows, no light.

"Unlock the front door
Step into the dark
No smell of something cooking
No silly dog to bark."

Her head jerked up. From the corner of her eye she thought she had seen a movement among the spruces. Immobile, she blinked rapidly as if experiencing the onset of snow blindness.

Probably a squirrel. Or the damned Harrington-Clark deer on the loose again. The mention of Talbot's last name. Whenever she had a moment's peace, something happened to bring back the agony.

Although the snow was soft, it took a long time to open a path between the shed and the door. She finally managed to clear a wide enough path to ferry logs, three or four at a time, up to the front porch. When she decided she had enough, she began working on a path to the driveway. The Point was private land but the road up to their driveways was public and kept plowed. She'd have road access to the world once the town plow came through. Her car was nearly invisible at the top of the rise, a larger lump of white.

Less than a quarter of the way to the road, the light began to fail. She was exhausted. Returning to the shed, she hung up the shovel and went back into the house. She hung up her outer clothing in the front hall and dialed Steve Schwartz' number.

"Where were you?" he asked as soon as he heard her voice. "Jogging? Swimming? I've been trying to reach you."

"Where do you think I've been? I've been coping. Clearing a path."

"That's my Sport alright. How're you fixed for food?"

"Everybody's worried about my caloric intake."

"You've been talking to your mother?"

"Well, actually no. Maybe she tried while I was out. I still haven't installed an answering machine. It was my older sister. Not a whole sister. A half-sister."

"Which half belongs to you?"

"She's the dearest person in the world but – "

"Oh oh. Whenever somebody says 'the dearest person in the world but' they generally mean the person is a pain in the butt."

"Not this one. She's the most loveable person in the world, but she's a . . . uh . . . what I'm trying to say is that when Sarah goes to heaven – which without a doubt she will – but not for hundreds of years, I hope . . . ." Sport knocked on the wooden counter. "She'd still find something to worry about. Like maybe God was being a little harsh when he sent Adam and Eve to . . . ."

"So you have enough wood if the power goes off? As it undoubtedly will."

"Hey, Doc, suppose I don't? What are you going to do about it?"

"Strap on my snowshoes and head out to rescue you."

"It'd take you about a week. Besides, you rescued me once. I can't keep counting on you to rescue me every time I'm in need."

"I can't think of anything I'd rather do."

Sport was about to speak but instead shut her mouth. There was a brief silence until once again, Steve rescued her. "I called the highway department – such as it is – to remind Bill about the one resident still out on the Point, but they have a lot of plowing to do closer to town before they can get to you."

"I appreciate it, Steve, but really, I'll be ok. Keep in touch. I'm a little bored with talking to the birds and taking potshots at the squirrels."

"You shoot squirrels? For food?" He sounded as if he was almost ready to believe it.

"Not to worry. I have lousy aim."

When she'd hung up, Sport began preparing for a siege. She found a flashlight on the shelves that lined the side of the stairs to the living room, and in a kitchen drawer, a trove of treasures: half burned candles, Sterno cans and souvenir matches which, Sarah, a non-smoker, always collected on trips. Lastly, she built a fire with newspapers, kindling and wood, but didn't ignite it.

While she puttered, she couldn't dispel the impression of being watched. Her mother didn't believe in curtains. ("Why live on 'the coast of light' if you're going to blot it out?") The windows were now rectangles of absolute blackness.

To make up for the lack of something palatable to eat, she prepared a tray with a linen mat and napkin, dried roses in a vase and silver cutlery which had no purpose. She examined her father's stock of liquor and chose an expensive sherry which she poured into a crystal tumbler. She arranged the crackers coated with peanut butter on the tray and tried to concentrate on reading *The Tin Drum*. She couldn't remember anything that she had read before Talbot's death and the book made almost no sense to her.

When she had cleaned up, she turned on the outdoor lights and saw that the path she had cleared was coated with a fresh layer of white. The thick white flakes drifted slowly earthward as if they were moving according to the moon's gravitational rules. The lights illuminated only a short radius around the house, intensifying the surrounding gloom.

She flipped through the few channels she could get on the TV without cable, imagining how interesting it would be to find one of those reality shows set in a northern climate. But of course, that could never happen; not enough opportunity for skimpy bathing suits. At that moment, the power failed.

Congratulating herself on her foresight, she found the flashlight, lit a candle, and turning off the flashlight to preserve the battery, headed upstairs. She peered into unlit corners of the balcony as if the loss of electricity had made her more vulnerable to danger. The flame sent her shadow skittering up and down the walls. In her bedroom, she collected pillows and blankets and returned to the living room. First, she lit the fire and then she tested the telephone. It was still working and she dialed the electric company to inform them of the failure, but evidently others were doing the same. The line was busy. The only thing she had forgotten to do was to fill the tubs and sinks with water but she could bring in snow to melt if this went on for any extended period.

Too restless to sleep, she sat on the sofa and peered out the windows, hoping to see the headlights of the snowplow, but the windows remained completely black. She walked over to the steps between the entrance hall and the living room and, with the aid of the candle, began flicking though photograph albums. There was a picture of her mother's wedding. Her beautiful mother at age twenty dressed in a demure calf-length white dress; her father still handsome if a bit heavy at age forty, beaming down at his second bride. Snapshots of seemingly interchangeable infants, then toddlers, birthday parties, Christmas, skiing, sailing, picnicking, windsurfing, swimming, playing tennis. She flipped the page to a studio portrait of Talbot at age sixteen. The latter showed a squarish face, forthright expression, well-formed features and fair hair.

Talbot fixed in time. Never to be tainted by age.

She turned the page. An announcement of Sport's birth, school report cards, a series of stories about a blue leprechaun she had written in third grade. Something bothered her about the albums, and after a moment, she realized that what it was. There were almost no photographs of Sarah. Whose fault was that? Her father's? Her mother's? Or the fact that Sarah hated to be photographed. Always shying away from the camera.

A lined sheet of cheap paper fell out from between the pages of the album. No envelope. The salutation and signature ripped off. As if someone had been loath to throw the letter away, but didn't want it identified.

"What can I tell you about here?
You're the one with things happening. Here it's the same old things. Same
old July 4 picnic at Fork's Head Beach, same old people, work and more
work. See you next holiday."

Sport stared at the note for a long time. It had clearly been written by someone on the island given the reference to the town beach, but who had written it? And to whom was it addressed? For all she knew, maybe she had written it as a young girl to a friend back home one summer and had forgotten or decided not to send it. Although it looked like a man's writing. And why would she, or anyone else in her family for that matter, be complaining about work while vacationing up here?

She replaced the albums on the shelves and tried to go back to her book. But the combined effect of the letter, Talbot's photograph, and the difficulty of reading by candlelight, made her give it up. Putting on her outer clothing again, she dropped the flashlight in her pocket and went out to fill two buckets with snow for drinking, cooking and toilet-flushing.

Some people were most exhilarated by moonlit summer evenings, others by brisk autumn mornings. For Sport it was snowy winter nights. She inhaled deep lungfuls of the cold air, lifted her face to the drifting flakes, and picked up a handful of snow to put into her mouth.

From a dark stretch of woods came a sudden fluttering commotion from some unidentifiable bird in the bushes. So far as Sport knew, birds, with the possible exception of owls, were rarely awake at night. She flicked on the flashlight and directed the beam at the scene of the disturbance. The chickadee, she could now see, was zigzagging frantically but there was no sign of a predatory animal. What there was, however, were fresh snowshoe tracks that had been made a short while ago, just before the most recent snow.

*   *   *

From the battery operated weather radio a voice sputtered erratically. "...record inches of snow . . . since nineteen-fifty-two when Route One was shut down . . . . Thorofare frozen solid and all ferry services have been suspended . . . . Coast Guard out all night breaking up the ice . . . ."

It was morning and the fire had turned to ashes. Sport struggled out of her nest of blankets and pillows and began building another fire. She looked out of every window but there were no new tracks.

When she'd spotted the tracks the night before, she'd latched the windows and locked the doors. But then reason had taken over. The only people within reasonable snowshoeing distance of her house were Edith and Johnny Wright. It was conceivable Johnny had come over to make sure she was alright, and having seen the firelight, had been reassured and returned home. This was believable behavior on the part of morose and taciturn Johnny. Or it could have been Edith. For Edith, any bizarre behavior was possible.

Sport checked the telephone and discovered that it too had given up. Opening a window slightly, she let some of the cold air seep in although the house was quickly becoming cold. With the exception of the green undercoats of the spruce branches and the tree trunks, sky, ocean and land flowed into one another without definition. The world was wrapped in celestial cotton. No birds, no animals, no humans, no boats.

She opened the window further and scooped up some snow with a fondue pot. Setting fire to the Sterno can under the pot, she boiled water, added a tea bag and sipped slowly, warming her hands at the same time. She was tired of peanut butter, so she breakfasted on dry crackers. She built the fire up again. Then, dressing in layers of outdoor clothing, she made her way to the shed for snowshoes and started slogging down the driveway. A large birch tree had fallen across it. Maybe she could persuade the town to plow the driveway if she got rid of it. She returned to the shed.

The five-gallon can of gasoline was full, and consulting the chart on the yellow plastic bottle of Pennzoil, she saw that she needed a mixture of one part Pennzoil to twenty-five parts of gasoline. Shrugging, she added a few drops of Pennzoil to a quart container of gasoline and poured it into the chain saw gas tank. "Close enough." Next, she pressed the starter button and pulled the cord. The first few times it snapped back without springing into life, but accustomed as she was to this kind of recalcitrance from dinghy motors, she persisted until she won out.

She kicked the snow off the tree in the middle of the driveway and cut it roughly in the middle. Then she started sawing off two-, three-foot sections. Occasionally, she stopped to rest. It was easy to see how even seasoned woodmen could become baffled in a snowstorm and die of exposure a few hundred yards from shelter. All landmarks were obliterated.

The isolation, the hushed stillness punctuated only by the clamor of the saw, the crackling of overloaded branches and the whisper of falling snow, the shimmering timelessness of the day all conspired to make her lethargic. She felt a nearly irresistible desire to lie down and have the snow enclose her in its deceitful embrace.

Abruptly, she stiffened into awareness.

A flicker of movement? A hint of sound? Or something beyond the range of her normal five senses? She had the distinct impression she was under surveillance. She pivoted sharply trying to catch an unwary movement. Nothing. As she stacked the birch logs by the side of the road – they wouldn't be dry enough to burn until next winter – she longed for the sound of a plow, the ring of the telephone, the purr of a plane, but there was nothing.

Back in the house, she lay down on the sofa and fell into a deep, exhausted sleep. When she woke up, she was confused, uncertain if it was late afternoon or dawn of the next day. Groggily she consulted her watch. Ten to four and already getting dark. She lit a candle and built up the fire again. She fixed herself a whiskey sour with the aid of a powdered mix. Then she opened a can of oysters and placed one on each of ten crackers. She ate, staring at the fire, then brushed her teeth, banked the fire, set the alarm to wake her in the middle of the night so she could add more logs to the blaze, and still wearing her daytime clothing, settled back into her nest.

An unidentifiable stimulus snapped her to a sitting position.

"Wh – what?"

Nothing had changed. The fire was still sizzling. The snow was still whispering against the windowpanes.

A sudden panic pierced her drowsiness. If her impression of surveillance was real, why did the person watching her have to be on the outside? She had left the door unlocked while she had been sawing wood. True, she hadn't noticed any tracks other than her own and last night's snowshoe tracks, but she might not have noticed them. Besides, the relentless flakes had kept reglazing the surface of the snow.

Her eyes circled the room. She picked up her flashlight and began a search. Holding a poker in one hand, she peered under and behind furniture, tucked the flashlight under her arm to open closets, went up the stairs to the second floor. Then down the stairs to the game room. Finally, there was only the attic.

The crammed, spider-webbed, low-ceilinged space had never held any attraction for her. Unlike other children who loved to scrounge through ancient trunks, Sport had always considered the attic dusty and dull.

Perhaps she could skip the attic.

But no, if she did, she'd keep wondering what was up there.

She opened the door and peered up the narrow, dark passageway. Then she listened. Nothing. Finally she forced herself to start up. Putting down the flashlight, she lifted the trapdoor. That was when something – someone – from above slammed it back down.

*　　*　　*

Sport Abbott sought out and courted danger on the ski slopes and in all sports involving water. However, she had never been stalked by another human being. In fact, she had never completely believed in her own mortality. The slamming of the trap door changed all that. For a moment all the blood in her body seemed to well up in her throat, and in the movie of her mind, she glimpsed Dede windsurfing in a peaceful cove; Whitney speeding along a deserted Connecticut road; Talbot crossing a crowded New York City street.

"Nevah, I didn't mean for it to happen. Nevah, it wasn't my fault. Nevah, please forgive me."

Like a fly injected with a spider's paralyzing venom, Sport was completely immobilized for a moment. But then she heard a whisper of sound from above, a creature moving along a bare floor.

Her torpor snapped. Dropping the poker and grabbing the flashlight, she ran down two flights of stairs, snatched her coat, hat, mittens and boots, stuffed the flashlight in her pocket, and bolted out into the snow-mantled night.

She stopped at the edge of the woods, gasping, and realized she was above her knees in snow. Getting back to the cleared path, she went to the shed, grabbed her snowshoes and snapped them on.

She decided to go down to the beach because it would be washed clean of snow and she would leave no trail. In addition, if she was right in thinking that it was low tide, she could walk along the shore, cross the road and get to Heather's house.

At the back of the house near the edge of the bluff, concealed by snow, the old picnic table sent her sprawling. She wasn't hurt, but the snowshoes got in the way of her righting herself. Taking them off, she peered through the dusk over the bluff's edge. Right. The tide had cleared a path. She hooked the snowshoes on one arm and then catching hold of the rope which had been secured to an oak branch years before, she slid down the steep slope to the shore. Out on the bay she could see ice floes drifting in blocks with the current. But no seabirds diving for food, no boats hauling lobster pots, no sign of life.

Protected from observation by the bluff, she began traversing the slippery rocks on the beach. It was hard, slow going and she fell several times but she heard no sign of pursuit. It seemed to her that every element in the universe was pitted against her. Until now she had been too intent on escaping, but now she was aware of her wet feet, of the stinging pain in her fingers and toes. She had to get to shelter soon or freeze.

When she reached the road where it came down to the beach, she could see lights on in the Wright house to her right. She put her snowshoes back onto her wet and frozen boots, crossed the still unplowed road and headed up the road on the other side towards Heather's house.

She was exhausted. She wanted to give up, lie down and die. Emitting soft, animal-like whimpers, she started to take off her snowshoes again so that she could climb up the front steps to the door and then paused.

Could the stalker have anticipated her destination and arrived before her? She turned on the flashlight and studied the stark cottage and the surrounding terrain. As far as she could tell there were no disturbances in the snow. She had to stop, to get to shelter and lie down.

Exhausted, numb with cold, she rattled the locked door knob on the off chance that someone had forgotten to secure it. Then she moved back and swung a snowshoe at the window to the left of the door. She was shaking so uncontrollably that the blow was ineffectual. She closed her eyes, took several long breaths and swung again. The glass shattered. Gingerly, she reached in with her mittened hand, unlatched the window, raised it, and cleared away the broken shards. She climbed through.

Heather's living room was nearly as cold as the outdoors, and the sheet-shrouded furniture gave the house the appearance of a mausoleum. Which, she thought, it might become. She fumbled her way to the fireplace, and blessed whoever it was – ironically, probably Johnny – who had carefully placed foot long matches, newspapers, kindling and logs. And then she remembered. Although the windows and draperies were closed, the smoke from the chimney would give her location away.

God, you must really be mad at me.

She pulled off her mittens and blew on her icy fingers. Then she took off her boots and wet socks and rubbed her toes. As sensation returned, needles of pain stitched through her nerves. She went to the downstairs linen closet and pulling out a pillow, stuffed it into the broken window. Then she took a down comforter and the fireplace poker up the familiar stairs. She found dry socks, pants and a sweater in Heather's drawers. She unlocked the window so that she could jump down the ten or so feet into the snow if necessary. Then, too tired to consider any more possibilities, she curled up inside the comforter with the poker within reach.

Never again, she thought, would she feel enchanted by a snowy night.

Fifteen

The squealing of the gulls awakened Sport. She seemed to be in a lighthouse, the sun shafting through cracks in the clouds, sky the color of ivory, birch tree branches moving in a slight breeze shaking off the snow. The snow had stopped falling. Sitting up, she saw no sign of life except for the seabirds. Waves were frozen to the rocks by the shore. Again, Sleeping Beauty's castle came to mind but where was the prince to wake them all up?

Scattered in the deep blue sea.

She had gone to sleep with all of her borrowed clothes on and all she had to do was put on her hat and some boots Heather had left in a front hall closet.

Apparently it had snowed only a short time after she reached Heather's house and she could still see traces of her own tracks. But no evidence of pursuit. With the whole island shimmering with light, she could barely recall the terror of the previous night. Who was the intruder? Was he or she still there? Why would a would-be murderer huddle in the attic? To wait for her to fall asleep?

What was she going to do now? Return to the house, take the poker and check the attic? If the house was deserted, she could lock the windows and doors, start the fire, wait for rescue . . . .

And if the house wasn't deserted . . . .

It was the hardening of the snow that decided her. The snowshoes would hardly sink. She could walk. The next islander's house past the Wrights was about a mile down the road. She couldn't recall who lived there but it would be warm. She'd have to come up with an explanation for why she hadn't gone to the Wrights.

Her snowshoes crunched on the crusty surface, her breath was audible and visible. When the sun intermittently slid behind a scurrying cloud, the woods and ocean turned a uniform lead color. The loneliness of the landscape was intimidating, deepening her sense of having been abandoned to an endless existence of solitude. A different kind of hell. Her former life was a distant memory. She had lived in this void forever. She longed for the sight of another human being. At the same time, she longed for her own living room, a crackling fire, hot soup.

The sound of the truck didn't immediately penetrate her blunted senses. When it finally did, she felt almost hallucinatory. And then, like a great yellow prehistoric monster, a huge snowplow came towards her, spraying arcs of snow onto both sides of the road.

"Sport!" a voice yelled, "You ok?"

For a moment Sport stood in amazement, as if she'd been marooned for years instead of days. She didn't know if it was tears or snow stinging her eyes. The snow plow driver was waving at her. She waved back hesitantly.

And then she caught sight of Steve's Jeep behind the plow. The spell broke. Laughing and shouting, "Dr. Schwartz, I presume?" – a hackneyed joke she never would have resorted to under ordinary circumstances – she scrambled around the stopped plow, opened the passenger door of Steve's Jeep and fell in. The blast hit her like the warm air of the tropics when stepping out of a plane in mid January.

"Where were you? Why didn't you get here sooner?" she asked illogically. Her voice was rusty and she felt as if she could easily disintegrate all over the seat like the melting snow.

He took her hands and removed her mittens. Then he began blowing on her icy skin. "Jesus, you've got some frostbite in your finger tips. How're your toes? The roads were impassable. But if I'd known you were this bad off . . . ." He broke off, frowning. "I could have skied over."

She wiped the moisture off of her face with the edge of her sweater and leaned toward the car heater. She didn't want him to think she was crying with joy over the sight of him. At the same time she had a nearly irresistible urge to burrow against him, to have him encircle her with his arms and kiss her. Instead she turned and pointed to the paper bags on the backseat. "Hey, is there food in there?"

Appalled, he said, "You mean you haven't eaten in two days?"

"It's only been two days?"

"You had no food at all?"

"Oh sure. Smoked oysters galore. But I'm dying for steak, potatoes, ice cream, hot cocoa." Her voice had regained its customary flippant tone.

"I would have thought you'd love toughing it out without electricity or a telephone."

As they followed the slow progress of the plow, she told him about her two days in the blizzard. In the warm car, with Steve beside her, it was hard to recreate the fear she had felt when the trapdoor slammed shut and she had fled across the frozen beach to Heather's house. She was still talking when they came to her driveway. In the spirit of community that typically followed bad weather on the island, the snowplow continued down the private drive and turned around at the house while they waited at the end of the driveway. As the plow came back towards them, Steve shouted his thanks, then parked the car in front of the house and picked up the groceries.

"I knew you'd be able to cope," he said, indicating the shoveled path with his chin.

"You sound disappointed."

At that moment, lamplight blazed into life at the curtainless windows. "Wouldn't you know. The electricity is back on. I can't seem to get the hang of this hero-rescue stuff. What an anti-climax."

Sport was bending over the partially obliterated tracks of snowshoe tracks. "These aren't all mine. My snowshoes are shorter than these tracks."

Steve walked past her and waited at the front door while she unlocked it. After depositing the paper bags on the kitchen counter, Steve headed out of the kitchen. "Stay here. I'll check the house."

Sport watched him a moment as he disappeared down into the playroom and then she began unpacking the groceries: a cooked chicken, potatoes, iceberg lettuce, a cucumber, cheddar cheese, eggs, apples, a bottle of wine.

She put the potatoes in the microwave and was setting the kitchen table with plates, utensils and paper napkins when Steve returned from his search. "Nothing. Nobody. I looked up in the attic." He started slicing the cucumber Sport had left with a knife on the cutting board.

"You believe me, don't you?"

"Don't be an idiot. Besides, I saw the tracks."

"I can't tell you how glad I am you're here," she said.

Steve's eyebrows arched slightly but he said nothing. She winced at the thought that this comment might be misinterpreted.

"You didn't have to bring wine," she continued. "Liquor is the one thing I'm up to my ears in."

She took out a salad bowl and placed it beside the cutting board. "Ok if I go upstairs and take a bath? Help yourself to a drink."

"A bath?"

"You've heard of baths."

"It'll take hours."

"Why should it? There isn't that much of me to wash."

The upper rooms were still cold, but when she switched on the hot water, steam began filling the room. Quickly she pulled off her clothes and stepped into the tub. Immediately she shouted, "Damn!" and hopped out again.

"What's the matter?" Steve shouted from below.

"The water's boiling."

"Want me to come up and blow on it?"

Not bothering to answer, Sport shut the door, adjusted the water temperature and sank into the tub. For a few moments she luxuriated in the heavenly warmth and then she scrubbed her hair and body. Leaving her hair wet, she put on a sweater, jeans and slippers and went downstairs.

Steve had cut up the chicken, opened the wine and was taking the potatoes out of the microwave. "Wow!" Sport exclaimed, "Will you marry me?" Now, for some reason she could not identify, she was being deliberately provocative and was ashamed.

He frowned at her flushed face and her damp hair curling around her shoulders. Then he asked, "Were you the one responsible for chopping all that wood beside the road?"

"Yup," she said with some pride.

"Did you clear the path all by yourself?"

"Who else?"

"Ok, I'll think about it."

He poured wine for the two of them and they sat down at the table under the bright fluorescent lights. She noticed with a hint of irritation that he had put dark meat on her plate without asking her for her preference. She didn't like dark meat and the iceberg lettuce with the cucumbers and some bottled dressing poured over it didn't look appetizing, even as hungry as she was. She thought back to her dinner with Whitney. Why hadn't she bothered to make a fire and set the table in the dining room? It wouldn't have been any more trouble. What was her subconscious up to? They ate in silence for a few minutes until Sport's hunger had subsided some.

"So who do you think was in my house last night?"

Without hesitating, Steve said, "Edith. Edith Wright." He looked up from his plate at her.

Sport was silent a moment. She didn't show any surprise. Then softly: "Yeah, it could have been only poor, disturbed Edith. Turned on by the snow like werewolves are transformed by moonlight. What an idiot that makes me."

"No, it doesn't. You were all alone – "

"In a cabin in the woods – "

"Exactly. Anyone would panic under those circumstances."

"Abbotts aren't supposed to panic."

He looked down into his wine glass and was silent.

"What are you thinking?" she asked.

"I was thinking that Abbotts go scuba diving in the middle of the night."

The moment the words were out he looked stricken. The blood left Sport's face and carefully, she placed her wine glass on the table.

"I'm sorry," he said.

"How did I offend you by saying Abbotts aren't supposed to panic?"

"You know us day-trippers. Sensitive."

"I didn't mean anything."

"I know you didn't." He poured some wine into his own glass and looked at her inquiringly. She shook her head. "Sport, considering everything, why do you insist on living here alone so close to the Wrights?"

She picked up her wine glass again. "I don't know why any longer. I'm thinking of leaving after Christmas. But then again, Whitney had his so-called accident in Connecticut and Talbot was . . . it doesn't matter where I am. If they want to get me, they'll get me. "

"In addition to which, you've been corroded by guilt all these years and you want to punish yourself."

"Which your crack about scuba diving did nothing to help."

Again there was a period of silence as if no subject were completely safe. The kitchen was completely silent except for the sounds of their forks clinking on the edges of their dishes.

"I think you're right about Edith," she said finally. "Over the years I've had this kind of sixth sense that Edith is always watching me."

"Maybe it's your fifth sense. The one that sees."

"Not with malice exactly, but – you'll think I'm crazy – with hopefulness. As if in some recess of what's left of her reason, is a memory of Nevah and me hanging out together and she thinks maybe he's only gone temporarily. That he's wandering alone somewhere, lost and afraid, in the dark, and that I'm the one who will find him for her."

Steve stood up, walked to the window, and watched a squirrel foraging in the snow.

Almost dreamily, as if she'd forgotten Steve was there, Sport continued. "When a person loses someone she loves very much, she can't accept the fact that he's really gone forever. I mean, the one left behind keeps searching all the places associated with the lost one as if she could find him again."

The squirrel Steve was watching had been joined by a second one. Undeterred by their lack of success, the two scrabbled energetically.

She broke off, startled to see Steve walking towards the front hall. Sport jumped to her feet. "Hey, what're you doing?"

He pulled his coat off a hook and reached for his boots.

"I've got to get to bed. I'll need an early start tomorrow morning. Nothing like an emergency, or even the prospect of one, to make people get sick. Just the merest hint of an impending hurricane can set off an epidemic."

"Do you really have to leave so soon? I made chocolate soufflé for dessert."

"No you didn't."

"Ok, so I lied. I think there's another tin of smoked oysters. Don't leave yet." Sport circled around him, blocking the doorway. She tried to get him to look at her, but he was putting on his gloves.

"Suppose I'm in danger again tonight?"

He finally looked at her. "What about tomorrow night? And the night after that?"

Sport had been leaning against the door. She stood there, completely still, for about ten seconds while they stared at each other, both of them expressionless. Then she shook her shoulders as if loosening tight muscles. Stepping out of the way, she said, "Thanks for the food Steve. See you around."

He hesitated a moment. Then he said, "I'm sure it was Edith. Anyway, lock everything up when I go."

When the sound of the Jeep had died in the distance and she was certain he wouldn't change his mind and return, Sport started cleaning the kitchen. The telephone rang.

"Darling, I'm so glad the telephone is working again," her mother said. "Is the electricity back on?"

"Hi, mom. Everything is back in working order. Did you guys get snow?"

"Just a foot or so. You're alright? You had enough wood?"

"I'm fine." She had no intention of telling her mother about the last two days. Her mother would insist she come home, and although she was beginning to think about leaving, she intended to do it on her own schedule.

"How's the renovation coming along?"

It was the wrong question. Ever since Talbot had died, her mother, always moody in any case, had alternated between anger nearly as unpredictable as her husband's and bouts of what appeared to be silent depression. Sport had suggested that her mother see a psychiatrist – as she herself intended to do on a regular basis when she left the island – but her mother hadn't even bothered to respond to the suggestion. Her mother harked back to an older generation that didn't believe in or discuss psychiatric treatment. You just buckled down and got on with your life. Sport recalled a time when her mother's brother had been dying of colon cancer and Anne would only say that her brother was very sick since it was also impolite to discuss cancer, much less colons, in public.

"Those damn contractors. They're robbing your father blind. First they delivered soft pine instead of the hard pine we ordered for the hallway and then they charged us twice the estimate for the tiles that will go into the sunroom – "

It seemed that her anger was finding an outlet with the contractors.

"When are you coming up for Christmas?"

Her mother was silent as if surprised by her own behavior. Then she sighed.

"God I don't know. I have so much to pack and with this chaos, I can't find anything. I have to figure out how to get the gifts shipped up there, and the ornaments – I know we'll have breakage – and then the Spode china for Christmas dinner. I think I'll bring that in the car."

"You don't need the Spode china for Christmas dinner," Sport interrupted.

"As a matter of fact, I do," her mother snapped back.

This seemed excessive, even by her mother's usual standards of compulsive order. Sport sighed, thinking of what an ordeal Christmas would be with all of them decorating Christmas trees, making wreaths, stringing popcorn and cranberries for the birds, hanging the customary mistletoe in the front hall, wrapping gifts, all as if nothing had happened. Her mother would undoubtedly insist that they roast chestnuts over the fireplace.

She felt a pang of empathy for her mother. She knew that Anne had probably made nearly as many plans for her daughter's life with Talbot as Sport had. Although Sport didn't know much about her mother's youth, she knew that her mother had grown up in Central Maine without much money. Everything that was knowable about Anne Abbott was the product of her marriage to Henry Abbott: the houses, the friends, the clothes, the jewelry, and Sport. Sport's marriage to Talbot would have been the culmination of all her efforts and plans. Sport saw how very bourgeois this plan was at its heart. She suspected that her mother saw it as well, but there was no stopping the drive behind it. Human societies used social status as an organizing principle. It was, after all, only another way of figuring out who was the fittest to survive. Different cultures at different points in history measured social status in different ways, of course, but in the end it always came down to who killed the biggest woolly mammoth or had the biggest plasma TV. How, exactly, was Anne going to try to reorganize Sport's life to ensure the survival of her gene pool? Sport felt bone-tired at the thought.

There was more discussion about the renovations before her mother finally seemed to have exhausted her nervous energy.

Sport hung up with relief and had just finished cleaning the kitchen when the phone rang again.

Lifting the receiver, she snapped, "I'm fine, Sarah. The roads are plowed and power is back on."

Silence. Unable to move, she stared out at the all white world. After a moment, she said, "Hello? Who is this?"

When the voice did come on it was unrecognizable at first. Not because it was whispering or attempting to disguise itself, but because it seemed to come from an infinite distance away. A distance having nothing to do with ordinary dimensions.

"Sport, it's me, Sport."

Sport stared at the wall beside the phone in horror. She opened and shut her mouth several times before she could speak. "Edith?"

"I come t' see you last night. I looked all ovah' the house but I couldn't find Eddie. What did you do with my baby, Sport? Where'd you hide him?"

Motherhood. Another biological imperative. Sport didn't want to be cruel to poor crazed Edith, but she felt that if she didn't hang up, she would become just as deranged. With trembling fingers, she replaced the receiver and went upstairs to bed.

Sixteen

After another long day of sitting in front of her computer, watching the snow melt while the screen saver reappeared over and over. She had changed the screen saver from a picture of Sport and Talbot sitting side by side, sailing an antique Hereschoff, to one from about ten years ago of Sport on a ski vacation with her parents in Aspen. The ski picture had absolutely no reverberations for her since she could barely recall the trip. Suddenly, she stood up and picking up the phone, dialed the Wright's number grimly. It was her habit and her need to confront the thing she most feared.

Johnny answered.

"Hi Johnny. It's me, Sport."

"You weathered the storm alright? I saw the doctor headed down your way right after they plowed so I figured you were ok."

"I was fine, no problem. Hey, I'm getting a little stir crazy and I was wondering if I could join you and Edith for dinner tonight."

There was a pause, Sport couldn't tell whether from surprise or reluctance, but then he said, "Sure Sport. Come on down. It won't be fancy but you can come for dinner."

"Thanks Johnny. Around six, ok?"

"That'd be fine Sport. See ya then."

After that, she was able to work a bit before she started walking down the road to the Wrights. As she walked, she recollected how Edith had, in her own fashion, celebrated all holidays as aggressively as Anne. Although the summer families did not often spend Christmas on the point, Sport recalled one Christmas when she was about eight when all the summer families on the Point had gathered there for the holiday.

Of course, the families on the Point had decorated their houses with care and taste. Anne had decorated the Abbott tree exclusively with antique ornaments and real candles that were lit only on Christmas Eve. The Harrington-Clarks had arranged for someone to bring over a Welsh pony to pull a small sleigh. One morning that week there was a fresh five-inch snow just perfect for the sleigh. The weather was almost always perfect for the Sheep's Head Point families. Or at least that was how it seemed in Sport's childhood memories. Maybe because when it wasn't perfect, the kids had played indoors and that had been equally fun. In any case, before the plows had gotten out to clear the roads, their parents bundled up some of the children and Johnny drove them into town on the sleigh where they had cocoa at Elliott Barnett's store. In the late afternoon, after the roads had been plowed, their parents had come in cars to pick them up. It was only years later that Sport realized that the parents' main incentive had probably been to get the kids out of the house while they wrapped gifts. It also occurred to her that it must have been a cold and dreary six-mile sleigh ride back to the house for Johnny.

As wonderful as that had been, the kids had been even more awed by the festivities at Nevah's house. There had been eight, life-size inflated plastic reindeer on the front lawn pulling an inflated life-size sleigh and Santa. The roofline of the house had been outlined in colored Christmas lights and there had been two spruce trees lavishly covered with silver tinsel in the living room. Edith had arranged a party for some of the kids from the Point and about ten island kids. It was utter chaos and one of the most fun parties Sport could remember from her childhood. The kids had run roughshod over the house, wrestling, playing in the kitchen with Edith's pots and pans, watching TV and eating chocolate. In the living room no less. Edith had taped hundreds of tiny candy canes to the ceiling and Johnny kept holding up one child or another and letting them grab a candy cane.

She remembered only one Easter at the Wrights but that had also impressed her. There had been a six-foot-tall inflated bunny sitting in a puddle of muddy snow.

She and the other summer kids on the Point had always loved playing at Nevah's. In the summer, there was usually a junk car without tires in the backyard. The five of them would sit in the car and pretend, for reasons Sport no longer recalled, that they were driving to France. There had also been a lobster boat propped up on a wooden cradle in the front yard with a hole through the starboard side of the hull and a ladder leaning against its side so the kids could climb on board. They played pirate for hours. There were piles of tires and rotted firewood to use as walls for pretend houses, and Edith's homemade cookies for snacks.

Inside the house, Johnny had cut down the legs on a round wooden table and made a table only one foot high with miniature chairs to match. When Sport and Dede could persuade Tal, Whitney and Nevah to participate, the five children would sit there eating Edith's cookies and pretending that the chocolate milk was tea. They would use a set of doll china that Edith had kept for just this purpose. The china had been covered with tiny pale pink roses and light green vines. Sport had been enchanted with the tea set. Each time they finished their "tea", Sport would stand on a chair and wash the tiny dishes in Edith's sink. After drying them, she would put them back in a wooden box lined with cotton. One time she had asked Edith if she could have the dishes when Edith died and Edith had picked her up, hugged her tight, and assured Sport of her inheritance.

Nevah's birthday was on July 4. Since Nevah was the only child on the Point who had a July or August birthday, Anne had made it an annual occasion for a group birthday party for the children on the Point. Anne would prepare an elaborate treasure hunt and the children would be divided into teams of four or five kids each. Each team would follow a series of five or six clues written on pieces of different-colored paper. The clues were all in rhyme and there would be a prize for each child as they solved each clue and arrived at the next. The prizes were good: beading kits, watercolor sets, small model sailing boats and Lego toys. Whichever team got to the end first got the grand prize. One year it had been a huge tube that was used to tow the kids behind the Mako all summer and the winners also won the right to decide who got rides first. Another year it had been a log cabin playhouse that the other kids could use only at the express invitation of a grand prize winner.

As Sport approached the Wrights' house now, the debris on the front lawn looked like a series of miniature hills and mountains under the piles of snow. The house looked dark. However, when Johnny opened the door at her knock and she walked in, the first thing she saw by the light of a dim lamp in one corner were hundreds of paper valentines, some small, some large, most of them crayoned with Valentine greetings, suspended from the same ceiling where once the candy canes had hung.

"How 'ya doin'," Johnny said and then following her glance towards the ceiling, he added, "You know Edith's birthday is on Valentine's. All the Island kids made these for her."

Sport nodded and walked into the living room.

"Have a seat Sport. Can I get you a beer?"

"That would be great," she said although a cold beer was the last thing she felt like after coming in from the chilly outdoors.

She looked around the room. The Cape-style one-story house had been built in the 40's. The large combined living room and dining room had one large plate-glass window overlooking the bay. It was, quite literally, a million-dollar view that might have been Johnny's except that the Harrington-Clarks had bought the house and the land under the house from Johnny's parents about twenty-five years ago. Johnny and Edith had lived there rent-free since the purchase.

There were two large brown La-z-Boy armchairs placed directly in front of the plate-glass window. This might have been for the view except that there was also a large flat-screen TV planted in the exact middle of the window. As a child, Sport had always had the vague impression that the Wrights must have more money than her own parents since Anne did not allow a TV in the Abbotts' house until Sport went away to college. Not knowing anything about TV shows had, in fact, set Sport at a social disadvantage that she made up for during her freshman year in Chicago by watching four or five hours a night while she did homework. By the end of the first semester she had felt as if she deserved an extra four credits for the effort.

There were two bedrooms off to the right of the Wrights' living room with a bathroom in between. The kitchen was over to the left just beyond the dining room table.

While the yard had always been filled with Johnny's equipment, the house, as Sport recalled it from her childhood, had usually been clean and even neat if there wasn't a crowd of children around. There had been a sofa and two wing chairs back then and brightly colored rag rugs on the floor. Now there was only one small rug left, grey with dirt, and the room was dusty and gave off a musty smell.

Sport could see into the refrigerator past Johnny's shoulder. There didn't seem to be anything in there except for a couple of six-packs of beer, a carton of milk, a carton of eggs, some ketchup, pickles and mustard. Sport wondered what the dinner menu might be.

At that moment, someone opened one of the bedroom doors and walked in. As dark as the room was, it startled Sport because she could tell at once that it wasn't Edith.

As the person approached she saw that it was a tiny elderly woman that she finally recognized as Hope Lantagne, Edith's mother. Sport knew that Hope lived somewhere near Augusta but she hadn't seen her for several years. Sport estimated that she must be at least in her mid-eighties.

Hope was bent over in the shape of a comma, but she walked briskly over to Sport.

"Oh, it's you. Anne Abbott's girl. How are you?" Her voice was a caricature of an old woman's voice: squeaky and high, she spoke quickly. In fact, her question sounded more like a demand.

Hope sat down on the edge of the one of the chairs. She was dressed in surprisingly youthful clothes: jeans, a white turtleneck, a bright blue pullover sweater that came down nearly to her knees, and what looked like new hiking boots.

"I'm fine, Mrs. Lantagne. How've you been?"

"Nevah' ask a ninety-fouh' yeah' old woman how she is if you don't want to heah' a long story. I'm fine. I've been helping out Edith heah'. She's not quite right these days, you know. I've been cleaning down cella'. Figure there's some folks as could use some of the junk down theah'. Old toys, clothes, those so't of things."

Sport was impressed, not only by the thought of this tiny creature hauling junk up and down the steep steps that led to the cellar but also at the generosity implicit in this task. This seemed much closer to the spirit of giving than all the charity balls her parents and their friends were always arranging and attending.

Johnny came back into the room with two beers and stood since the two chairs were occupied.

"How's your family, Sport?"

"Oh you know, as well as can be expected. We were all pretty hard hit by. . . ," her voice trailed off.

Johnny nodded.

"They'll all be here for Christmas, you know."

"Yup, next week I guess."

Sport winced. Of course Johnny would know they were all coming up. It would fall to him to make sure the furnaces were working, the water was turned on, the driveways were plowed, and there was plenty of wood for the fireplaces.

Johnny looked out the black window as if there were a view there.

"I was remembering your father today, Sport."

Sport looked at Johnny quizzically.

"The summer I was sixteen. He was, oh I'd say, thirty-five or so. He decided to teach me race sailing. I don't know why. On his Ensign. We raced maybe fifteen times that summer. God almighty, that man could yell and carry on."

He paused and then continued. There was no malice in his voice, just a slight hint of quizzical wonder, as if the memory surprised even him.

"We won a trophy that summer. Your father gave the trophy to me but it was a rotating kind of thing and I had to give it back the next summer."

So Johnny had been a summer "project" for Henry. Henry viewed most younger people as projects, the way other people viewed gardens. As something to cultivate with a view to showing it off to others. Some sort of Pygmalion complex except that Henry was easily disappointed and tended to cut short his losses with less successful projects. Like Sarah. He had probably been disappointed with Johnny's sailing prowess. Otherwise, who knew, maybe Henry would have loaned the money for Johnny to go to college.

Johnny asked after Dede and Whitney, staring out the window as Sport described the ways in which they were adapting to their handicaps. Hope appeared to be listening although Sport suspected that either her hearing was less than perfect or she wasn't up on the local news since at one point she asked whether Talbot was coming up for the holidays as well. Sport said no and Johnny did not elaborate. Meanwhile, Sport nervously wondered where Edith was.

After a while Johnny stood up and went back into the kitchen. He took a frozen pizza out of the freezer and a minute later Sport could hear the whirring of the microwave. He came back with the pizza, four plates and some napkins. He placed them on the table and walked over to knock on one of the bedroom doors. Hope walked briskly, if stiffly, to the table. She sat politely with her hands folded on her lap looking down at her pizza.

"Dinner, Edith."

The door opened and Edith emerged. She was wearing what looked like a pair of Johnny's pajamas and she seemed to have just woken up because her short grey hair radiated out from her head like spokes.

But her face broke into a smile when she saw Sport.

"Oh Sport. I didn't know you was heah'. I fell asleep."

She sat down in one of the chairs and started eating.

"How's your mothah', Sport?"

"Oh fine." This was no time for either details or the truth. "She'll be coming up for Christmas next week."

"You don't say. Why, that's real nice. I'll look fo'ward to that."

There was some talk about the blizzard and how it had affected Augusta. Hope grumbled that it had kept her out of her car and housebound for three days. Sport glanced at her with surprise, wondering how this tiny person could even see over a dashboard. There was talk about people on the island that they knew in common, or that Sport at least pretended to know. Then Edith asked after Whitney and Dede. Sport, again omitting the details, said they were all fine and looking forward to coming up for Christmas.

"And Talbot? He'll be heah' I'm sho'."

Johnny didn't even bother to look up from his plate.

"Oh yes," Sport said, her voice catching only a little. "He'll be here." It was easier than anything else she could think of to say.

"Good, that's good," Edith said, nodding her head and smiling at Sport.

Hope, who had been cutting up the pizza with her knife and fork into tiny squares and enthusiastically shoveling it into her mouth looked up with surprise.

"I thought you said Talbot wasn't coming up for the holidays," she said indignantly as if Sport had somehow tried to trick her.

Sport looked over at Johnny. These were his women after all. Let him deal with them. But Johnny just stood up and cleared the plates, waving Sport back to the table with his hand when she started to stand up.

"I'm sorry. I forgot. You're absolutely correct, Mrs. Lantagne. Talbot can't make it."

Hope nodded, but Sport had the sense that Edith's mother would have a lot more questions for Johnny as soon as she left.

Johnny came back with five Fudgesicles still in their wrappers. He put one in front of Sport, one in front of Edith, one in front of Hope and took the last two back to his seat.

The already-dying conversation lagged further while they ate the cold sticky dessert. It tasted to Sport as if it had been in the freezer for a long time. She excused herself to go the bathroom, breathing through her mouth while she was in there to avoid the rank odor.

As she sat in the bathroom, she wondered how she could ever have been scared by these sad people. Surely she would feel it if they held any malice towards her. But she felt nothing even close to it, no matter how well deserved it might have been.

"Well, I better be going," she said as she emerged. Edith looked up, startled, as if she had forgotten Sport was there.

Johnny only nodded, as if he had been expecting her to bolt at the first opportunity. Then Hope spoke up.

"Oh, no, stay put a while. We can play a little Scrabble."

Hope scurried across the room and pulled an ancient and tattered Scrabble box down from the shelves, returned to the table and started putting out letters with her tiny wrinkled hands that reminded Sport of a dried crocodile foot Henry had once given her.

Johnny turned on the TV and watched a basketball game and Edith simply sat at the table and stared at its empty surface while they played.

Hope was an excellent player and beat Sport soundly although there were one or two occasions on which, if Sport had been playing anyone else, she might have demanded a dictionary check.

When they were finished, Sport stood up and thanking them again, started determinedly towards the door, reminding herself of a prisoner in a movie making a desperate break across the prison yard to the gate. As she was going, Edith stood up and somehow managed to fold Sport into her arms. Startled by the feeling of Edith's bony body pressed against her own, she forced herself to hug Edith back, although Edith smelled very much like the bathroom.

"I'm sorry you missed Eddie, Sport. He'll be broke up he wasn't heah' to see you. You come back next week and he'll be heah' for sho.'"

Sport closed her eyes and patted Edith's back.

"That would be great, Edith," she said, "I'll look forward to it."

Johnny was standing by the front door, holding her coat out to her.

She took it and, afraid that she might not be able to maintain her composure, waved to Johnny as she walked out, not daring to say good-bye.

Seventeen

"How about this one?" Anne Abbott pointed to a narrow six-foot spruce.

Not even bothering to look at it, Henry continued past.

"What's wrong with it?"

Neither Sport nor her father answered and Anne, who never stooped to unimportant battles, continued following them. Bringing up the rear in the hushed woods was Sarah, who made no attempt to voice a choice. It occurred to Sport that Sarah was a mixture of immaturity and maturity, the maturity stemming from the verbal buffeting she had endured over the years from Henry; the immaturity from the resulting lack of confidence.

"This one isn't bad." Henry Abbott stopped in front of a nine-foot white pine.

It was not easy for them to move through the knee-high snow and Sport suspected that Henry's choice was attributable more to his reluctance to continue than any aesthetic sense, but of course, Henry could never admit to any weakness, no matter how trivial.

"No, I don't think so," Sport said, half because she didn't like white pine for a Christmas tree – the branches were too weak – and half because she wanted to both provoke and please Henry. Sure enough, Henry followed his younger daughter, rolling his eyes and grinning.

It was an automatic reflex on her part to show how tough she could be in front of Henry. How pathetic that she still felt this need. Then it occurred to her that without Talbot or any immediate job prospects she would be financially dependent on Henry for the foreseeable future. A wave of depression rolled over her at this thought. Oh God, hadn't she earned enough A's by this point in her life? Actually no, not if she couldn't support herself.

"When do we meet your doctor friend?" Sarah asked.

"Tonight." Sport stopped in front of a tall thick-branched Douglas fir. "I invited him to dinner tonight."

Shielding her eyes from the hard bright sun, Anne looked up to the top of the tree. "Are you planning on cutting a hole in the ceiling?" she asked politely.

"The living room is two stories high."

"Do you expect me to drag that monstrosity home – " Henry started, but Sport interrupted him.

"What do you mean *you're* dragging it home. We're *all* dragging it home." Hesitantly, and without hope, Sarah said, "How about the spruce beside it? It's much more manageable."

"That's such a loser," Sport said and right afterwards, looked stricken, afraid one of them would pick up a connection between the word "loser" and Sarah. None of them did.

"I prefer the spruce," Henry said just to provoke Sport.

Anne raised one eyebrow. "Sarah, we're about to find out what happens when an irresistible force meets an immovable object."

There was always a brief period of adjustment at the start of a visit between Henry's first daughter and second wife, but eventually their desire to get along always overcame the awkwardness of their relationship. They were, in any case, so very different from each other: Anne was so directed; Sarah so willing to accommodate.

"I'm more irresistible than she's immovable," Henry said, proving his point by giving Sport a shove with his elbow that nearly sent her sprawling in the snow.

"Stop being such a pain in the ass!" Sport picked up the axe and walked toward the Douglas fir.

Grinning, Henry watched her. His affection for his younger daughter manifested itself in a constant, affectionate bickering.

After a short time, Henry took Sport's place at the tree, and then Anne and Sarah took turns.

"Why the hell didn't we bring the chain saw?" Henry grunted as he took the axe from Anne. Despite his complaints, he was easily the most effective.

"You don't cut down Christmas trees with chain saws," Sport said. "It isn't traditional." As usual, she was turning thorny after a few uninterrupted hours in Henry's company.

"Timber!" yelled Sarah, who tended to say such things, and they all scrambled back. The tree, however, fell exactly where Sport had planned for it to fall.

Henry grabbed the trunk and the other three distributed themselves where they could be the most effective along the trunk as they headed back to the house. The sun hung low and silvery in the sky, radiating light without heat. The snow was past its prime, resembling encroaching greyness on an ageing head. A northeasterly wind stung their faces. Softly, in a sweet, true voice, Sarah began singing "Noel, Noel" as she tugged and yanked at her section of the tree trunk. It took them almost an hour to get the tree back to the house.

"I knew it!" Henry yelled as they tugged and pulled it up onto the front porch. "We'll never get the damned thing inside."

Sport assessed the situation. "We'll set it up on the porch. That way we can decorate it with cranberries and popcorn and it'll be for the birds." Seeing Henry open his mouth, she added, "Don't you dare!" and he laughed instead of coming out with the obvious.

"We could have saved ourselves a lot of trouble," Anne pointed out, "if we'd decorated one of these outdoor trees in the first place."

"And the life of this tree," Sarah added.

"Oh for God's sake, let's just get it done," said Sport in exasperation, with a painful realization that they were just going through the motions, pretending that this was just an ordinary Christmas.

They hauled the tree the rest of the way onto the porch and into the living room. Sarah went to the shed for the stand while Sport and Henry sawed the bottom into a narrower shaft. Anne went into the house with Sarah to start preparing their traditional Christmas Eve dinner of clam chowder served with French bread and salad.

By the time the first guests arrived for the supper, they had the tree set up in the living room and decorated with the antique ornaments Anne had been collecting for nearly a quarter of a century. It had all been done in such a rush that things were, at least by Anne's standards, a bit haphazard. The tree was still dripping melting snow and they had forgotten to bring in wood for the fireplace. They had had to make the salad with wilted lettuce from the island store since they had forgotten to bring fresh baby greens with them from Rockland and they hadn't had time to wrap the evergreen roping around the stairway banister. Even Anne, coming down the stairs to greet her first guests, looked as if she had been decorated a bit too quickly. She hadn't had time to do her makeup and Sport spotted a run in her mother's stocking that started just below her calf-length velvet red skirt.

The first to arrive were the Harrington-Clarks. Sport was starting down the stairs behind her mother when she saw Timmy, Talbot's twenty-year-old brother, coming through the front door. Talbot and Timmy had been like the reverse sides of woven cloth. Whereas Talbot had been serious and responsible, Timmy had always been insouciant and easy-going. Talbot had worked hard at each endeavor, while Timmy succeeded through charm and natural ability. Talbot had been ambitious, while Timmy only wanted to own a snowboard shop.

However, from twenty feet away, Timmy was a replica of his older brother: the same height, build and coloring. Sport turned on her heel, went into the bathroom and stood standing over the sink, shaking and wondering if she was going to throw up.

"Sport," Henry shouted from below, "Where are you? Everybody's arriving."

Sport looked up into the mirror and washed her face. Then she carefully applied lipstick and combed her hair again. It didn't make her look any less drawn and strained.

Notwithstanding their haste, the downstairs had been transformed from Sport's solitary writer's sanctuary into a Dickensian set piece. Anne had brought her Philippine housekeeper with her from Connecticut and the housekeeper had been hard at work all day. Sport wondered what the housekeeper, who had only been in the States for six months, made of all these elaborate preparations. There were fake battery-operated candles in all the windows, a dozen poinsettia plants in pots, a red tablecloth on the dining room table with green napkins, tall white candles in holiday candlesticks on the table, a flower arrangement with cyclamen and, of course, the Christmas Spode china. Since there was no proper mantelpiece over the living room fireplace, a Nativity scene of Hummel porcelain figures – bought during Anne's last trip to London – had been set up on a bookshelf.

As Sport came back down the stairs, Anne and Sarah were standing in the front hall in their velvet holiday dresses, greeting their guests, heaping coats and boots in Sport's study and stacking tinseled, glittering gifts in a corner of the living room. In addition to Talbot's parents and brother, there was his older sister, Claudia, Claudia's husband and their two small boys. Henry, dressed in a red plain vest over his white shirt, kissed the women, punched the men on their shoulders, swung the little boys in the air. Sport was careful to avoid any emotion-charged glances between herself and Marilyn and Spencer, but nevertheless noted the changes. Unable to insulate themselves from despair by money and class, they seemed fragile, almost insubstantial, and held up by a hard plastic coating of pride. Marilyn was heavily made up, her hair tinted gold, and she wore a winter white wool outfit as if she were in Chinese mourning. Spencer, who had always looked younger than his years, had suddenly aged beyond them. It looked as if the bone structure in his face had melted down, leaving behind sagging and puffy flesh. Spencer had one hand under Marilyn's elbow as if he thought she might collapse without it but Marilyn was smiling bravely and talking to Henry about their plans to go to Costa Rica in February.

They sat down on the sofa together, something they would never had done before Talbot's accident. It seemed to Sport that usually one spouse was much more gregarious than the other, but this had never been true of the Harrington-Clarks. They seemed equally outgoing and happy at parties. It then occurred to Sport that she had never heard them argue or fight. It seemed the result of true compatibility, not just repressive good manners. They were, after all, the only adults on the Point who were still with their original spouse. Sport recalled Talbot telling her that his parents had gone out to dinner by themselves once a week all his life. Sport's eyes teared up.

Whitney, Heather, and Whitney's younger sister, Sabina, had arrived. Whitney's guide dog managed to lead Whitney successfully around the obstacles in the room, allowing only one branch of the Christmas tree to whack Whitney in the head. Henry, who always pretended that neither Whitney nor Dede were disabled, tried not to watch as Whitney put out his hand to touch the big armchair by the fireplace that had always been Whitney's favorite.

It called to Sport's mind a summer evening, right after she graduated from high school. Sport's parents had gone to some picnic or other. Whitney had sat in that chair with Sport on one knee, both of them drunk on Henry's gin. That was the summer that they often acted out skits about their parents' personal histories. At Dede's suggestion, Whitney had been pretending that he was Henry – it was easy to imitate Henry in one of his irritatingly jovial good moods – trying to choose between his first wife, Thora, and Anne. Sport had played Anne and Dede had played Thora.

For some reason, Dede had used a squeaky voice with an English accent to imitate Thora although Thora's voice was actually rather throaty.

"Oh Henry, you'll so-o-o-o regret this. You know dahling that I'll go on to marry Chuck who's much richer than you dear and when he dies – so unfortunate," she paused for effect, "I'll be ever so much richa' than you," she finished by poking her finger in Whitney's chest.

"Dear, dear Hen-n-n-n-ry," Sport had stage whispered into Whitney's ear, mussing his hair, "You really *must* get away from that aging hag. My God! She's nearly forty. Where are your eyes, man! Thora can't possibly accommodate your many manly needs so well as I!"

Looking back, Sport saw the scene as her and Dede's pathetic teenage attempt to cope with the lava-like shiftings of their parents' marital allegiances, although in fairness to Dede's father, Dede's mother had already been dead for years before he went off to Italy to live with his second wife.

Sport couldn't recall where Talbot had been at the moment. This was not, in any case, the sort of horseplay that he was likely to engage in, even when drunk. But it was at this moment in the skit when Sarah had walked into the room. They had all frozen but Sarah had only said, "Dad will know you took that gin," and then walked back out of the room.

That memory dissolved into the present where Whitney had now taken center stage with a story about strolling along Fifth Avenue with his dog, when he had nearly fallen off the curb. He had been caught just in time by a beggar pretending to be blind.

"How'd you know he was pretending? Or that he was a beggar?" Timmy never believed Whitney's stories.

"He told me."

Although the others laughed, Heather was not amused. She refused Henry's offer of a hot rum toddy and went to the bar to fix herself a scotch and water. She was a small, pretty woman, but lines of dissatisfaction had etched themselves into her forehead and around her mouth years before Whitney's accident. Since then, it was as if she had a taken a vow of angry depression.

A car horn blasted the night air. Sport went to the door. Johnny Wright, standing at the passenger door of his pickup, was holding Dede's crutches and helping her out of the truck.

"Hi, everybody," Dede shouted as she took Johnny's hand. Henry and Timmy ran out to help. Dede looked pretty in her bright red parka but she had put on still more weight since Sport had last seen her at Talbot's funeral.

"I'm ok, all of you. Just give me my crutches." Breathing heavily, she was making an effort to sound cheerful.

"Thanks for the ride, Johnny."

"Johnny," Henry said, "Come in for a hot rum toddy."

"Can't. Edith's not good."

"How was your trip?" Sport asked, kissing Dede gingerly so as not to upset her balance.

"What's wrong with Edith?" Henry asked.

"The trip was ok," Dede said, now making an effort not to sound irritable. "A cab took me from the airport to the ferry and Johnny met me at the ferry."

"She caught a cold," Johnny said shortly, then got back into his pickup and drove away.

Inside the brightly lit house, the air was fragrant with the scent of pine needles. Glasses tinkled, voices rose and fell as if with the rhythm of the invisible sea, while Henry distributed alcoholic and non-alcoholic beverages appropriate to the ages of the recipients. Sarah passed platters of cheese and crab canapés while Anne and the housekeeper laid the buffet dinner out on the sideboard. Talbot's little nephews bickered over a chest full of old toys and Sport wondered if Edith's illness was a result of Edith's night-time meanderings.

Since she had been waiting for it, Sport heard the Jeep motor first. Without putting on a coat, she ran out into the bitter cold. "I'm so glad you're here," she said with uncharacteristic humility.

Steve, bareheaded and wearing only a bulky sweater, reached into his Jeep. His voice muffled, he said, "Why wouldn't I be?" He emerged with a large, brightly wrapped parcel. Dismayed since she hadn't thought to buy him a Christmas gift, Sport fleetingly considered which of the items she had ordered for Henry might be most easily transferred to Steve.

"Well," she said, "the last two times I've invited you over, you were too busy poking into people's ears and throats and what-nots."

The bulky package under one arm, Steve straightened. He started to respond with a quip, but then at the sight of Sport's face, apparently changed his mind. He looked her in the eye for a few seconds and then quietly, he said, "Hey, Sport, you can't help it if you're in love with a dead man."

Sport folded her arms across her chest as if she'd just become aware of the cold. She began to shiver uncontrollably. Steve dropped his package and put both arms around her, presumably to stop the shivering. His arm moved along her back. "God, I'm sorry. We can't seem to stop hurting each other."

"Sport!" Henry yelled from the doorway. "Who's out there with you?"

Steve picked up his package and the two of them went indoors.

"Henry, I'd like you to meet the man who rescued me from that man-eating deer last fall." Sport's voice was firm.

"Don't you believe it, Mr. Abbott. Your daughter will never need rescuing."

"That's for sure," Henry agreed with a pleased laugh. He shook Steve's hand and led him to the bar. "Rum toddy or something stronger?"

"Rum toddy would be fine." Steve placed his gift in a corner next to the two little boys. "For me?" one of them asked. Steve grinned and shook his head. "Next time. I didn't know you'd be here."

"It's ok," the other said kindly, "We'll get lots tomorrow."

The chatter died down as Sport led Steve around the room to make the introductions. The older Harrington-Clarks shook hands politely but their expressions were questioning. Sport imagined their thoughts. *You haven't found a replacement for our son already, have you, Sport?* Heather, lost in her own unhappy thoughts, nodded indifferently. The younger crowd – Talbot's brother, sister, and brother-in-law, Whitney's sister – were all friendly. Dede and Sarah were openly curious.

"What did you say your name was?" Whitney asked.

Steve studied the vacant eyes. "Steve. Steve Schwartz."

Whitney offered his hand and Steve shook it. "I hear you're the new doc on the Island. Well you've certainly come to the right place if you're looking to expand your practice."

Steve smiled politely while a thoughtful expression appeared on Whitney's face as he remembered something else about Steve. Something about a baby.

The chatter resumed. People walked back and forth to the buffet, filling their plates and glasses, moving around to speak with each other. It sounded like any other party they had ever had in that house. It was the sound of a houseful of people murmuring to each other and occasionally laughing. There were no loud voices, no loud laughter, no ribald jokes or obvious drunkenness. It was the soothing, pleasant sound of an affluent New England dinner party.

Sport was telling the two little boys how she and the other kids used to slide down the bluff behind the house to the dock on snow saucers at Christmas. They would climb back up using the rope that was strung tree to tree down the incline. Whitney, who was listening, dared Sport to do it again tomorrow and Sport laughed and agreed that she would if Whitney would go first. Whitney said he would if he could use the guide dog and then Dede said she'd go also if Whitney did that. Timmy said he'd go down on a snowboard and the twins clamored to be allowed to go down on the new sleds they had been promised for Christmas. Sport solemnly swore that she would take them sledding Christmas day to calm them down.

Steve sat down on the floor next to Dede and the two began discussing her disability and how she coped with it. Sarah joined them on the floor and the conversation shifted to her hyperkinetic students.

By now Talbot's small nephews were beginning to exhibit their own signs of hyperkinesis. Having spread all the ancient Abbott toys on the floor, one was beating on a drum, making conversation impossible, and the other was pointing a rifle at the grownups and taking deliberate aim at one head after another.

Abruptly, Steve got to his feet. Surveying the buffet table, he removed one of the red napkins and tied it around the head of one of the astonished but willing little boys. Then he told the one with the drum to continue banging. He placed the rifle on the shoulder of the other, and he himself, limping, played on a pretend flute. The three of them began marching around the room.

Henry was the first to catch on and burst out laughing. In a moment Sarah joined him and ran to get her camera.

"What's happening?" Whitney complained. "Will somebody please tell me what's happening?"

Dede explained and Whitney remarked laughing that it was a good thing that he and Dede were so damned insensitive. While the others laughed delightedly at the sight of the three militiamen, Sport's eyes roamed around the room. Talbot's brother, Timmy, and Whitney's sister, Sabina, were seated on the floor together, almost like a reenactment of Sport and Talbot years ago. Sport hadn't noticed until now how pretty Sabina had become. Her face, which had seemed too long and gaunt as a teenager, now looked classic with its high cheekbones and pale coloring.

For the first time in her life, Sport felt old.

She looked away to watch the Harrington-Clarks clapping their hands in time to Henry's whistling of Yankee Doodle. Talbot's sister Claudia was wiping a tear away but smiling at the same time. In a moment everyone was clapping except Heather. Sarah took some more pictures.

Hardly knowing what she was about to do, Sport jumped to her feet. She started with Whitney, kissing him on his mouth, and then circled the room, hugging the little boys, kissing Steve's cheek, embracing everyone else. No one seemed surprised. They all responded with kisses and hugs, and Talbot's brother-in-law patted her shoulder as he brushed her cheek with his lips.

"Everything's going to be fine from now on," he promised and right then, it sounded like something that could be true.

Eighteen

Forgive me Father, for I have sinned.

Where the hell did those words come from? She wasn't even a Catholic.

As she lay in bed early Christmas morning, Sport's thoughts were as scattered as the skeins of cirrus clouds in the grizzled sky.

I never meant to kill Nevah. Take me. But wait, that's a sin too, isn't it? Heedlessness. Maybe that's my greatest sin. I feel like Sisyphus, each morning rolling a whole bag of sins up a hill only to have them fall back onto my head while I sleep. Like the time that I ran the Grady White onto a rock of Fish Point and Sarah decided to martyr herself and tell Dad that she had been driving, and I just let her lie. Or the time when Mom backed the Volvo through the garage door and I made Dede invite me over for the weekend so that I wouldn't have to hear Dad yelling at Mom all Saturday and Mom slamming doors and crying all day Sunday. Or the day Grandfather Abbott died and I went to a dance the same night . . . .

I'm only depressed because it's so gloomy out this morning. Actually, last night was one of the first times I've felt a bit lighthearted since Talbot . . . . Maybe it will happen again today. It could. We'll go to that ecumenical service at the Baptist church; we'll have a big breakfast of eggs, bacon, sausage, biscuits, fruit, coffee and what not; we'll open scads of presents all day; I'll be totally surrounded by all the people I love. Well, almost all.

Her thoughts skittered to lying in a hammock with Talbot behind Talbot's house discussing the logistics of commuting between their two colleges. Her sixteenth birthday party when Anne had thrown a barbeque party for most of the island's summer people and she had gone searching for Talbot only to see him drive by with another girl. A temporary aberration. She sighed, got out of bed and dressed.

Except for Steve, everyone who had been over for dinner the night before was back for breakfast. It was chaotic but cheerful. The little boys insisted on making the fried eggs and burned most of them. Henry was annoyed because the bacon was overcooked. Whitney told a story about a girl he met at a crowded party at the Dendur Temple at the Met who hadn't realized he was blind and kept pointing out interesting aspects of the Temple to him until she noticed his dog sitting behind him. Dede told a story about a girl who had recently lost the use of her legs. Dede had met her for the first time in a physical therapy class a couple of weeks ago. The girl was still in what Dede referred to as the "despair in the chair" phase and at the end of the session, the girl had driven the electric chair straight into the physical therapist and knocked her down. There was nothing funny about the story and it created a vacuum of silence around Dede that spread through the dining room so that the room was uncomfortably silent by the end of the story.

When they were done eating and were just sitting in front of their empty plates, they started placing bets on how long it would take Sport to slide on the saucer from the top of the incline to the edge of the beach. Henry took the bets and recorded them on paper. Then Timmy dared Sport to do it in her swimsuit and Sport disappeared and came back downstairs in her wetsuit, a ski hat, a bright yellow nylon slicker, and winter boots so then they had to take pictures of that.

By the time they had found the saucer in the shed and were standing on the top of the bluff it was almost ten and they were in a bit of hurry in order to get changed and make it to church by ten thirty. Although the snow in back of the house had been well packed down by their feet by now, there was still too much snow for the saucer to slide easily over the gradual incline that led to the edge of the bluff so Sport floundered through the snow to the edge of the bluff. Grasping the rope that was strung from tree to tree down the bluff, she began the gymnastics of sitting on the saucer while still holding onto the rope. There was something about the slicker that made it almost impossible for her to stay on the saucer and everyone laughed as she kept slipping off first one side, and then the other side, of the saucer.

And then, once again, what should have been a minor accident spun out of control. When the rope broke, Sport started to slide, half on and half off the saucer, down the still snowy bluff. She wasn't even going fast. In fact, it looked almost like slow motion as she slid and bumped along although she was unable to quite stop herself. But then, a hidden spruce stump under the snow caught the slicker so that she hung for a couple of seconds at the edge of a small cliff near the bottom of the hill, right above the beach. When the slicker tore, she was suddenly airborne for the last five feet before landing on her head on the snow covered rocks below.

There was an instant when, having rushed to the edge of the bluff, before they could see what had happened to Sport and before they could start down the incline, that they all were staring at the rope. It had clearly been cut by a sharp knife. All except for one thin strand.

PART 2

One

"'Pears t' me she'd be better off dead."

"No call for you t' think that way, Lucy. Fact is you're earnin' a sight o' money."

"Fact is, I'd have earned a sight more if I'd gotten off this island and finished college and nursing school."

"You could have been a doctah' Lucy, you had the brains."

"If I'd had the brains, I should have figured out how to get outta' this place."

"You think Anne will evah' get ovah' this?"

"No, I don't. Wouldn't surprise me if she went as nuts as Edith."

The two voices mingled with the booming of the sea against the ledges and the screeching of the herring gulls gliding along the air currents, diving for mackerel. As if she'd developed gills, she seemed to be breathing under water. The reflection of the waves shimmered overhead, the room surged back and forth with the tides, the brininess of the ocean filled her lungs.

> *Nevah was scared but he tried not to show it.*
> *Talbot said, "There's nothing to it. To inflate,*
> *you push this button. To deflate, this one."*

The snow was never going to stop. It whirled off the tops of the trees like smoke from a chimney. It fell hour after hour, day after day. Sarah said, "In the spring they'll dig us out and we'll be perfectly preserved fossils caught in our last act on Earth. Like the guys in Pompeii."

*"Johnny, do you still hold it against us?" And Johnny said, "He
wasn't dumb, though give him two choices, like as not,
he'd pick the wrong one."*

"It's worse than the blizzard of fifty-two," Dede said. "At least that's what Johnny told me. That time Route One was completely shut down."

Whitney said, "I heard that they're driving quarter ton pickups across the Thorofare."

The snow went on and on. It covered roads, scrubby undergrowth, the lower limbs of trees. All landmarks had disappeared. So the voices said. Chickadees grubbed forlornly for food, scrabbling their tiny, branch-like scrawls into the snow. The electricity went off, the telephone died, the world stood still.

*Steve said, "I allowed a new born baby to die. Intentionally."
"What was wrong with the baby?"
"You name it."
"I killed Nevah Wright."
"We're just a couple of murderers, you and I."*

The voices, like the snow, went on and on and she couldn't tell the difference between now and long ago. The bedpost moved, came closer and hit her head.

"Oops," Lucy said. "I'm sorry, honey. I slipped on the rug." The ceiling changed from the bedroom to the bathroom skylight. She could feel the water warm against her body. It splashed in her eyes and the towel took it away.

"I have a theory," Whitney said.

"If it's anything like your last one – " Dede interrupted.

"During certain epochs of time," Whitney went on, "the firmament develops a crack, and evil presences, festering beyond our powers of perception, slither through and entangle us in their slimy clutches."

"I knew you'd be the first among us to develop cabin fever and go nuts."

The weather radio sputtered to life. "Average seas of three to six feet and variable winds offshore."

"My theory is," Dede said, "that there's too damn much inbreeding on this island – summer and winter residents both – and someone who got a raw deal in the genetics department is on a rampage."

Whitney's voice was sad. "If only one of us had gotten sick that night. If only our parents had caught us in time, the one time we actually needed them to."

The letters on the poster hanging on the wall across from her bed were clear, but she couldn't form them into a message. And it had been there most of her life.

Why couldn't she read it?

"Sarah, what's a stepsister?"
"What makes you ask that, Sport?'
"Dede said you're my stepsister."
"Being Dede, she got it wrong. You're my half-sister."
"What's a half-sister?"
"Same father, different mothers."
"How come?"
"Dad liked your mother better than mine."
"That means Daddy likes me better'n you?"

Pretty soon the snow would creep past her upstairs window, cover it, swallow the whole house. And herself with it. Along with Mommy, Dede, Whitney and Lucy. No, they could escape any time they wanted to. Only she would be trapped. How long would it take to smother to death?

She'd lose her mind if the snow didn't stop. She forgot. She'd already lost it. It was like saying, "I'd give my soul for . . . ." People were always giving away their souls. Forgetting it could only be given once.

A black-capped chickadee perched on a branch of the spruce outside the window and peeped. The voice on the radio said, "The Ospreys are still feeling their way and stand seven-six in the middle of the Western D ranking. They finished up with an eighty-one, sixty-two against Vasalboro on December sixteenth but after Christmas they fell back again . . . ."

The sun slipped away and there was only a pool of light on the bedside table. The ocean pulsated and smashed against the granite ledges. Lucy said, "Now don't you sorrow, Anne. I've heard about many that were a sight worse'n her and now they're good as new."

A fly buzzed on the window sill, stupidly trying to escape. Not knowing it was five degrees out there. It circled the room and buzzed against her ear. She tried to lift her hand to brush it away. Her hand wouldn't lift. She tried to call for Anne but her lips wouldn't call.

"It's Nevah 's birthday next week," Dede said. "What should we do?"
Sport said, "let's get him something neat. Something his parents couldn't afford. They don't have much money."
"They have money," Whitney said. "They have our money."
"I have an idea," Talbot said.
"What?"

"We'll pool our money, buy him diving equipment and teach him how to scuba dive."

The station sputtered with static. ". . . reported missing for two days . . . police traced him to his foster home . . . the number one growth industry in France is wine . . . number one consumer is a young, upwardly mobile executive earning over . . . six degrees going up to fifteen today . . . I live in a house that looks over the ocean. Please come to L.A. I'm the number one fan of the man from Tennessee . . . cracks in the cabin bulkhead caused the plane to crash . . . for only nine-ninety-nine you can live like a king . . . ."

After the dark the light would come back, a little at a time. First the edge of the bed would appear, then the outline of the window, and then the spindly branches. As the sky turned grey, the world came back like a photograph developing.

Her head hurt. She needed to get a pill. She needed to shoo away the fly. She needed to go to the bathroom. She needed . . . .

From down on the beach she could hear them singing.
The moon was an orange ball that a mermaid was lifting
out of the water. Sarah was playing the guitar.
"Your leaves they will wither.
Your roots they will die.
And all will forsake you.
You'll never know why."

Two

"Mornin', Barnett. I have a hankerin' for that ice cream with the nuts and marsh-mallows. Get some in?"

"Heavenly Hash. The truck ain't come ovah' yet."

"You heard Sport Abbott's goin' t' be paralyzed for life?"

Barnett Elliott, concluding correctly that the hunger for ice cream was second-ary to a hunger for news, said "Too much talk goin' on. I heard nobody knows for sure."

"You think it was an accident?

"Accidents happen."

"You believe that, you'll believe anything."

"I need a post cahd stamp, Barnett. I'm sendin' a recipe t' my niece ovah' t' Southwest Habah."

"How ye be, Nanci? Heard tell anythin' new?"

"I was ovah t' Bob's and he's kin to Lucy Clayton who's lookin' aftah' Sport, and Lucy tole him there weren't no change."

A voice further back in the line said, "Hey, Nanci you going to stand there all day? Some of us need stamps too."

*   *   *

"How's the new boat coming along, Emory?"

"The ownahs' 'll have it by May." Pause.

Then, "Three maimed for life and one dead."

None of the three men and one woman admiring the half-built thirty-six foot lobster boat sitting on its cradle in the shed had any difficulty following the drift of the non sequitur.

"I figure Talbot was the luckiest of the lot."

"It's a shame. That Sport allus had a nice word for everyone."

"How come the Abbotts ain't takin' her t' the best doctahs' in the country?"

"They said nothun' else to be done, at least for now."

"Henry thinks the sun rises and sets on that Sport."

"Pays no mind t' the othah' one, Sarah."

"Paid no mind to Sarah's mothah' neitha'."

"He fell hook, line and sinker when Anne appeared."

"Who'd a thought Anne would marry Henry?"

"Me. I'd a thought. That girl nevah' slackened up from the moment she washed up on this island. Knew what she wanted and went for 't."

"I allus said Johnny Wright was a deep one."

"You sure it was Johnny that did it?"

"Edith mebbe. She set a mighty stoah' by that little Eddie."

"It was hahd on Edith, waitin' all those yeahs' afore she finally got a baby and then losin' him to such foolishness."

"I nevah saw the like, the way she looked aftah' that boy. In bad weathah', she had him so bundled up you could hahdly see him."

"The trouble with little Eddie was he was all adrift. Not belongin' t' us, not belongin' t' them."

"He belonged t' us alright. Johnny's and Edith's kin bin around these parts three hundred yeahs'."

"Ayuh, but he was takin' ovah' by the summah' kids. He'd a bin fine, he'd stayed away from them."

"That were Edith's fault. Wantin' the best for him. Started the minute she was carryin' him. Kiting' off t' her mothah' in Augustah months afore her time in case the ferry couldn't get out when her time came."

"Leastways, it's company for Anne havin' Dede and Whitney stayin' all wintah'."

"Nothin' else they kin do."

"I hear she's a pretty good painta'."

"What kin that Whitney do?"

"Doesn't need to. Has all the money from his grandfathah'."

"My cousin's daughter went to law school at Cornell. Said she had a blind professor taught her contract law."

"All Whitney could teach would be jumpin' outta' planes. Climbin' mountains. Scuba divin'. He won't be doin' much of those things any moah."

"Who was t' give him the name Nevah? Not that 't weren't apt."

"Sport. She was a great one for nicknames."

"Best I recollect he was a nice kid, little Eddie. Fierce t' go."

"That was his undoin'. I remembah' once Johnny and me took him out lobsterin' and him only a mite. Waves high on fifteen feet, but would he let on he was scairt? No way."

"Do you remember the time Mike Hudson hauled one of Johnny's lobster pots by mistake and Johnny nearly killed him? Johnny always had a terrible temper."

"Poor Mike had no luck that yeah."

"Everyone pitched in and brought them suppahs."

"How could Johnny get to Connecticut and New York City and nobody the wiser?"

"He has a car, boats. Knows how to fly the Harrington-Clark plane they leave here. He could easily take a boat down the coast, tie up somewhere, rent a car, smash up Whitney and Talbot and be back in no time."

"At least it's over now. All four of them had more than their share."

Three

Henry Abbott threw an old New York Times crossword puzzle he had found in the kindling bin on the floor and said, "If I knew for sure it was Johnny who was responsible, I'd skin him alive and boil him in oil." He was sprawled on the living room couch.

"Could Johnny have been brooding about revenge for nine years?" Dede asked, cocking her head sideways to examine her painting from another angle.

"Nine years is nothing. Think about *The Count of Monte Cristo*," Whitney said in an authoritative tone.

All morning Anne Abbott had been listening to the other three but saying nothing. In the past she had always nurtured her natural good looks. Now her hair hung limply, new lines had appeared on her face, her body appeared to have gone slack and she was indifferently dressed in jeans and a sweatshirt. Every now and then she forgot that she was half-heartedly tidying the bookshelves that lined the steps leading from the entry hall down to the living room and paused to examine Dede's painting. It was a self-portrait in oil; a view of Dede standing in a barn, seen from the outside through a cracked window. Although she was indoors, her dark hair was flying about her frightened face. She looked doomed, a creature who would never escape the wind that howled around her. The painting fascinated Anne and she kept returning to it.

"I have a new theory," Whitney announced. Since he happened to be standing at a window, a stranger would have thought he was admiring the winter view. "My theory – "

"Johnny Wright is exactly the type to brood for nine years," Henry said, sitting up and retrieving the puzzle, "and Edith is crazy enough to do anything."

Finally breaking her silence, Anne said, "Edith wasn't always crazy. Only after she lost Eddie." She left off gazing at Dede's portrait and went up the steps to the kitchen. She began chopping garlic and onions. Occasionally she lifted her eyes to the clouds, changing from pale grey to yellow to slate. Her expressions were as unsettled as the weather. Spasms of emotions crisscrossed her features. She worked slowly, as if any abrupt movement could prove fatal in her fragile world.

"About my theory," Whitney began again when Henry interrupted with, "Can a word of farewell be a vale?"

"Don't be ridiculous," Dede said as, outdoors, they heard a car approach and a moment later, a plain, short, stocky woman in her fifties entered carrying brown paper sacks. Placing them on the kitchen counter, she removed her parka and hung it on a hook in the entrance hall. "There weren't any grapes, Anne, so I bought frozen berries." She began stowing the groceries in an efficient manner that bespoke many years of kitchen labors. "Everyone was askin' about Sport. I could have spent the whole day answerin' questions. You can sit. I'll take ovah' in the kitchen now."

"That's ok, Lucy. I'll take care of dinner if you'll look in on Sport."

With a quick glance around and sensing that she was interrupting something, Lucy nodded and headed for the stairs. Henry's eyes followed her and then became riveted on the ceiling as if he could see through plaster and wood into Sport's room. Hauling himself off the couch, he went to the shelves and removed the dictionary.

"Here it is. Vale. Low lying country – "

"Ha!" said Dede.

" – earthy life in contrast to heaven or salutation of leave-taking. Ha yourself."

The telephone rang.

Making no move to answer it, Henry lay down again. "What's a Banff rebuff? Three letters."

Anne picked up the receiver.

"Hello?"

"Anne? I had no idea you were all back in Maine. I just called Dad's office and his secretary told me you'd picked up Sport from the hospital and gone back to the island."

"Oh Sarah, I'm sorry." Anne's voice was a blend of exhaustion and guilt. "It all happened on the spur of the moment. What with the doctors agreeing that – well, you know – nothing could be done – and the house still turned upside down with the renovation, we decided – "

"Why didn't somebody let me know?" Sarah wailed. Her tone was not resentful, only distraught. "I called and there was no answer and I nearly went out of my mind with worry. And on top of it all, I couldn't get in touch with Dede or Whitney – "

"They're here, Sarah. I can't tell you how sorry I am that I didn't call you. I wasn't thinking straight. With so many things on my mind – "

"You simply forgot about me." Sarah said in a failed attempt to make this sound lighthearted. "Is Dad with you?"

"Yes, he's here, and as I said, since Whitney and Dede – "

" – happened to be at loose ends at the moment," Dede interrupted dryly.

" – heard we were coming, they decided to come up with us. They've been marvelous. They're helping to keep us all sane."

"Isn't that an awful lot of work for you, Anne?"

"Oh no. I have to keep busy. Besides, Lucy helps me look after Annie and when I need it, I can get extra help in the village. It's not exactly the height of the season up here."

"I wish I didn't have to go to work."

"There's nothing you could do here, Sarah."

Pause. Then, "Does Dad want to talk to me?"

"Of course, Sarah. Hold on a minute." Pressing the mouthpiece firmly against her chest, Anne said to her husband, "Henry, Sarah wants to talk to you."

"Oh Christ. The last thing I need is Sarah blubbering all over – "

"Henry." Anne's voice was soft, but her eyes bore into her husband's.

"Give me the damn thing." Henry lumbered off the sofa and went up the steps from the living room to the kitchen. Anne kept the mouthpiece covered until he snatched the telephone away from her.

"Hello, Sarah."

"How are you, Dad?" Sarah asked in a tentative voice, immediately realizing that it was the wrong question under the circumstances.

"Great. Super. We're having a ball."

Sarah automatically moved into a comforting mode. "The doctors said it wasn't hopeless. That she could recover spontaneously any time."

"And a pig could sprout wings and fly."

Another pause. "How long are you going to stay up there, Dad? Don't you have to get back to work?"

"Actually I'm due to fly to Lima, Ohio tomorrow. I'm flying out of Portland. I'm sure as hell doing no good around here."

"Tell Anne I can take off from work if she needs me."

"Ok, Sarah."

"I may fly up for the weekend in any case."

"Only if it is convenient, Sarah." Abruptly, Henry sagged against the wall and his voice rumbled slightly as he said, "Take it easy, Honey."

That was all Sarah needed. She began to weep. "You take it easy too, Daddy." It was the first time she could recall calling him Daddy since he had left her mother for Anne.

When he had hung up, Henry remained where he was. His finger drew curlicues with water on the kitchen counter. "It *is* stupid for me to hang around here when there's nothing for me to do."

"Right," Dede agreed. "The only ones it isn't stupid for is me and Whitney now that our official job titles are 'hangers-on.'"

Henry's dull gaze flickered into awareness. His eyes traveled from Dede's pretty face to her no longer thin body and then to her painting. Going back down the steps, he bent to study the painting as if seeing it for the first time. After a moment he kissed Dede's cheek.

Whitney, who hadn't heard him descend the carpeted steps, looked in the direction of the kitchen and said, "Now may I tell you my theory?"

Henry sat down on the couch and nodded. Anne stopped stirring the garlic and onions in the pan and waited.

"Isn't this fun?" Dede said, clapping her hands together lightly, "I feel like we're in some Agatha Christie novel. You know, a bunch of rich people holed up in a country house trying to solve a murder mystery." She looked expectantly at Whitney.

Although none of their waiting attitudes was apparent to Whitney, he said, "My theory is that our – uh – incidents were not necessarily connected to Nevah."

"Yeah, they were just a remarkable string of coincidental accidents," Dede scoffed.

"Nor were they coincidental accidents. Instead of the four of us having a common enemy, only one of us has. And this enemy, wanting to divert suspicion from himself – or herself – attacked all of us so we would never suspect who the real target is."

They waited, expecting more, but when nothing followed, Dede reached behind her for a pillow and threw it at Whitney, hitting the guide dog who jumped up, stared indignantly at Dede and then lay down again.

"You've been in the dark too long, Chapin."

Whitney felt along the floor until he located the pillow and then threw it back in the general direction of Dede's voice. It hit Henry.

"This enemy," Whitney continued, "decided to use Nevah's death as a cover-up so he could pretend to be after all four of us."

Dede returned to her painting. "That's even worse. This enemy didn't have anything against three of us and look what he did. Or she."

Whitney had a new thought. "Exactly! There was something half-hearted about these attacks. I keep thinking about what happened to you, Dede. It was as if whoever did it, happened to be passing by, caught sight of you and tried to give you a scare. If you hadn't held on to the board . . . I don't know. There was something . . . well, spontaneous about it."

"What about the attack on you, Whit?"

"Well it didn't kill me, did it? If whoever it was wanted to kill me, he could've come back and finished off the job."

"And Sport?"

"She should have just rolled down that hill in the snow. The attacker couldn't have foreseen she'd hit that rock just that way on her head."

"Careless sort, this murderer," Dede replied. "So Talbot was the real intended victim?"

Whitney was silent. Three pairs of eyes studied the one who couldn't see. After a moment, Whitney said, "Hey, why isn't somebody saying something?"

"Nay," said Dede.

"Nay?" Whitney repeated. "You don't agree with me?"

"I'm talking to Henry. A Banff rebuff. There's a Banff in Scotland. N-A-Y."

Henry consulted his crossword puzzle.

"It doesn't fit. The third letter is E."

"Ok. Have it your way. N-A-E. Scottish spelling, I suppose."

Four

She was rising to the surface from a dive so deep and so prolonged it was not measurable by ordinary standards. Surrounded by a pale, vacuous light, she could see the tides ebbing and flowing far beneath her like a huge expanse of heaving and swelling blue sheets.

"Her eyes are open, Lucy."

"Makes no difference, Loreen. Keeps them open half the time."

"Do you think she knows we're talkin' 'bout her?"

Lucy shrugged. "I'm glad you're here, Loreen. Not only for the work, but for the company."

"As long as Anne's willin' to pay me. She want the sheets changed?"

"Ayuh."

"Seein' Sport like this does so carry me back to when she was a mite."

"She was a cute little kid. She used t' pick me bouquets of violets and dandelions when she was in town waitin' for her mothah' to finish shoppin' or visitin' and I was volunteerin' at the library. She could talk my eah' off. She was always going on about these little squabbles she'd had with Dede. Dede said this, then I said that, then Dede did this . . . on and on. I used to call her Little Miss Mini Motormouth. I was always tellin' her she should be a lawyer but then, with Henry for a fathah', I guess it didn't seem so attractive."

"What do you mean?"

"Oh, you know. He can be charmin' but he's a real taskmastah', that man."

The sun bounced back and forth on the white wall, the yellow and green quilt, the dried Japanese lanterns in the vase, the beams on the ceiling. An airplane droned in the distance, the noise increasing as it approached the public air field. The wall, the quilt, the vase and the ceiling settled back into place. Lucy and Loreen went away.

The evangelist on the radio said, "I know what makes men immoral, my friends. It's spelled f-l-e-s-h. Every third person in this great nation of ours is carnal. Yes, c-a-r-n-a-l. Every eighth person is homosexual. H-o-m-o-s-e-x-u-a-l. Every fifth person has indulged in sex this morning, my friends. And many of them with people who aren't their legitimate partners. Matrimony, The Book of Common Prayer tells us, is not to be entered into unadvisedly or lightly, but reverently, discreetly, advisedly, soberly and in fear of God."

From the direction of the road a voice yelled, "Get that truck the hell outta' here." God. G-o-d.

She had just spelled God. How come she could spell God but not read the words on the poster hanging on her bedroom wall? It'd been there all her life.

Chair legs screeched like chalk on a blackboard. Footsteps grated on her nerves like sand in her teeth. And that voice on the radio sounded like a crow. Loreen had forgotten to turn it off again. Waves boomed closer and closer, trying to clutch the house with slate-colored claws, smash the foundation and suck the inhabitants to the bottom of the sea. Back and forth the tide thundered, orchestrated by a celestial baton. Other times the swells slid along the ledges slyly, lulling everyone into a false sense of security, sedating them into lowering their defenses.

Someone was sitting on the side of her bed, nagging her. "Can you feel that? Does it hurt? I'm holding up my fingers. How many? Blink to show me how many."

> Talbot said, "Maybe I'll join the Peace Corps, help the underprivileged."
> "Last week," Sport said, "you were going to be an astronaut."
> "I know. So many things to do and so little time in which to do them."

He had no idea how little time. Why wasn't Talbot sitting on the side of her bed? Maybe he was in the Peace Corps helping the underprivileged.

"Alcohol is a disease," the evangelist said, "It's the only disease contracted by one's own will. The only disease bottled and sold over the counter. The only disease that is habit-forming. The only disease advertised on billboards and in magazines. The only disease that can cause accidents. The only disease which will keep you out of heaven. Jesus, and only Jesus, can help you break the spell of alcoholism."

Machinery rumbled somewhere. Unspeakable activities taking place under the house's foundation. Beings, unknown to the legitimate inhabitants, manufacturing a product too hideous to be imagined.

"I wish the road crews would finish their repairs and get back to wherever they go when they're not disturbing the peace," Dede said.

"Do you think I could work on a road crew?" Whitney said. "I could certainly manage a shovel. Or else, how about broom-making? Blind people often make brooms. And license plates. No, that's for convicts."

"All over the world," Dede said, "blind people teach, practice law, write books, compose music . . . ."

"Go in for brain surgery. You could use a bit of brain surgery, eh Sport?"

" – and all you can come up with are shovels and brooms."

The ceiling rolled and circled and then water was pouring over her and soap was stinging her eyes. Lucy said, "Oops, I'm sorry, Sport" and after a while the room settled down and she was warm and dry.

Sarah said, "Oh Sport, I love you and I don't want anything bad to happen to you." "How can anything bad happen to me when I'm all alone in the woods?" And Sarah said, "You could get into trouble anywhere."

The sun shot shards of gold across the bedroom walls. Childhood drawings of landscapes and stick-figure self-portraits were reflected in the mirror. The fragrance of stewing beef wafted up from below.

Lucy was folding laundry. She sighed and said, "I recollect your mothah' once telling me, befoah' she married your fathah' that there wasn't any way she was going to spend the rest of her life in Maine. I was about ten years older than her. She kinda thought of me as an oldah' sister that first summah' when we were both workin' at the restaurant. And I said, oh, we all think we're goin' to get out of heah'. Well, I was part right. She still spends every summah' heah'."

Lucy, along with a lot of other people, was different now. Said things she would never have said if she wasn't sure Sport couldn't hear them.

Sport could see the letters on the poster but she couldn't make sense of the message. Maybe it was in a foreign language. Maybe someone had replaced the original with an optometrist chart. Maybe there was something wrong with her head.

"Millions of common folk are high on drugs," the evangelist said, "Our politicians sniff and smoke drugs. Our nation is in the shape it is in today because corrupt government officials condone the use of marijuana. Marijuana is addictive and encourages immorality. Sure as I'm talking to you, the men who run our government are damned to eternal hellfire."

Lucy never sat still. She moved furniture so that she could scrub every corner of the floor. She took down all the books and dusted each one. She removed fireplace ashes after every fire. When she could think of nothing else, she knitted, sewed patches on Sport's jeans, replaced buttons. "I remembah' when you bought these jeans at the Grange fair. Money was scarce at the Zebbs and they sewed cut-out flowers on old pants and sold them. You bought everythin' they sewed to help out."

"Whether I shall turn out to be the hero of my life or whether that station will be held by anybody else, these papers must show."

Mommy was reading to her. Just the way she used to read to her when Sport was a little girl. It made Sport feel safe. The words sounded familiar. Which novel was it? Some day Lucy would tire of dusting and sewing patches and bathing a vegetable. And Dede and Whitney would get bored. And Daddy would be too busy to come up weekends. And even Mommy would disappear. They would go back to Connecticut or New York and not even notice that she was missing. Mommy would straighten up one day and say, "I have an uneasy feeling that I've forgotten something. Something important."

> *"It's a dark road*
> *But it'd be a darker road*
> *If I had no one*
> *To come home to."*

Sport's eyes snapped to the foot of her bed. A flutter of movement. What? A mouse? A large insect? But then she realized what it was. Her own toe. It was moving.

Five

Dede and Whitney were walking back and forth across the small patch of open ground behind the Abbott house. It was a relatively warm day for that time of winter and the ground behind the house was clear of snow for the first time since the previous autumn. Whitney placed each foot carefully, trying not to trip over protruding rocks and downed branches. His eyes flickering as if flinching from expected blows, he eased along as if each step might be his last. Soon I'll get better at this, he kept reminding himself.

"Look, Whit!" Dede pointed with her chin. "There's the lobster boat Emory Ames built for those people what's-their-name. Black? Maybe Brown. Or was it Green? Isn't she a beauty? If I weren't, well you know, I'd like one of those myself."

Whitney nearly tripped, flung out his arms and recovered his balance.

"Hey! I think I just spotted a rough-legged hawk. At least it has those kind of mitten marks on its wings." Dede placed her crutches under her armpits, and resting on them, lifted her binoculars.

Warily, Whitney scuffed the ground sideways to make sure he wasn't near the edge of the bluff.

"God, it feels good to get out of that house. There's a pine that must have been split by the storm this winter. It looks inhabited, as if a squirrel might be living inside."

"Dede, do you mind paying a little more attention to my physical well-being rather than my aesthetic one? I should have brought the dog."

"I'm much better company, and I'd never let you go over the side, Whit. I'm keeping an eye on you."

"It's true," Whitney said glumly, "You're a big improvement over that other bitch."

A brisk southwest wind was brushing the sky clear of clouds. Out on the water, the dark choppy waves were crisscrossed by the weaving wake of the lobster boat.

"God, it's a gorgeous day. You don't mind my telling you it's a gorgeous day, do you, Whit? I mean if we're going to be spending so much time together, I can't be watching my step, metaphorically speaking, every minute, can I?"

Whitney lifted his face to the wind and inhaled the fragrance of balsam. "We *are* spending a lot of time together, aren't we, Dede?"

Taking her eyes off a gull diving for its breakfast, Dede shoved Whitney out of the path of a broken oak branch with her elbow. She smiled. "The halt leading the blind."

"I was hoping you'd never sink to that. You know, Dede, you can't let me go into the drink. I'm probably your last hope for a husband."

"Gosh, that's romantic. Anyway, don't kid yourself. Some men like looking after the handicapped. Makes them feel superior, saint-like. Look at Steve. He's over every day to check on Sport."

"Do you think we ought to get married, Dede?"

"That depends. Do we love each other?"

Abstracted, Whitney momentarily lost his nervousness about dropping off the side of the ledge and walked more briskly. Head down, as if studying the terrain, he asked, "Do you remember Chris McMahon?"

"How could I forget?" Dede rolled her eyes disdainfully. "What brought her up?"

"I was nuts about her."

"No kidding?" Dede's voice was incredulous, not jealous. "She was an awful asshole."

"How was she an asshole?" he asked, sounding defensive.

"Her reading matter consisted of *Town and Country* and the Sotheby's catalogue. Once I caught her carrying around an actual hardcover book. Know what it was about? Bungee jumping."

"Sounds like something I loaned her. Anyway, she was gorgeous."

"About her interests. Let us count the ways: who was who socially. Who owned the most expensive everything. Where to go for lunch. Twenty-one or . . . ."

"You're jealous. Anyway, soon as she heard I was blind she got engaged to Desmond Lowell."

"She would."

"What's that suppose to mean?"

"Assholes like Chris always get married immediately after their first choice becomes unavailable."

"How's that different from us?"

Ignoring that, Dede said, "Anyway, Whit, it's lucky you didn't marry her. None of us could stand her and it would've split up the four of us."

"Yeah, would have been a shame to break up the team before we started getting killed and maimed."

That silenced her. No longer enthusiastic about boats, birds or the weather, she shuffled along on her crutches in silence. After a moment she said in a matter-of-fact tone, "I had the hots for Talbot in the worst way for years."

Whitney stopped in surprise. "You did?" He reached out to touch her but his hand met only air. "I'll be damned! I never once suspected it."

Dede turned away as if to conceal the expression on her face from the sightless Whitney. "Nobody did. Just goes to show what a cool cat I am."

"You are, Dede. You always were. But it must have hurt."

"Not as much as if he'd thrown me over. I always knew he and Sport were joined at the hip."

"Dede . . . ." He hesitated. "When Talbot was killed . . . ."

"Look, Whit! There's some kids on the beach down there. A little early for shorts, I'd say."

"When Talbot was killed – don't get mad at me for saying this – did you, well, did you feel the littlest bit, I don't know . . . . I mean, since you couldn't have him, were you well, relieved, that nobody else . . . ." His voice trailed away.

"They're wading! Tough little things."

"In my case, when I heard about Chris and that Lowell guy, I was kind of relieved that I wouldn't have to keep on seeing her day after day. But you would've had to keep watching Sport and Talbot be together for the rest of your life."

"Whitney, look at this." At first he thought she was still trying to change the subject. But then something in her voice told him it was more than that. He sniffed, as if trying to catch her scent. "Where are you, Dede? What's happening?"

"Don't come any closer." Dede had propelled herself carefully to the edge of the bluff and was peering intently at the ground.

"Answer me, Dede."

"Wait a minute." She bent over the edge of the bluff and picked up something.

"For Pete's sake, Dede, will you please tell me what the hell is going on?"

"Down there is where Sport was found."

"What are you talking about?"

"Remember how the rope had been cut?"

"Yeah."

"Well, here's the knife that the person used I think." She held up, to no purpose, a stainless steel knife.

"So what else is new? No one really thought it was an accident."

"I wonder if we should show it to that deputy, what's-his-name."

"Is it a common type of knife?"

"I don't know. It's one of those folding deals with a pair of pliers and a knife . . . . I've seen lots of them."

"Probably a Leatherman. They're very common."

Dede looked down at her hand. "Maybe I shouldn't have picked it up."

"Probably not. The fingerprints would be gone but the deputy might have wanted to see how it lay on the ground."

"Well, maybe there's some way to prove that it belongs to Johnny."

"Hey, Dede, if the police arrest Johnny or Edith who'll we get to do the dirty work around here? You know what my mom is always saying about how good help is so hard to find."

"You're as big an asshole as Chris. Come on. We're going back to call that guy."

Six

From the open door of her bedroom, she could hear snatches of their conversation. "It isn't much to go on. Just a common knife." She recognized the voice of Deputy Sheriff Coombs.

Dede said, "I know that was the knife that was used to cut the rope."

"No way o' knowin' when and by who."

Whom, Sport corrected silently, unconsciously.

"Can't you, well, ask Johnny Wright if he has a knife like that?"

"What would that do? You're watching too much TV."

"Can't you do anything? Did you ever question him? Find out where he was Christmas morning? And at the times of the other attacks?"

"I'm not goin' to go down and ask Johnny a question like that. He'd either laugh or shoot me with a shotgun."

A new cold front was coming down from Canada, the weatherman said. The ground swell and the northern winds met at a different angle, causing treacherous currents for the scallopers. Powdery gusts of snow blew along like smoke, and the frozen branches tinkled like crystal chandeliers.

Time was fluid, night and day flowing into each other without boundaries. Voices, people and events swirled around her in no chronological order and she lost track of what was now and what was then.

Eyeless in Gaza.

How could she remember Huxley's *Eyeless in Gaza* and be unable to read a poster?

Steve was sitting on the side of the bed. "I think I fell in love with you the first time I saw you. No, not sitting up in a tree under attack by a deer. No, I saw you first as a child. Or at least I think I saw you once. Diving off the dock at the Yacht Club. You were pushing a boy into the water. Maybe it was Talbot. Maybe it wasn't you. Who knows. At the very least, it was the idea of you. Tan, athletic, golden hair, great figure, impeccable background . . . . What in hell is an impeccable background? Does that mean mine's peccable? An old family. What the hell is that? Every family is old. Some just are better record-keepers than others. Anyway, it rarely takes more than four or five generations to get from riches back into rags."

Like a transfusion, warm, liquid contentment coursed through her veins. Almost, but not quite, the way she used to feel when she saw Talbot the first time after he'd been away at school for a few months. Or when she stood positioned on top of a steep, snowy ski trail, readying for the run. Or when sailing on a Laser, wind abeam, racing the waves.

* * *

Sarah said, "Do you remember the kite, Sport?"

Kite? What kite?

"A fifty-cent kite and Dad carried on as if I'd lost the family jewels. The one that caught in the tree."

Oh yes. *That* kite. Henry had been such an asshole about the kite.

> *"Damn it, Sarah. It isn't just the kite.*
> *Any idiot can see it's too windy today to fly a kite."*
> *"I said I'd buy you another one. What else can I do?"*
> *"You can climb the tree and get it."*
> *"What! It's fifty feet up."*
> *"Sport, you do it. Get the damn kite out of the tree."*
> *Mommy said, "Sarah 's right. Forget the damn kite."*
> *"It looks awful up there. Mars the view. I'd do it myself, but I'm too heavy*
> *for those branches."*
> *"For Christ's sake, Henry. Stop it! This is my only daughter. What are you*
> *thinking?"*
> *But Daddy persisted. While they waited in nervous silence, he went up*
> *to the house and came back in a few minutes with a slicker, boots and*
> *gloves so that the spruce needles wouldn't scratch her. As soon as he*
> *returned, Sarah started back up to the house, avoiding his gaze.*
> *Mommy was beside herself.*

"Henry, I can't let you do this. I won't."

"It's ok mom," Sport said, "it's no big deal."

"Jesus Anne, you're raising her to be a coward. That's no way to go through life."

Mostly to stop the argument, Sport began climbing, placing her feet next to the tree trunk where the branches were strongest. No big deal. She wasn't afraid of heights. Now if it had been a spider that Henry wanted her to retrieve, that would have been a different matter. Sport remembered that Sarah used to have a spider collection as she moved up the trunk. When she reached the kite, she tried to untangle the string, but she couldn't do it without using both hands.

She stiffened her grip on the trunk with her knees and yanked at the string. And nearly fell over backwards.

Mommy screamed.

But she caught hold, dropped the kite and came down safely.

Mommy was crying.

Daddy said, "That's my Sport. I knew you could do it."

He gave her a squeeze around the shoulders. Sport couldn't figure out if she felt proud or ashamed.

Sarah said, "Nothing I ever did was right. You were always his favorite."

The frigid iron grey front crawled down from the land of the icebergs, snaked along the open wastes of the Arctic, and settled on the northeastern shore of North America. The window was glazed over with frost. A bell buoy moaned.

So far no one had noticed that she could move her toes, and now her fingers as well.

*   *   *

Mommy said, "I didn't always love this island. In fact, I almost hated it when I was working as a waitress here summers. I was one of the island girls."

Mommy seemed to be speaking to herself. For all she knew, she was.

"You ever notice the way Heather Chapin speaks to Edith and Johnny? To other islanders? That exquisite politeness of hers? Like velvet over ice? That's the way she used to speak to me when we were both in our teens."

Poor mommy.

"I was a great one for Horatio Alger stories. Swore I would go to college, become successful in some unspecified career, and return in glory to the island."

She went to the window to open it a crack. The cold blew in as sharp as a knife's edge and the curtain fluttered.

From below, Lucy called out, "Anne, you want t' buy Girl Scout cookies?"

Mommy shut the window again and went away. She could hear wheels swishing on the frost-covered roads. A radio rumbled somewhere. The soup was hot, full of beans and vegetables, and she wanted more, but Lucy didn't know that and took the bowl away. Voices whispered and called out, murmured and prattled, engaged in soliloquies and dialogues. People told her their secrets, their innermost thoughts, failings and successes. Confiding information they would never have revealed to a fully cognizant Sport. Convinced the information would be "interred with her bones." Where did that come from? Conversations fused like water colors, losing their outlines and their proper place in space and time. Trying to focus was like trying to fix binoculars on a distant object in a heaving sea.

* * *

Sarah said, "I was always jealous of you when you were growing up, Sport. My smart, capable, beautiful little sister. Half-sister. I don't know why I don't hate you, Sport."

Because I love you so much, Sarah?

* * *

Mommy said, "When I was at Orono – it was the only college which gave me enough financial aid to attend – I couldn't get interested in any of the boys. I was determined to land one of the 'summer boys'. The ones who arrived with the robins and left with the geese."

* * *

Steve said, "Do you know what you meant to me the first time I saw you? You were the indifferent beauty I was going to awaken to my assets with a kiss. The pot – if you'll pardon the expression – at the end of the rainbow. But of course I knew that, as far as you were concerned, I could've been part of the wallpaper."

Snowflakes formed kaleidoscope patterns on the windows. Nothing was stationary. Shadows flitted across the ceiling, over the rug and into the hallway. One moment the sun lit up the top of the bureau; the next, a lower drawer. Had she slept for hours without being aware of it? Sometimes all the furniture in the room was sharply outlined; other times objects blurred .

"Hey, Sport, enough already. Who was it who saved you from that insane deer? Who came through snow and sleet to rescue you when the power failed?

Who brought you real food when you were subsisting on smoked oysters? All I'm asking for is a blink. One lousy blink. Well, make that two. One for yes. Two for no."

The faces grew large and then disappeared. Sometimes the spoken words were as indecipherable as the message on the poster; sometimes clear as the proverbial bell. She was running along a corridor past closed doors, each one with an indecipherable number on it. A wind gusted along the passageway, propelling her towards a destination she didn't want to reach. Her feet barely skimmed the floor as she fought the current. All around her was an odd droning, bodiless voice whispering unwanted knowledge to her.

* * *

Whitney said, "I never saw the Taj Mahal or the Cape of Good Hope or the Seychelles or the Himalayas. Hell, I never even saw Yellowstone National Park."

I see London, I see France. I see Dede's underpants. And she did, the way Dede was sitting with her legs on Sport's bed and her short skirt hitched up. Her legs looked awful. Heavy, with no muscle.

Dede was crying, tears sliding down her cheeks and on to her turtleneck. "I never finished climbing all forty-six peaks in the Adirondacks. I'll never be a 46'er."

"Who would want to?" Steve said. "But I tell you what. I'll take you both to all those places. I'll be your eyes and your legs."

Whitney said, "Our own in-house doctor, or rather out-house doctor."

"We'll sail on the good ship *Hopeless,*" Dede said, smiling a bit.

"We'll take along *Baedeker for Basket Cases,*" Whitney added.

"May I come with you?" asked Sarah.

"No way. You have all your parts."

"What about Steve?"

"Well, we have to have a doctor, don't we?"

Poor Sarah. Always odd man out.

> *"I hate you, Sport. I hate you.*
> *He gave you a ring and me a goddamned typewriter.*
> *Who wants a typewriter?"*
> *"Me for one. I'm going to be a writer when I grow up."*
> *"Then take the damned typewriter. It's all yours."*
> *Sarah threw the typewriter. Not at Sport. At the floor.*
> *The shift handle flew off.*
> *Daddy said, "That's the last present I'll ever buy for you kiddo."*

*   *   *

She was flying over the surface of the bay, a huge lifting wind behind her. It would have been wonderful but it was making her seasick. She thought she might throw up. "It's a local lesion," Steve said. "Called Broca's Aphasia. The rock hit you right here, the front lobe, just anterior to your lip, tongue and mouth area. Non-fluent aphasia. What they can't understand . . . there's no sub-arachnoid hemorrhaging, no lesions in the cranial nerves which serve the speech organs . . . ." After a while his voice faded and disappeared.

*   *   *

Mommy said, "I never intended to break up anyone's marriage. I never even really noticed Henry at first. He might have been one of the summer boys at one time but he was twenty years older than I. His hairline was beginning to recede by the time I met him. The way it all started was, right after I graduated from college, I got a job as a temp paralegal in New York. By the merest chance I happened to be assigned to Henry's law firm one week. He knew me from the island, of course, and one day he invited me out to lunch. It was odd. I had been his waitress dozens of times on the island and then, suddenly, I was sitting across from him and someone else was the waitress."

A pale sun threaded in and out of the clouds. She could hear the waves down at the beach, slapping themselves silly against the rocks. The wind crawled through every crack and cranny of the house, chilling her insides.

"After that he began inviting me out to dinner. Then for a weekend at an inn in Vermont. God, did that make me nervous. He told Thora he was visiting his brother. There was a bad moment when the innkeeper referred to me as Henry's daughter. He told me he had only married Thora because both sets of parents expected it. He and Thora had grown up together – like you and Talbot – except that of course you and Talbot loved each other . . . . What was I saying? Oh yes. He and Thora were in the same social circles, attended the same dances, went with their parents on the same vacations and, of course, spent their summers here. So it was a marriage they had simply fallen into."

The voices surged and retreated like the tides. Sometimes she drifted along with them; sometimes they left her high and dry on the beach of her own consciousness.

"In those days Henry's work called for a lot of traveling. After a while I stopped working and traveled with him. Thora never suspected anything. She was terribly naïve, accepting his excuses even over holidays. I don't know how long it might have continued that way – Henry talked the usual stupid nonsense about not wanting to hurt his wife and his daughter by getting a divorce . . . ." Pause. "But then I got pregnant."

So what does that make me, mommy?

"And that concludes today's installment in the saga of Anne Abbott: local girl makes good as career girl, wife, mother."

Hey, Anne, you left out a category. How about adulteress? And you have the wrong order. Mother first. Then wife.

The sky was a speckled mix of salt and pepper. Every time she shut her eyes, the earth reeled alarmingly on its axis. From pepper and salt, the Western sky turned into bands of rubies, jades and sapphires. And the people metamorphosed as much as the weather.

Lucy: "Poor Edith. Wanting a baby so bad all those years and then losing him in such a careless stupid way."

Sarah: "I'll never forget the night Dad told my mom he was leaving her. She sat rocking back and forth on her bed, holding her head in her hands and sobbing. Why'd she let me hang around and see that?"

Whitney: "If only one of us had been sick that night. Or if only the weather had turned bad. Or if only our parents had caught us in time. Talbot and Nevah would be walking the earth. Sport wouldn't be a vegetable. And I . . . ."

Who're you calling a vegetable?

Daddy: "Why you, Sport? Why did it have to be you?"

Did you have another candidate in mind, Daddy?

Lucy: "Oh Sport, honey, I do sometimes wish I had figah'ed out how to get off this island. I love Bobby and the kids but still . . . . I hope my son sticks it out in Boston. There, you're swallowing much bettah' now. Oops, hold onto that soup and don't make me a liar, ok?"

Steve said, "I'm going to hang this chart on the wall next to your poster, Sport. This one's nothing but an alphabet. If you recognize an 'A', give me a short blink followed by a longer one. For a 'B', a long blink followed by three . . . ."

Whitney said, "Jesus Christ, Steve! She doesn't know her ass from her elbow and you're trying to teach her Morse Code!"

Voices droning on and on. Coming from the radio or the TV or from downstairs or from the side of her bed. From everywhere and nowhere. From inside her head or outside. From long ago or right now. Or tomorrow.

The world was frozen solid. Diamonds coruscated along the tree branches. The sky was the color of ice. Not a branch, not a bird, moved.

Only people were malleable, changing constantly, revealing more than they had ever imagined.

Steve: " . . . lost the power of speech due to an injury to the centers which con-

MILDRED DAVIS AND KATHERINE ROOME

trol it in the brain . . . . higher of these centers, having to do with speech, lies on the surface of the cerebral hemispheres, particularly on the left . . . caused by a destruction of part of the brain owing to a rupture of a blood vessel or a blocking of a blood vessel or by clotting . . . the inferior frontal convolution on the left part of the brain in right-handed people may be impaired although intelligence may be unimpaired . . . Boca's convolution, which governs the movements of the mouth and the tongue and larynx . . . all sorts of varieties such as something colloquially called 'word blindness' . . . may only last a few hours or a few days . . . . due to the passing congestion or to a block in circulation . . . functional aphasia . . . resulting from hysteria . . . a spontaneous recovery is possible at any time . . . ."

Seven

The sign said DUMPING ON TUESDAY AND SATURDAY ONLY. Steve drove down the bumpy dirt road, around the mounds of wood and metal waste, to the recycling bins. There were separate bins for colored glass, clear glass, plastic milk jugs, other colored plastic, clear plastic, recyclable plastic bottles, newspapers, cardboard, magazines, and tin cans. It was the most complicated recycling center Steve had ever seen.

On the one hand, there was something refreshingly old-fashioned about the laborious task of sorting garbage into the appropriate bins. If it wasn't exactly getting back to the land, at least it involved nineteenth-century types of skills. On the other hand, Steve sometimes suspected that the whole set-up was an elaborate joke on the summer people and the full-time residents just threw their trash into the ocean when the summer people – or the doctor in his case – weren't around.

Once they were done with the sorting, he and Sarah lugged the large, black plastic bags of miscellaneous trash, the authentic garbage as Steve thought of it, to the edge of what had once been a secluded lush glen and was now a gorge filled with human swill. They added their own contribution to the defacement, watching as the bags bounced down the slope.

They walked towards the Jeep past the small house that housed the compactors, nodding to the other garbage-disposers chatting inside. This was, Steve thought, the true social center of the island.

"The valley of the slops," he muttered as he climbed into the driver's seat.

"Well, what do you want us to do with our garbage?" Sarah asked.

"The dell of the dregs," was Steve's only response. "Ok, what's next?"

"Anne wants us to stop at Black's garage to see if they put the new spark plugs in the Chevy wagon."

"We'll leave that for last because we'll have to separate if the wagon is ready. What else?"

Sarah consulted her list. "The flea market at the Grange. Anne wants us to pick up a stepladder."

As he drove, Steve kept swiveling his head to admire different ocean views, the snow-covered fields, and the limpid sky. He kept telling Sarah to take a look at this or that feature of the landscape. Sarah's head moved back and forth under his direction as if she were watching a tennis match.

"You really love this island, don't you?" she remarked as he pointed out what looked like a perfectly nondescript stand of pine trees.

"Don't you?"

Sarah turned away, her eyes following a path through the woods that meandered off towards a hidden beach. Then she glanced at a modest double wide that had just been deposited onto a lot outside of the village for one of the island families. It was surrounded by ice, mud, half-demolished spruce trees and debris. "Half and half."

"What does that mean? You love it in the summer, hate it in the winter?"

"No, I wouldn't say that."

They drove in silence for a while and then: "My mother used to love it here."

Steve waited for her to go on, but when she didn't, he asked, "Does your mother come here much?"

They turned off the middle road and headed for the Grange.

"Off and on. Her main purpose in coming since the divorce is to show Henry how little she cares about his leaving her. And to flaunt all her money in front of Anne."

Something in her voice made Steve glance at her, but her face was averted again.

"When I was a kid, my mother was always jet-setting around, leaving me with nannies. I usually stayed with Henry and Anne during the summers. Anne would arrange sailing lessons for me, beach picnics, swimming lessons, play dates. I think she felt sorry for me. I went away to boarding school when I was fourteen. When I came home for holidays my mother mostly just took me to restaurants or I stayed home while she went to parties."

"Poor little rich kid, eh?"

"Actually I think I got a lot more enjoyment out of being rich then than I do now. Still, it wasn't a happy childhood. I started spending more and more time in Connecticut with Henry, Anne and Sport. Anne took Sport and me to plays, shopping, visiting museums, bike riding."

Sarah paused and then smiled at Steve. "My wicked stepmother."

They parked in the lot beside a large, white clapboard building. It looked as if a large proportion of the island's winter residents were crammed into the building, intent upon exchanging their own unwanted possessions for others'. Sarah and Steve squeezed their way into the warm, crowded room, chatting with friends and acquaintances as they wandered up and down the aisles past rough wooden tables covered with appliances, tools, odd assortments of china and glassware, lamps, books, magazines, toys, knickknacks, crafts, clothing. It occurred to Sarah that eventually all of it would probably end up, sorted or unsorted, over at the dump.

A woman in her twenties, two small children entwined around her legs, was sitting behind the craft table with her wares.

"I knitted this sweater with Sport in mind," she told Sarah, "but of course, she won't . . . ." The rest of the sentence drifted into the noisy room.

Sarah picked up the female of the two tow-headed children. "How're you doing, Sharon?" Sharon regarded her warily and didn't answer. It was her older brother who told Sarah, "Tomorrow's my birthday."

"What a coincidence!" said Sarah. "I just happened to pass a Lego set. And you know what? I was wishing I knew someone exactly the age you're going to be tomorrow to give it to."

Flushing, the young mother said, "Todd, it isn't polite to tell people it's your birthday."

Bringing back the Lego set, Sarah continued, "Sport's birthday is coming up too. I'm going to get her that sweater."

"Hey, wait a minute, Sarah. She won't have any use for it now."

"Who says so? She'll be going out soon as the weather warms up."

"That's a great-looking sweater, Sarah," Steve commented as he left off sifting through a pile of books to join them. "It goes with your eyes."

He examined the hand-knitted sailboat that jauntily cruised across a bright blue sea of yarn.

"She doesn't want it for herself," the young mother pointed out. "It's for Sport."

Steve glanced from the sweater to Sarah's bent back as she made out a check for a hundred and forty dollars. She placed it, face down, on the table.

Catching sight of the little girl's face, now less wary but still anxious-looking, Sarah said, "C'mon, Sharon, I saw a great looking picture book – "

"It isn't her birthday," her mother protested.

"Sooner or later it will be," Sarah said firmly, "I'd hate to be caught unprepared."

"I don't want a book," Sharon said, taking Sarah's hand. "I want the blue stuffed tiger."

They ran through the cold back to the Jeep with the sweater, two nineteenth-century medical books Steve had found, a knitted cap for Sarah and a garden tool for Anne. They hadn't been able to find the stepladder. Steve drove to Barnett Elliott's market. Sarah quickly collected groceries among the three short aisles on the ground floor while Steve conducted an out-of-office consultation with an elderly man who wanted Steve's opinion of a growth on his hand. Sarah, as instructed by Anne, put the groceries on the Abbott account, and they drove out of the village and headed back past the fields, the balsams and firs, and the silvery seascapes. In the short time since they had left the house, Sarah's generally pale face had lost its tenseness and her skin was tinged with pink.

"Hey, the tide's out," she exclaimed as they started across the thin neck of land that led to the Point. "Let's get us some mussels."

"We don't have boots. And we don't have anything to carry them in."

"You sound like somebody from away. We Mainers don't need L.L. Bean boots and fancy hods to get us a mess o'mussels."

Shrugging resignedly, Steve parked on the side of the road and the two of them scrambled through low rose shrubs and tall grass to the marshy flats. Sarah found a discarded plastic bag and headed for the water. Indifferent to the icy cold creeping up above her running shoes, she pushed back the sleeves of her parka and peered into the clear shallows. Reluctantly, Steve followed, but soon got caught up in the hunt. Since Sarah knew where the mussels were thickest, they quickly collected a tangle of black shells encrusted in barnacles.

"We'll clean them when we get – " Sarah began and then broke off, squinting at a distant figure ambling along the beach. Steve's eyes followed hers to the stark silhouette moving against the cloud-shredded sky. As the figure approached, the faint strains of a hum reach their ears.

> *"Dance, then wherever you may be; I am the*
> *Lord of the dance, said he, and I'll lead you*
> *all wherever you may be, and I'll lead you*
> *all to the dance, said he."*

"Edith!" Sarah called out. "What in the world are you doing here?"

Edith stopped singing in her thin high-pitched voice and watched as Sarah and Steve stamped their frozen feet and dried their hands on paper toweling pulled from the grocery sacks. She was dressed in an enormous black parka that must have been Johnny's and incongruously bright yellow boots. Edith smiled happily.

"Well theah', Sarah, got yourself some mussels?"

"Did you walk here, Edith?"

"I allus walk. Got t' shed o' folks sometimes."

"C'mon. We'll give you a lift home."

Sarah was beginning to shiver with cold as the three of them headed back to the Jeep. Dropping the mussels in the back behind the seats, she removed her muddy shoes and climbed in the back seat behind Steve and Edith. As Steve started the motor and turned the heat up high, Edith began to sing again.

> *"I danced on the Sabbath and I cured the lame, the holy people said it was a shame; they whipped and they stripped, and they hung me high, and they left me there on a cross to die.*
> *Dance then wherever you may be . . . ."*

It made Sarah and Steve cringe with embarrassment until suddenly Edith broke off to casually remark, "Little Eddie weren't mine, you know."

Her tone was so nonchalant that Sarah almost missed the significance of what she'd heard. But then it penetrated.

"What did you say, Edith?"

Steve took his eyes off the road to glance at Edith.

"'Pears it's brewin' up some weathah'," Edith remarked.

"Edith, what do you mean? Did you say Eddie wasn't your son?"

Her head weaving back and forth as if to the rhythm of the hymn, Edith regarded Sarah with clouded eyes. Steve slowed down so that they wouldn't reach the turnoff to the Wright house too soon.

"Edith, what are you talking about?" Sarah said, "Eddie wasn't your son?"

"He were Johnny's though. Even if Johnny allus said he weren't."

Steve and Sarah looked at each other. When they got to the Wright house, Edith climbed out and walked towards the house without either thanking them or saying good-bye.

"What do you make of that?" Sarah asked.

Steve made the turn out of the Wright's driveway and shrugged. "Nothing."

"Nothing?"

"Hey, Sarah, consider the source."

"Why would she say Nevah wasn't hers but was Johnny's?"

He stopped the car in front of the Abbott house and began gathering up the bags in his arms. "Could be to lessen the pain. Come on, my feet are completely frozen."

"Lessen the pain?"

"If he wasn't her own son, the pain is easier to bear."

Doubtfully, Sarah picked up the rest of the sacks. "Shall we tell Anne what Edith said?"

He shrugged again. "What for? It just churns up the whole mess again."

Eight

Again and again Sport plunged the knife into Nevah's back while Talbot held him down for her. Nevah's face was contorted in agony and fear as he struggled in Talbot's grasp. "Die!" Sport wept, unable to bear Nevah's pain. "Why don't you die?"

"I'm taking you out for a ride," a voice said.

Sport struggled out of her nightmare back into her bedroom. The sunlight nearly blinded her as it shot into the room from a velvet blue sky. This was not a new dream. Even in her confused state she knew that much. What made her do that in the dream? She had loved Nevah. Was it an extra-sensory perception of what Nevah had suffered as he struggled against the immovable rocks, as he'd felt his lungs bursting with the torture of trying not to inhale?

The tears rolled down her cheeks.

Steve's face hovered above hers. It wasn't unusual to see tears running down Sport's cheeks, but he never knew what they meant. Was it a reaction to something specific or a meaningless response to eyestrain?

"Hey, we don't *have* to go for a ride if you don't want to. Forget I ever suggested it."

"Do her good t' have a spell of fresh air." Lucy was tugging Sport's outdoor clothing onto her: the new sweater, sweatpants, socks, boots, parka, a knitted cap. Lucy's face lurched back and forth, the ceiling moved up and down, they were helping her down stairs which made the entire house rock, and the line of slickers on the front hall pegs zigzagged. Then Steve and Lucy were settling her into blankets and pillows in the front seat of Steve's Jeep. With the seat pushed back as far as it would go and the seat belt fastened firmly around her, she could ride in the Jeep and even see out the window. Assuming, of course, that she could actually see and register what she was seeing.

Bare branches crisscrossed the sky, whipped about by gusts from the Canadian hinterlands. The sunlight stitched in and out of the sea like silver needles. A scallop boat plunged and crested, and an empty osprey nest at the top of a dead tree swayed in the wind.

"What a great day!" Full of enthusiasm, Steve turned the Jeep down the driveway to Dede's house. The snow had melted and the dirt roads had turned to black mud. The car jounced and bucked on the rough road which made objects bounce up and down in what had become a perfectly normal fashion for Sport.

The road continued past Dede's house to a bluff overlooking the north shore of the point. Parking on the side of the trail, Steve got out and peered over the side of the escarpment.

Then Steve's face appeared at the open window, his elbows resting on the door. Although his face was shadowed, Sport's face was in full sunlight, the blue of the sky reflected in her eyes, her cheeks whipped rosy by the breeze. Before he knew what he was about to do, he bent and kissed her on the lips. Then he examined her expression intently for a reaction. There was none. After a moment he sighed, opened the back of the Jeep and began fiddling with an object.

When he straightened up, he was holding a black chrome cylinder bristling with knobs, tubes, lenses and filters. He began assembling the parts on a tripod beside the Jeep.

"You are observing Questar, the ultimate snooper."

Bending over, he began rotating bars for adjustment. While he fiddled, he kept up a constant, ebullient patter. "Isn't she a beauty? This marvel represents one broken bone, four cases of the flu, a heart attack, a suspected onset of colitis, a D. and C. for Mrs. – hey! What am I doing? I can't be mentioning names. If I know you, you'll blab it all over the island."

He poked his head in the car again to grin at her, this time his expression reminding her of one of Talbot's little nephews tearing open gifts on Christmas morning.

"It weighs only twelve pounds! Pretty remarkable for what it can do. I can carry it anywhere. You aren't going to believe this. It has a focus control from less than ten feet and all the way up to infinity! I told you, you wouldn't believe it. And there's a built-in drive that neutralizes the rotation of the earth and holds the stars motionless for viewing. It's almost worth what I had to do for Mrs. – oops! I mustn't give away professional secrets."

The sun warmed Sport's skin and colors shimmered past her eyelids in non-representational shapes. It seemed to her that, for the first time since her fall, she felt a flicker of peace, of something approaching contentment.

> *"Rule one," Daddy said, "Is don't sweat the small stuff.*
> *Rule two is it's all small stuff."*
> *Mommy made a face.*
> *"And if you can't fight it," Daddy went on, "flee.*
> *And if you can't flee, flow."*
> *"King of the cliché," Mommy said.*
> *She was standing behind Daddy's back. She put her thumbs in her ears*
> *and wiggled her fingers.*
> *Sport began to giggle.*
> *"Change what you can," Daddy went on, "accept what*
> *you cannot, and be smart enough to know the difference."*
> *Daddy caught on to what Mommy was doing and the two of them began*
> *to wrestle.*
> *Sport got between them and joined the fun.*
> *But Sarah, to whom the lecture had been addressed, stood*
> *apart and watched.*

Steve was still chattering. "And moreover, the filter protects my eyes because only one part in fifty thousand of the light enters the scope. Now, please, try to contain your excitement Sport."

Sport drifted gently with the air currents, the small waves out on the water, the cadences of Steve's voice, all of them merging into a pleasant rhythm.

"First, I use the power finder. Then, I adjust to finer focus. Third . . . ." He led her each step of the way as if they were in a classroom and she would be required to demonstrate mastery of the telescope any minute now.

"I can see an insect ten feet away or I can take a solar photograph . . . wow!" He began adjusting the knobs frantically. "Look at that! A male Barrow's goldeneye crossed with a common! I've never seen a cross on this island before."

He dragged the tripod closer to the Jeep, and after resighting the telescope, he brought her face close to the lens by supporting her with his arms. "Can you see it, Sport? Down there. Near Dede's beach . . . ."

She had a blurred vision of grey rocks, slate-colored water and images she couldn't define. Without thinking, she lifted her head for a clearer view.

Steve hadn't noticed. He was busy, as usual, thinking up the next trick or exercise that he should try to further Sport's recovery. As he had explained it recently to Sarah, trying to solve the riddle of Sport's muddled brain had become almost an obsession for him, something that caused him to wake up in the middle of the night, or to reach for a pad and pencil in the middle of a consultation with another patient. At this particular moment, he was scanning their surroundings for interesting sights to point out to Sport. And as a result, he missed the most interesting of all.

Sport's head was filled with the surprise of this new control over her muscles. But oddly, instead of joy, she felt only shock. And fear.

Before she could analyze the source of her fear, Steve tucked the blankets more tightly around her. "I'm going down to the beach to look around. I'll be back in a few minutes." He grinned at her. "Don't go away."

The combination of the clouds scuttling by, seemingly on the run, and Steve's temporary abandonment gave her a deep sense of urgency, of impending disaster. Further disaster. Her skin tingled. It reminded her of the stinging sensation of blood returning to limbs that have been asleep for a long time. She willed her hand to move but nothing happened. She tried to lift her head again but couldn't.

"It's not that I set myself above the rest o' folks here, but I gotta get away."

The words, clear and close by, were so startling that for a moment she thought they came from inside her own head. Then she recognized the voice. Mingling with the roiling of the tides and the screeching of the shore birds, she heard Johnny Wright say, "I wasted a heap of my life and I want something for myself before I die." Pause. "The money's nothing to you."

The words, imagined or real, blended and separated. The Johnny Wright she had known all her life had never been particularly friendly, certainly not obsequious, but he had always been, well, civil. Neutral. But this Johnny Wright was someone else. It was as if a great weight, pressing him down all these years, had suddenly been lifted to reveal another person beneath.

He was on the trail behind her, out of sight and apparently unaware of the Jeep or its occupant.

"I'm not talkin' about you and me. I'm talkin' about murder."

Sport's fear changed from a disturbing trickle to small rivulets and then, as the channel widened, into a raging flood. She was sitting – no, she was trapped – in a car parked at the edge of a steep cliff, listening to an exchange between an apparent blackmailer and a murderer.

The other voice was far more restrained, a whisper, pitched far too low for her to distinguish the words or identify the speaker. Impossible to say even if it was a man or a woman.

"Ok. I'm not in a hurry. Waited this long, what's a couple of months?" The tone was flat, but the threat was clear.

Twigs cracked. One set of footsteps crunching on the scattered patches of snow faded away. The other set grew louder, approached around a turn in the path, and then stopped abruptly. The Jeep had been spotted.

Sport was accustomed to immobility, to drifting inside her head from one moment to another without lines of demarcation. It was easy to shut her eyes and pretend unconsciousness. No footsteps, no twigs crackling. A presence leaning over her. Blackmailer or murderer? Then she smelled Johnny's brand of pipe tobacco. Blackmailer. For the first time since her accident, she was grateful for her immobility.

"Hey, Sport," Steve called out from the direction of the beach, "do ring necks have this sort of white spur on their sides?" His voice grew louder as he approached. "And if they do, why is this one back from vacation so early in the season?"

The smell of tobacco faded.

"I wasn't away too long, was I?" Steve asked, his face bending over hers. "I got carried away."

Just as well. What would have happened if the blackmailer and murderer had thought Steve overheard them?

As Steve disassembled the telescope and repacked the parts, Sport's fear became sharply delineated. It was as if her fear had suddenly come into focus through the sights of Steve's telescope. What would happen if she recovered completely? What if the person who had been stalking the four of them – Talbot, Dede, Whitney and herself – realized that Sport Abbott had not yet paid the piper? Would the faceless avenger make another stab at balancing the ledger?

And another thought.

If she recovered, what about Dede and Whitney? What would their reaction be? Bitterness?

And what about Sarah, the underdog? Her temporary ascendancy would be gone.

And Steve? Did he really want her to recover? His docile, helpless, always available doll-cum-science-experiment would no longer be under his control. He would be back to being the poor substitute for Talbot.

Only Mommy's and Daddy's happiness would be unadulterated. But they wouldn't be able to keep the news to themselves. It would be all over the island. Sport Abbott – the only one of the four to get off scot-free.

In the distance she could hear a buoy keening. If it wasn't Johnny or Edith avenging Nevah, then who?

Keep away, the buoy wailed. Keep away.

Nine

"My God!" Sarah groaned.

"Yours. Mine. Everyone's." Daddy was laughing. Sport hadn't seen him this cheerful since Christmas Eve, the day before her accident. "C'mon, Sarah, show me how smart you are."

"If I haven't accomplished that yet, what makes you think I can start now?"

'Atta girl, Sarah.

It was Sport's twenty-third birthday, and vegetable or not, her mother and father were throwing her a party. Talbot's parents, brother, sister and sister's family, Whitney's mother Heather, a few other summer people there for Easter week to open their houses, and some all-year residents had been invited. The weather was still chilly, but Sport could see scattered purple, yellow and pink crocuses poking up here and there among the rocks. The afternoon's entertainment, conceived and nurtured by Henry, was a treasure hunt. Only a few of the guests were participating. The others were eating and drinking, playing badminton or baseball.

"'Down in the meadow where the black hawk goes, up on the crosspiece where the Picea grows. There you will find it if you're light and fleet. But woe to you if you're not steady on your feet.'"

Reading the clue aloud, Sarah looked accusingly at her father. "Who's responsible for this crap?"

"Who's the only one clever enough?" Henry retorted.

The other treasure hunters, conferring in whispers, began to disperse.

"May I look up Picea?" Sarah inquired.

"Not cricket."

"That's not the name of this game."

Uh, oh, Sarah. Mistake.

Daddy frowned.

In an effort to take the heat off Sarah, Dede said, "Some birthday party! Reminds me of a funeral. Everybody can enjoy it except the guest of honor."

"Who's enjoying it?" Sarah mumbled.

Daddy looked around for a drink and found only a half empty can of Sprite someone had left on the deck railing. Holding it aloft, he said, "To Sport, may she enjoy her next birthday with all of her faculties intact."

If I'm still around at all.

Underneath the knitted throw her mother had tucked around her, Sport exercised her fingers. Every day, when unobserved, she did her "workout," moving her extremities. Each day she considered confiding the good news to her mother and father, to Dede, Whitney and Sarah.

And each day she postponed it.

Why?

They would surely let it slip. Particularly to Lucy. And once Lucy knew, the entire island would know.

And then, whoever it was, might try again.

Mommy held a glass of champagne to Sport's lips and Sport sipped.

"'Pears t' me," Lucy said, "It's not right to give Sport alcohol in her condition."

"Why?" asked Whitney. "She pregnant?"

Impatiently, Daddy said, "Think, Sarah. Or one of the others is going to beat you to it."

> *"I had this dream," Sarah said. Daddy groaned. "Not another of your long winded dreams."*
>
> *"I came home from school and you were all gone. The next day when I came home, all my belongings were gone. The day after the food was gone . . . ."*
>
> *"Sarah," Daddy sighed, "If you're going to list the things that disappeared in your dream, item by item, I'm going to have to sit down."*
>
> *"On the last day, there was nothing left but me.*
> *I lay down on the floor and waited for them to come for me."*

"Do you like your sweater, Sport?" Sarah held up the hand knitted pullover with the sailboat on it.

It's beautiful, Sarah. And some day I'll tell you how beautiful it is.

"I wish I could tell you that I knitted it myself, but you know what a chump I am when it comes to knitting."

Daddy opened his mouth but Sarah snarled at him, "Now don't *you* say the obvious."

Daddy laughed. "All I was going to say is, quit fooling around and solve that clue."

"I wish Steve were here," Sarah said. "I bet he would know what the damned thing is about."

Mommy clapped a hand to her forehead.

"I wonder if I remembered to invite him? I know I called but he wasn't there. Did I leave a message on his machine?"

She went off to amend her mistake.

"Maybe I ought to hop in the car and check out a few of his haunts," Sarah said. Daddy grabbed her wrist. "Oh no you don't. You're not getting out of this that easy."

"'Down in the meadow where the black hawk goes . . . .'" Sarah repeated, frowning with concentration.

They could hear shouts of laughter and frustration from a group down by the beach. From behind them in the field, the baseball contingent was whooping with joy over a home run. And from the direction of the newly erected badminton court came an argument about whether the shuttlecock had landed outside the boundary line.

"To discourage all my would-be guests," Heather was telling Talbot's sister, Claudia, "I tell them, 'Yes, do come up. The plumbing's really not a problem; it's just a short walk down the road. You're not allergic to bees are you? And would you mind bringing a few perennials with you to help with this little garden project I've got going?'" Heather laughed. "I had only one visitor all last summer."

Claudia's reaction was an uncomfortable smile.

Dede hobbled over to Sport on her crutches and sat down on a wrought iron chair. She held up a watercolor in front of Sport. Sport saw a stretch of blue-grey ocean lapping against a cliff. On the face of the cliff was the hint of an opening. A cave.

"It's your birthday present, Sport. Do you recognize the scene?"

Talbot was lying crossways in the rowboat, feet on one gunwale, head on the other. A strip of pale flesh showed over the top of his swim trunks in sharp contrast to the rest of his bronzed skin. Suddenly he sat up. "Look at that, you guys." He pointed to a black hole that cleaved the rocks. "It's a cave!"

Dede exclaimed, "Let's explore it."

"How?" Sport asked.

"We'll go to the top of the cliff, tie ropes around ourselves and slide down."

"Yeah ?" Sport said doubtfully. "When should we do it?"

"When we're feeling really stupid," Whitney said.

"Why are you crying?" Dede said in alarm. "The picture isn't that bad, is it?"

They had never explored the cave. And now, of course, they never would.

Mommy and Lucy and two hired helpers were setting out platters of meats, cheeses, jellied fish, salads and breads on the outdoor table. A bartender was distributing drinks. The treasure hunters were coming up from the beach, apparently still stumped by the clue. Mixed sounds of triumph and defeat came from the badminton court and the baseball field.

"There aren't any black hawks on this island," Sarah snapped.

"Sarah, think, for Pete's sake," Daddy snapped back.

Black hawk. Picea. Down in the meadow. Which meadow? The one where Mommy reaped her wild strawberries? Or the one where she and Talbot used to lie in the tall grasses, hoping no one would see what they were doing? Maybe the one leading to the sea behind Whitney's house.

"It won't fly," one of Talbot's nephews was complaining. He was gyrating furiously on his thin, stick-like legs, trying to lift a kite off the ground.

"There's no wind," Claudia told him. "You'll have to try another day."

*"Damn it, Sarah. It isn't just the kite.
It's everything you do. Any idiot can see it's
too windy today for kite flying."*

Black hawk! A type of kite!

Involuntarily Sport emitted a sound. Daddy whirled around to look at her. Then he bent down to examine her face intently. "Sport, are you trying to tell me something? I'll bet anything you've caught on. You know what the clue means, don't you?"

Over Daddy's shoulder, Sport could see Sarah's face. She reminded Sport of a defendant in a murder trial watching the jury file in.

"Sport, baby, blink! One quick little blink to show me you know what I'm talking about."

Sport stared vacantly into the distance, making sure she didn't blink. Her motivation was vague even to herself. Was she protecting Sarah from scorn? Or herself from the amorphous danger of her recovery?

"Jesus, Sport, for a minute there I could swear you were trying to tell me something. If you don't make an effort, you'll never recover."

"Dad, stop that," Sarah said sharply.

Sport's eyes remained vacant. Caressing her cheek with the back of his hand, Daddy said, "I'm sorry, Honey. I didn't mean that."

Suddenly Sarah let out a shriek. "I've got it!"

Daddy, clicking his fingers above his head like castanets, began dancing around. "I think she's got it! I think she's got it!" he sang in a fair imitation of Professor Higgins.

"Picea!" Sarah shrieked. "I just remembered. From a nature walk. Picea is a spruce. A black hawk. Is it a kind of kite? Sport, remember when I lost the kite and you . . . ." She broke off and her eyes widened with dismay. "No! Oh no! You're not going to make me climb that tree!"

Daddy grabbed Sarah around the waist, whirled her around, and continued singing. "I think she's got it! I think she's got it!"

"No way. If you think I'm going to . . . ."

"Don't be a chicken. I'll catch you if you fall."

"You'll be on the ground and I'll be fifty feet up in the air. I'd crush you."

"I'll go get a slicker and gloves so you don't scratch yourself. Hurry up before someone else catches on."

"This is ridiculous. A sixty-something-year-old man trying to force a nearly thirty-year-old woman to climb a tree!"

"Sarah, do you think I'd let you do it if I didn't know those branches could support your weight?"

"Henry!" Mommy had just come out with a tray of butter and condiments. "What in the world . . . ."

"You can do it, Sarah! I know you can do it."

"Henry, do you want two daughters . . . ?" Mommy stopped and looked down blindly at her tray.

Sarah's eyes shot back and forth between her father and stepmother. Then they swiveled around to Sport.

"Damn it! Damn you! Ok, I'll do it. I'll climb your lousy tree and if I break my neck I hope you'll never forgive yourself."

"Sarah! No!" Mommy tried to grab Sarah's arm but Sarah brushed past her.

Sarah! No! Anne's plea echoed in Sport's head. Don't do it! The tree is thirteen years older. Spruce trees were dying of all over the island, some kind of tree disease, and the branches might be weakened. Besides, a grownup Sarah was heavier than a thirteen-year-old Sport.

But Daddy must have climbed the tree in order to place the treasure there. He tested the limbs. It's ok.

Then why don't I want Sarah to climb the tree? Am I jealous of Sarah? What a reversal. Sport jealous of Sarah.

> *"Sarah," Daddy said, "I told you the world was your oyster. I fished it*
> *for you. I opened it for you. What more can I do? Eat it for you?"*
> *"Who asked you? All I said was I wanted to be a teacher."*
> *"I didn't give you a hundred thousand dollar education*

*so you could waste your life wiping the noses of six-year-olds. At least, if
you have to teach, get a PhD. Teach in a university."
"I like little kids. And I think it's important to give kids – particularly
public school kids – the right start."
"In this world, Sarah, you either go up under your own power or you go
down by gravity."*

Down by gravity.
*Don't do it, Sarah. Anything could go wrong. You could step on a dead branch. You
could have a dizzy spell. An osprey could swoop down and make you lose your grip . . . .*

They were gone. Suddenly, she was all alone. The other treasure hunters had
gone off, pursuing other theories as to the clue's solution. The guests who had been
eating and drinking on the lawn had taken their plates indoors to avoid the slight
chill. Even the clamor from the badminton court and baseball field had become
muted. The stew in Sport's brain simmered. Ingredients blended, separated, swirled
and congealed. As always when she was temporarily alone, she began to envision
emergencies. A fire. An attack by the one she always thought of as "the avenger."
True, she could now move her fingers and toes, but run? Not nearly. Two days ago
she had tried to stand. She had tottered for a moment and then caught the bedpost
to keep from falling.

How long could she keep this up? Until Deputy Coombs captured the avenger?
That could take forever.

She needed a confidante, someone she could trust. Mommy would tell Daddy.
Daddy could never keep his mouth shut. Sarah would blab to Steve. Steve would . . .
she wasn't sure. He's probably let it slip to, well, somebody. Dede and Whitney? They
were hopeless.

And what would happen if she told the police that Johnny Wright was blackmailing somebody? Even if she could tell them, whom would they believe? A sixth
generation island native or someone with . . . whatever Steve had called it. Broca's
aphasia.

The afternoon was fading into dusk. A golden plover, back early from vacationing in the south, rested on the deck railing and peeped at her. A loon snickered out
on the water. Someone shouted, "You can't tell me that's out!" from the direction of
the badminton court.

And from the direction of the village, the town ambulance siren wailed. Fire?
Heart attack? Accident?

Or you go down by gravity.

Oh, God, no. No, God, no. Not Sarah.

In her mind she cold see the tall, spindly spruce, a tiny figure climbing higher
and higher, a weak limb cracking, snapping off, a puppet-like figure spinning round

and round as it fell.

Sport felt as if she were suffocating, gasping for breath, her lungs bursting with pain. Just like Nevah.

"Sarah!"

The scream exploded into the air. *Who had screamed?* It took her a moment to realize that it had come from her own throat. An agonizing spasm was shooting between her ears, into her throat and down to her chest.

Where was everybody? Somebody, help! Tell me what's happening. Tell me it isn't Sarah.

"Hey, Sport!" a voice called from the direction of the road, "I did it! I actually climbed that damn tree!"

Sport collapsed against the back of the chair, worn out by worry and strain. Tears stung her eyes. Thank you, God. Thank you. I promise never to be jealous of Sarah again.

Sarah hadn't heard the scream, didn't notice the tears. Flushed with excitement, she held out her hand to show Sport the proof of her climb: a tiny red, white and blue paper kite.

"She was super!" Daddy exclaimed. "You should've seen her! Climbed straight up like a monkey."

Sport wanted to throw her arms around her half-sister, tell her how much she loved her, how important she had been to her all of her life, how sorry she was for having always taken her for granted, how happy she was that she was safe.

"Sarah," Daddy was saying, "I knew you could do it. I had one prize prepared just for you." He reached into the pocket of his navy windbreaker and drew out a small box. Sarah stared but didn't reach for it.

"What if I hadn't climbed the tree?"

"I told you. I knew you would."

"What if someone else had gotten there before me?"

"Hey, I had lots of other prizes, but this one was just for you."

"What were you going to do with it if I didn't climb?" Sarah persisted.

Irritated, Henry snapped, "I don't know. Throw it away. Actually, I'd have saved it for your next birthday."

Anne Abbott came up behind her husband and said gently, "Don't spoil it by being an ogre, Henry."

Taking a deep breath, Henry said, "Sarah, do you remember when I gave you a typewriter and Sport a ring?"

> *"I hate you Sport. I hate you.*
> *I wanted the ring and he gave it to you.*
> *He gave me the typewriter."*

Mesmerized, Sarah stared at the box.

"Well, open the damn thing."

Almost inaudibly, Sarah said, "What I remember is that you told me you were never going to give me a present again."

"So I lied. You know I never stick to my word."

From the direction of the road came the shouts and laughter of returning treasure hunters. Still arguing, the baseball players and badminton competitors joined them. As they all began helping themselves to the buffet, Henry distributed prizes to those who had returned with proof of their successes. Lucy explained the ambulance; the Sprague boy had had an appendix attack. Talbot's brother-in-law harangued Heather Chapin with a description of people who "go to church but they aren't Christians; they run charities but they aren't charitable; they're do-gooders who do no good." Whitney, hearing a fly buzzing, said to the minister, "Hear that fly? It's alive. Which makes it better off than the most famous dead man in history?" The voices hummed and droned around Sport. For the most part the guests ignored her, forgetting she was there. Was she better or worse off than the fly?

And then, a new voice, loud and strong, rose above all the others.

"I've come to say good-bye."

Johnny Wright was standing in the middle of the driveway in front of the house. Due to the crowd of cars in the driveway, he had parked his truck at the end of the drive and no one had heard him drive up.

Sport's first thought was how handsome he looked standing there in the middle of the drive, tall and straight, with his weathered face and longish greying hair. He was dressed in a hunting shirt, jeans and a parka. His arms hung by his side. Notwithstanding the parka and his sneakers, he looked like a gunslinger, braced and ready for the final shootout.

"You folks are going to have to shift without me," he said in a loud, strained voice that caught Henry's attention. Henry, who had been vigorously explaining to Lucy how little he thought of the island's state legislator, turned to face Johnny, and never well attuned to others' emotions even at the best of times, waved a hand at Johnny, "Come on over, Johnny. Have a beer. I've been wondering where the hell you were. You should have brought Edith."

Sport saw Johnny's hands slowly fold into fists as he repeated, "I've come to say good-bye. I'm leaving."

Johnny's voice was an unstable compound of vindication and something akin to despair. Sport heard his words as both those of a man who had finally gained his goal over immeasurable odds and those of a man who wasn't certain that the goal was all that worthwhile. By now, the hubbub had diminished and the forty or so people standing on the front lawn turned to look at Johnny. Now Sport was reminded of the bad fairy showing up at Sleeping Beauty's Christening to announce her evil spell.

Henry had apparently finally realized the significance of what Johnny was saying and for once had nothing to say himself. It was Talbot's father, Spencer, who broke the silence. "What are you talking about, Johnny?"

"I'm leaving."

"What do you mean you're leaving? Where are you going? For how long?"

"Doesn't matter. I'm leaving you all a gift. A good-bye present."

By now, even the children were quiet as they regarded the stranger who had once been Johnny Wright. The only noise was from the direction of the kitchen: the tinkle of dishes and glasses, water splashing and voices exchanging directions.

"I'm leaving Edith to all of you. I took care of you folks for a lot of years. It was you that drove her mad and it's you who can take care of her."

Confused, benumbed, they waited.

"But I have something to tell you before I go. You folks – you island folks included – are a great hand at making accusations. Ever since Dede got attacked, you've been saying it's likely me or Edith was responsible."

Johnny's eyes moved slowly from face to face. He was clearly in no hurry now that he had finally reached this point. His gaze lingered longest on Sport, but she kept her gaze on the ground. After several seconds he turned away to look at Henry.

"Edith and me, we had nothing to do with what happened to Sport and the others. Nothing. So look somewhere else."

Like a professional actor who had delivered his final punch line, Johnny turned and headed back down the road to where he'd parked his pickup.

For a moment the silence continued. Then the reaction erupted. Exclamations. Speculations. Questions. Uninformed answers. The children tugged at grownup hands, wanting to know what was going on. Those in the kitchen, finally sensing that something unusual had happened, came out to look around with curiosity.

"Do you believe him?"

"Who else in the world would want to avenge poor little Eddie Wright?"

"I think he's just tired of taking care of Edith."

"Who'd ever guess he had all that anger in him?"

"Hey, how are we going to get along without him?"

"He'll be back. He doesn't have any money."

Only Sport and Sarah took no part in the ferment.

"Oh yes he does," thought Sport, *"Well, good for you Johnny, although it does still leave the murderer at large, and my neck on the line doesn't it?"*

Sarah only stared down bemusedly at the diamond and ruby ring in the small box her father had given her.

Ten

Just because you're paranoid doesn't mean they aren't after you.

The words popped into Sport's mind like a suddenly lit flare in the sky.

She had just read the message on the poster. For the first time since the rock had smashed into her head she could read. The symbols had finally coalesced into a meaningful message instead of what previously could have been a Jackson Pollock painting. She was back among the ranks of homo sapiens.

That idiotic poster she had put there when she was seventeen. Rather prescient, now that she thought about it.

She listened a moment. From below came Katie Couric's voice, apparently instructing Lucy about the ins and outs of making puff pastry from scratch. She had heard Anne say she was going out to get some groceries. Dede and Whitney were polishing up their halt-leading-the-blind skills on a walk. Dad and Sarah had left with the rest of the summer crowd that had come up for Easter.

Carefully she sat up. Then she stretched and flexed her muscles. She was in training. In training for what? She didn't know. She was like one of those militia weirdoes preparing for the apocalypse in the Rocky Mountains.

Carefully she swung her legs over the side of the bed. At that moment she heard a car motor below.

Quickly subsiding back against the pillows, she heard feminine footsteps clicking on the outdoor wooden boards, the door opening, Lucy greeting the newcomer. No surprise in Lucy's voice. Then the same footsteps coming up the stairs and entering her bedroom.

It was Thora Kemp, née Thora Bradley. Thora Abbott in between. For an instant, Sport had the impression she was seeing a slightly shorter version of her own mother or perhaps a sister of her mother's that Sport had never known existed. Same slim figure, same fair coloring, same well-molded features. But of course men married the same women over and over, didn't they?

Thora was twenty years older than Anne but Thora was exquisitely groomed and elegantly dressed in a grey silk pants suit with an Hermes scarf at her neck, whereas Anne had fallen into a state of unkempt depression since Sport's accident. At this point, they almost appeared to be the same age.

Thora exhibited a marked ambivalence about being where she was. She was an uneasy mixture of curiosity and resentment. Bending over the bed, she examined Sport as if she were a lifeless artifact. Then she turned her attention to the room: the bed, the chest, the pictures, the poster. Perhaps remembering when this had been Sarah's bedroom and she had been mistress of the house.

"I'm staying at the inn. Lucy and I arranged for me to see you when you were alone."

Not so surprising. Lucy and Thora must have been close in the days Lucy had worked for Thora. Sport was not afraid. Thora had no reason to bear a grudge against her, Talbot, Dede or Whitney.

The visitor pulled a chair next to the bed and sat down. "You're wondering why I'm here."

Right.

"Well, first off, I was curious to see how Anne had redecorated the upstairs. She thinks she has such exquisite taste but really, it's so . . . . . clichéd. All this chintz and antique desks around every corner . . . . I don't even need to go into her bedroom to know that she put high quality bird prints all over her bedroom walls with lovely botanical prints in her bathroom. After all, she has the *de rigueur* hunting prints all over the living room. It's so eighties, so 'by the book' that it's tacky."

Thora looked out the window and sighed. "It must kill her that she has this modern house instead of a traditional farmhouse like Marilyn and Spencer's. It makes all this English cottage crap look even worse. Well, I hope she's not thinking that Henry's going to build her a new house. He won't spring for it, our Henry. It must have killed her when Chuck died and I inherited all of Chuck's money with no restrictions. So there I am with all the money and no pain in the ass like Henry to live with. Actually, this house was designed by a very well known architect. I doubt Anne knows or cares. But then she always was provincial. Couldn't really escape her Maine roots after all."

Thora walked back to the bed and peered down at Sport again. Sport gazed back at her blankly.

"Sarah told me the doctors give you a good chance of recovering completely. She's even sure you know what's going on." Sport's enzymes, heartbeat, glands, pulse began working overtime.

Where was this leading?

"Henry once accused me of molding Sarah into my friend, confidante, psychiatrist all in one. According to Henry that's why Sarah never married. It's a ridiculous theory. I barely spent any time with the girl. I was a lousy mother – lousy wife too – and Henry wasn't much better at being a father or husband. But then that's hardly news to you."

It occurred to Sport that Thora's self-awareness of her many faults was her one redeeming characteristic.

Thora rose, went to a table and examined a photograph of Henry and Anne in a sailboat, taken by Sport from the dock. For an instant Sport imagined that she was going to hurl it at the wall, but instead, she gently put it back on the table.

"But of course Henry found fault with everything I did . . . , as he does with everything Sarah does and undoubtedly Anne as well. According to Sarah, the only one he's soft on is you."

She looked back at Sport. "I don't really give a rat's ass about you, of course, but Sarah loves you. Like a sister."

From below, Sport could hear Lucy, who had turned off the television, talking on the telephone. "Edith isn't the visitin' type, but folks are takin' care of her. Makin' certain she has plenty t' eat and choppin' her wood and such."

Thora returned to the chair next to the bed and Sport caught a whiff of the same Louis Feraud scent Anne used. She was quiet for a moment and then Sport realized that she was crying silently, the tears sliding down her face although she didn't seem to notice. She was staring at Sport again.

"What a shitty mess this is. Eddie and Talbot killed, Dede and Whitney maimed. And you . . . . God what a mess. You were all such cute kids. I didn't feel much for you other kids but I loved watching the five of you playing with Sarah.

"I did love Sarah, still do. It made me feel like I hadn't made such a sorry job of motherhood when you guys were so happy and playing together when I visited. You little kids were, I don't know, pretty. Beautiful really. It was like watching a Renoir painting come to life. All pinks and blues and pastels . . . . It was always summer when I visited. I wish I had a movie of the six of you playing badminton. Like six little tanned jumping beans, hopping up and down, missing the birdie, falling on the grass, rolling down the hill."

There was another long pause and then, "God, what a waste. What a God damned waste."

Thora sighed and reached for a tissue on Sport's bedside table.

"Sarah kept begging me to come up and warn you that if you start recovering, don't tell anyone. Not until we know for sure who's responsible."

There was a traffic jam inside of Sport's head, with images converging and overlapping. Thora's features morphed into a composite of Sport's forehead, Anne's nose and Sarah's chin. Her voice appeared to be coming from a distance, almost as if it were coming from a radio. Sport closed her eyes. "Nobody knows for sure who's behind the attacks, but I have a hunch."

Sport's eyes involuntarily moved to Thora's face but Thora didn't notice.

What the hell was going on? If Thora knew, why didn't she tell the police? And why wasn't she dead? It was common knowledge, wasn't it, that if a person hinted about knowing the identity of a killer, that person generally ended up dead. But in that case, why wasn't Johnny Wright dead? Perhaps he was. Nobody knew where he'd gone to.

"I told the police about my suspicions but they laughed at me."

Sport had to go the bathroom. The worst part of pretending to be in a vegetative state – no, far from the worst, but still a nuisance – was needing people to help you go to the bathroom. Recently, whenever she was alone and no one was around to hear the flushing, she had begun to use the bathroom on her own.

"Johnny and Edith Wright weren't the only ones who loved little Eddie Wright."

So what? Everybody had been fond of sweet-tempered, easygoing Nevah. Especially Talbot, Dede and Whitney. And herself of course.

"Edith has a mother who lives in Augusta. Hope . . . what was it? Lantagne, yeah, Lantagne. Edith stayed with Hope when Eddie was born. Hope could've easily driven to Connecticut and New York. Hope was crazy about that boy and she has a will of iron. She could be capable of it."

Sport thought back to her dinner at the Wrights'. That tiny little crone? Thora must not have seen Hope Lantagne in the last twenty years.

Thora stood up.

"Well, I did my duty. I can go back to Sarah and truthfully tell her that I warned you. Although frankly honey, I don't give your recovery a snowball's chance in hell."

And with one more glance at the photo of Anne and Henry, Thora left the room, her tall heels clicking quickly down the stairs.

Eleven

Slowly, the town began to shake off winter and emerge from hibernation.

The Yacht Club floats were put in the water, the town harbor filled with outboards and tenders, fishing boats were pulled up on shore waiting for a coat of antifouling paint on their hulls, lawns sprouted newly painted lobster buoys. On the Tuesday after Memorial Day, both islanders and summer people were on their way down to the twelve-thirty ferry; the islanders headed for the Mainland to shop and the summer people headed back home until July.

Sport sat in the front seat of her mother's Rover, propped up by pillows, imbibing the bustle. Both Steve and her family had been thrilled by the increasing range of movement in Sport's eyes, head, fingers and toes but they still didn't suspect that that was only the tip of the iceberg that was her submerged recovery. She had a bubbling desire to dash out and be part of the living again.

If you start recovering, don't tell anyone. Take care until it's known for sure who's responsible.

"Nineteen?" a voice asked. It belonged to a summer person Sport didn't know. She was reading the plaque on the fountain. "'This memorial erected as a tribute to the town in memory of the men who served in World War I. 1917-1919.' I always thought World War I ended in nineteen-eighteen."

"They sure took their time about erecting the memorial," answered her companion, "It couldn't have been done before World War II. Otherwise, how would they have known that it *was* the first World War?"

A lobster boat chugged in, circled the ferry slip and tied up at the town dock. Two men unloaded a wire crate filled with their catch. Claws waved feebly from between the wires. A few bystanders watched, enamored with the spring air and the sense of witnessing a nineteenth-century ritual.

There were two new voices behind Sport.

"You going to the Legion supper tonight?"

"Last time I went I had t' have the doctah ovah' t' the house."

"It could have been Hannah's beans."

"'Less it was Shirley's tuna casserole."

Laughter without any malice in it.

On a patch of yellow-green grass beside the gift shop, Sport could see an eleven- or twelve-year-old boy trying to feed a baby seal from a baby bottle.

"He was washed ashore yesterday," the boy was explaining to a mixed group of islanders and summer people.

"You aimin' t' throw him back?"

"No Sir. He'd die without his mother."

"Kin I have him?"

Sport lifted her head slightly when she heard the familiar voice. Edith Wright, on her knees beside the small, frightened creature, was petting it.

"Gee, no. He needs special care. My Dad called the Boston Aquarium. They'll be picking him up in a seaplane this afternoon."

"More fuss ovah' a seal than most kids," one of the onlookers muttered.

A woman patted Edith's shoulder. "You're coming to supper tonight over at the Legion Hall tonight, Edith. Don't you forget."

Edith didn't appear to hear, or in any case didn't acknowledge the invitation. Losing interest in the baby seal, she wandered onto the ferry dock.

The woman who had patted Edith's shoulder said to the girl standing beside her, "I'm thinking of asking Edith if she wants to move in with us permanently."

"Ok by me, Ma. If I ever catch sight of Johnny Wright again, I may strangle him."

"I never looked for Johnny to do such a thing. He was always straight. It does make you think how one bad thing leads to another."

Sport watched Edith standing at the edge of the ferry dock looking down at the water. Although Sport couldn't see it, she knew that particular area was probably littered with beer cans, food wrappers, crushed cigarette packs and a bit of oil slick from the ferry and small motor boats.

Nearby, a summer owner asked an islander, "How've you been? Did you have a good winter on the island?" Falsely hearty. Condescending.

"I had a bad turn o' fevah' this wintah."

"Oh, too bad. Over it now I hope?" Edging slightly away. Not wanting to hear the details.

"I have no strength t' call upon, but I'm gettin' on best I can."

"Well good luck. I have to board now."

Whitney said, "I can always tell who's a native and who's one of us."
"Wow. Big deal," Dede said.
"Hey, most of the younger ones don't have Maine accents," Talbot point-
ed out.
"I mean even if they don't talk," Whitney said.
"Even if it's a summer person and they're not in their L. L. Bean uni-
form?" Dede asked.
"Yeah."
"How?"
"They look different," Whitney said.
Dede laughed. "You mean like Louise Eliott?"

Sport could see Louise Elliott standing in front of the post office, chatting with a friend. Dressed in jeans and a pullover, she was a "native" easily mistaken for "one of us." That is, if "one of us" was well educated, intelligent, slim and exceptionally goodlooking.

"How do they look different?" Talbot scoffed, "A lot of my friends from
home dress in clothes from the thrift shop and they're grossly overweight
and they look like they live on the streets."
"I just can tell," Whitney answered stubbornly.
"You know what I think it is?" Dede said. "Maybe it's a matter of confi-
dence."

Then how to account for Sarah's lack of it?
Henry Abbott.
Mommy emerged from Barnett Elliott's store, blinking in the sunlight. Depositing two huge paper sacks of groceries in the back of the Rover, she said, "There! That should last us for a least, I don't know, one day." She laughed without much mirth in it. "I just have to run to the post office, then I'll be back." She walked off. Sport noticed that with no trips to her hairdresser's since January, her mother's hair had gone almost completely grey.

And which was Mommy? Born to old-time Mainers, but metamorphosed into a summer person, courtesy of the same Henry Abbott.

An old Chevy rattled to a stop in front of the house and a voice called
out, "Anybody home?" although you could see by the cars that plenty of

people were home. Mommy ran out of the house so fast Sport could hardly keep up on her short skinny toddler legs.

"How ye be, my darlin'?" Granny asked, snatching Sport up in her arms and hugging her.

"What'd you bring me, Granny?"

"Well, I had to go down to Rockport and I just decided to come on ovah' and bring you a sight o' donuts. And a big hug. Maybe you could come down to town with me Annie Bananie?"

Mommy acted funny. She kept looking over her shoulder at the house.

"Ma," she said, "Sure, go on, take Sport to town. I have the Chapins and the Harrington-Clarks here and it's a real mob scene."

Granny acted funny then too. She kissed Sport and said,

"Sure, come on Annie Bananie. Let's skedaddle."

The next year Granny was dead and Mommy cried and cried. She kept saying things Sport couldn't understand. Like how sorry she was and how she had always meant to make it up to Granny. Make what up Sport had wondered at the time? It wasn't Mommy's fault Granny died of pneumonia.

An osprey dipped low over the goose-pimpled bay, and the ledges were spotted with terns. The weather was its usual mercurial self: one moment clouds blurred the wharf to a drab grey; the next, the sun brightened the seaside cottages to white and the waves to silver. The first trucks began rumbling onto the ferry. Then a car, the standard summer person's Volvo with a bumper sticker: "If you don't like our winters, you don't deserve our summers." It occurred to Sport that the sticker made no sense on a summer person's car. Foot passengers followed the vehicles, hugging the stern railing and waving to those left behind, or disappearing into the port and starboard cabins.

One of the returning lobstermen offered Edith a struggling crustacean, but she shook her head and walked down the ramp towards the ferry. She carried no purse, and the decision to board appeared to have been a last-minute one. A ferryman spoke to her, and then smiling, punched her arm lightly and motioned her on. It was a gesture that embodied a lifetime of interactions between two people who had known each other from birth, attended the same schools, worshipped at the same church, worked on the same civic projects, contributed to the same July Fourth picnics, helped each other during bad times, celebrated together during good ones, comforted each other at funerals, congratulated each other at Christenings and, in all probability, had a common ancestor.

Take care until it's known for sure who's responsible.

How long could she take care? And it hadn't helped Whitney and Talbot to be off the

island. Suppose it was never known? Play possum for the rest of her life? Remain a veg-
etable? Make no decisions? Accept no responsibilities? Never walk, talk or laugh in public?
Take on a new identity like a squealer from the mob?

Cables groaned, the ramp creaked as it rose, the ferry began its slow chug backwards out into the harbor where it would turn around. Edith appeared on the starboard upper deck as the ferry's stern turned towards the ferry dock. She leaned over
the stern railing, watching the dipping, wheeling gulls. Due to the worsening weather, she was the only one up there at the moment. And, as Sport watched, she placed
her hands on the wooden bin that held the life jackets and lifted herself to a sitting
position. Then she stood. Her shapeless brown dress fluttered in the wind.

The skeins of vapor in Sport's brain became thicker and more turgid. Thoughts
bumped into one another. She felt as if she were choking. Something clogged her
throat as Edith stepped to the edge of the bin, teetered indecisively and clumsily
tried to jump over the rail at the stern of the boat.

With surprising agility, she somehow twisted in the air and caught onto the railing. Her legs kicked in midair. She had changed her mind.

No one noticed Sport's screams. It blended with a dozen others. Yells.
Instructions. Exhortations to Edith to hang on. Orders to those below to dash up
and grab her. Bellows to the captain to cut the engines. Pandemonium among the
passengers.

And a doll-like puppet desperately hanging onto a ferry railing.

A man appeared on the upper deck and made a grab for Edith's fingers. Her
body flapping, the brown dress fluttering, her legs kicking, she released her grip on
the railing with her left hand and reached out towards the man. Both of them
missed. The next moment she was falling, her dress flying up around her to reveal
skinny white legs and white cotton underpants, like a nightmare vision of Mary
Poppins, flying through the air without an umbrella, towards the ferry's stern.

Everywhere came the screams of bystanders, empathetic but uninvolved. The
next scream was different. It began in fright, crescendoed to panic and climaxed in
hideous agony. Sport had not been near enough to hear Dede, Whitney, or Talbot
scream like that and, of course, Nevah couldn't have screamed under water. So this
was the scream that would haunt Sport for the rest of her life.

While others spurted out of the boatyard, the market, the library and the post
office, heading for the waterfront, Anne Abbott bucked the tide and dashed for the
Rover. When she saw Sport's head safe on the pillow, she stopped dead, her breath
exploding in relief.

The ferry engines finally died. A Whaler set out from shore and circled the spot
where Edith had plunged. Even Sport could see the water changing color. One of
the two men in the Whaler leaned over the side and grabbed for an object in the

ferry's wake. When he brought it up, the woman who had patted Edith's shoulder fainted.

Twelve

Dede gave detailed directions while Whitney loaded the inflated dinghy with their life jackets and the picnic cooler. Then, leaving her crutches on the dock, Dede scooted along the dock on her bottom, and carefully moved sideways, settling on the plastic seat next to the tiller. She tugged on the starter cord several times before the motor purred into life. Whitney got into the dinghy, seated himself beside Dede, and feeling for the lines tied to the dock cleats, he released the boat with a few practiced moves. They puttered away from the dock.

"The gimp and the blind man went to sea," Dede recited, "in a beautiful pale grey boat. They took some honey and plenty of money, wrapped up in a watertight note. What kind of a note was it that they actually used? A ten-pound note or something? And why would you put honey in a ten-pound note Whit?"

"Hey, Dede, do you realize that this is the first truly adventurous thing we've done together since, well, since we took Nevah scuba diving?"

"Yeah, and you remember how well *that* turned out. I hope the weather holds."

"How does it look?"

"It looks ok but you know the old saying about Maine weather."

The sea rolled away from them like a swath of silver cloth, and the rays from the sun caught copper glints in Dede's hair, which Whitney couldn't appreciate, and chrysanthemum shimmers in Whitney's, which Dede could.

"I'm glad it's just the two of us for a change, Dede. I'm tired of being patronized and condescended to."

"You're full of it, Chapin. Nobody patronizes or condescends to us. Especially not Anne. She's been a brick. Taking us in for the whole winter, cooking for us, providing us with entertainment – "

"What entertainment?"

"Videos. Scrabble. Well, no scrabble for you, or videos for that matter . . . ."

"Actually I was thinking of Steve."

"What's your problem, Whit? Steve's been absolutely super. Looking after Sport . . . ."

"What a cutesy preppy you are, Dede. The words you use! Super. Brick."

" – giving me free medical advice, doing errands for Anne . . . ."

"What does he look like?" Whitney wiped spray off his face with the sleeve of his windbreaker.

"He's devilishly handsome. Slim, athletic, broody. A kind of Heathcliff."

"Sure. Think Sport would marry him? I mean if she ever recovers? Which doctors seem to think she will."

"Are you suggesting he's after her money?"

Whitney shrugged.

"Well, that's crazy if you think that's why he's hanging around," Dede said energetically. "Henry didn't inherit that much apart from the house here and he's just a lawyer. Steve will be a doc. He can do as well as Henry some day."

"Not if he hangs around here."

"He won't, not for long."

"You sound as if *you* want to marry Steve."

"Sure I would. But Sport always did get first crack."

"Well, I don't know, I think it may be 'even steven' at this point, if you'll excuse the pun. You a gimp. Sport a vegetable. Hard to say how that one might go."

Avoiding a lobster pot, Dede asked, "Which will it be? Cinder Island or Hallowell?"

"Don't ask me. You're the captain. And it doesn't make a helluva lot of difference to me. Did you check the weather?"

"I told you, the sky is powder blue. Whoever heard of blue powder?"

"Gunpowder? Let's head for Cinder. It's closer."

"What's happened to your spirit of adventure? You used to be such a wild man."

"Gee, I don't know. Maybe I'm just maturing."

"Whit! Look! A seal. Two of them actually. They're sunning on a rock like a couple of octogenarians on the porch of a seaside hotel. I adore seals."

"Know what you remind me of, Dede? A poem my English teacher at Andover used to read to us. Browning's 'My Last Duchess'. Remember? 'That's my last Duchess painted on the wall . . . .' The guy had her zapped because she loved everything equally."

"Your English teacher had her zapped because she loved everything equally?"

"Stop being a pain in the ass. The duke had his duchess zapped because she was like you. She loved everyone equally: her gardener, her cat, her duke. You show the same degree of enthusiasm for seals or sunsets or banana splits or me – "

"Now when did I ever show enthusiasm for you?"

Irritated at her mock incredulity, Whitney shut down. They chugged along silently for awhile, Dede involved in checking her plastic-coated chart and the cluster of islands overlapped against the smooth skin of the ocean. Whitney flipped through images of what he remembered of the landscape as if they were pages behind his sightless eyes.

After a moment he said, "I hear people fainted when they saw what was left of Edith after she was fell into the ferryboat propeller."

"Poor Edith. A lousy life and a ghastly death."

"Why do you say a lousy life?"

"Are you kidding? How'd you like scrubbing toilets, making beds, cooking – "

"They say parts of her are still showing up at the ferry landing. Her – "

"If you don't shut up, you'll be swimming."

Tucking the chart under her seat, Dede kept a lookout for lobster pots and sand bars as she steered through a narrow channel between two outcroppings of rocks. As they approached the tiny uninhabited island, only about four acres in size, she cut the motor, pulled it up, and coasted towards the rocky beach until the bottom of the dinghy gently touched the shore. Whitney stepped out at the front and dragged the dinghy up onto the beach.

"There's a rock you can tie up to about three paces straight in front of you and two paces to the right," she instructed. "The tide is coming in but it won't get up that far by the time we leave."

"Shit!" Whitney snapped, having found the rock with his shin. He tied the line around it, and following Dede's directions, unloaded the picnic cooler of plastic dishes, paper napkins, sealed bags of cold chicken, potato chips, pickles, two bottles of beer, an opener and two folded blankets.

"I wish I'd brought my sketch pad," Dede said after she'd crawled onto the blanket with Whitney's help. She looked around at the slight hill behind them topped by a few scraggly spruces. Then she looked out at the water. It was still only mid-June and apart from a few retirees who didn't boat much, the summer people had not yet arrived in force. There was no one on the water.

"I think it's been painted before," he said sourly, still smarting from her teasing. "But not by *me*."

"Too bad we can't explore, Dede. Remember how much fun it used to be to climb around the islands and find private coves for skinny dipping?"

"Me skinny dipping wouldn't do much for you Whit."

"Remember the time that guy appeared, like Friday in *Robinson Crusoe?* The one who was with Outward Bound and was supposed to survive on an island for a weekend?"

Dede began to laugh. "The one who was supposed to live on whatever nature supplied, but instead wolfed down most of our picnic?"

"Speaking of which, I'm starved. Is it time to eat?"

"It's always time to eat," she said, beginning to dispense the picnic. She laid out the food and then, arranging a few pieces of each item artistically on the plate, she put the plate in front of Whitney.

"You know, Dede, we're lucky to have each other."

"Mmm." Dede tossed a chunk of chicken to a hovering seagull. "Actually, we're lucky just to be alive. I feel like we've been through a war although only Nevah and Talbot actually died."

"You're not counting Edith?"

"Well, that was different. It was a suicide."

"What about Sport? You count her among the living?"

"Sport will recover. Sooner rather than later if I had to guess. Sometimes I catch her doing what looks a lot like rational thinking."

"Now what does that look like exactly?"

"You know. I'll see her eyes shifting from person to person while they're talking and she seems to be following the conversation."

There was a short silence while they ate. Dede sat back and sighed after a while.

"It does seem that the best people die young."

"You're not the first to have made that observation."

"Well, it's true. I wouldn't mind if I could choose the people who died young."

She opened a beer and handed it towards Whitney but instead of taking it, he seized her wrist.

"Get rid of this stuff," he said. The nature of his hunger had changed.

Dede laughed but it was a nervous rather than a mocking laugh.

"You're kidding, Whitney. After all these years, we've been dancing around each other. And now, you're finally getting serious?"

"Tell me why not, Dede?"

"I don't know, Whit. We've known each other since we were little kids. We're like brother and sister."

"How would you know? You don't have any siblings. I have a sister and trust me, I feel very differently about her. Anyway, we had a fling or two in our youth, you'll surely recall."

"I was so drunk or stoned I actually don't."

"And there I was, thinking the earth had moved."

Dede lapsed into silence for a moment, and then she shrugged.

"You know Whit, I'm not exactly pushing away suitors these days. You'd be surprised how hard it is to get laid when you're disabled in the way I am."

"Actually, I wouldn't be."

Dede pushed the food off of the blanket and lay down beside Whitney. It was surprisingly warm given the wind. She touched Whitney's cheek with the back of her hand. He pulled her towards him, encircled her with his arms and began to kiss her. His body was no longer that of an athlete at the height of his physical strength but still, it was the body of a young man. She was ridiculously delighted with this discovery. She suddenly felt more alive than she had since the accident as he kissed her and moved his hands under her sweater.

Out on the bay, a tag line of herring gulls swooped frantically in and out of the teal-blue sea as if hurrying to meet some deadline of nature. A northeasterly wind rippled the surface of the water, and the sun raced in and out among the fast moving clouds. The rubber dinghy began to stir and bob as the tide crept up on the beach. The air sweeping down from Canada caught a distant sloop, and it heeled over in the chop, while a tiny, yellow-slickered figure began tugging on the jib to bring it down. Dusk descended on the island.

Some time later, Dede said drowsily, "Wouldn't it be lovely if I became pregnant?"

It was hard for Whitney to discern if the words were ironic or sincere. With uncharacteristic gentleness, he said, "Nothing to stop us. We're young, healthy . . . in a manner of speaking . . . and we've both inherited enough to pay for whooping cough shots." He bent to kiss her again, the words nestled between them, growing like yeast dough under favorable conditions, or maybe like a hypothetical fetus.

Suddenly, Whitney's head rose up from the blanket. "Is it raining?"

Dazedly, Dede opened her eyes and became aware of the turbulent surface of the inlet, the sooty sky, some distant flickers of lightening, and the dinghy bobbing on the incoming tide. The terns and gulls had all vanished, and the stunted trees on the top of the rise were twisting and bending.

"Jesus!" Dede exclaimed.

"What?"

"Get dressed, Whit. We have to hurry."

Scrambling on the sand like a crab, Dede handed Whitney his under shorts, tee shirt, chinos, sneakers and slicker. Then she pulled on her bra and panties, shorts, tee shirt, and slicker. She started to gather the picnic paraphernalia, but glancing at the sky and ocean, she changed her mind. "Somebody can pick up this stuff another time."

"How come you didn't notice?" Whitney said.

"I was otherwise engaged. Think we ought to sit this out?"

"Do you see any shelter?"

Dede's eyes swept the few scattered spruce trees on the hill behind them. "Not really."

"This could last for hours."

"Hey, how about that old Maine saying? If you don't like – "

"Hell, it's a twenty minute run. We can make it."

Dede gave the line of low flying clouds another apprehensive glance. "I don't know, Whit."

"It's that or we die of pneumonia."

Whitney lifted her in his arms and carried her to the dinghy under Dede's instructions. Handing him one of the life jackets, she buckled the other one on herself. Whitney shoved the boat, which was already floating, further into the water and hopped in. He lowered the motor by feel, and a few pulls brought it to life. Dede took over on the tiller.

The rain began in earnest, pelting them with sharp, stinging needles. The cold penetrated their light slickers. Shivering, teeth clicking, Dede peered though the nearly opaque barrier to locate Ledge Island. They puttered out of the cove into open water and immediately the waves started rolling at them.

"Thank God we went to Cinder instead of Hallowell," Dede muttered.

"Hell, Dede, just last week I was reading about some guy crossing the Atlantic in a row boat. Surely one blind guy and one gimpy girl can cross a bay in a motor boat."

"Yeah, Whit, and not too long ago I was reading about some teenagers doing a little scuba diving and one of them drowned."

Thirteen

The ringing of the telephone downstairs awakened her from a shallow, incident-cluttered sleep. First she was trying desperately to reach the top of a ski slope, but everything conspired to thwart her: crowds of brightly dressed skiers pushing ahead of her; a faceless someone insisting it was far too late to attempt a run; a child tripping her with his pole. Then, with a skip in time, she and Edith were boarding a bus in a strange city and Talbot's little nephew was trying to cling to her hand but a stranger yanked him away. After that came a quick run of standard anxiety dreams: homework left undone for months; an abandoned baby sobbing for food; an endless, deserted corridor stretching out to nowhere.

The telephone was left unanswered and eventually it gave up.

Where was everyone?

Rain and wind slashed at the windows, making so much noise that she almost couldn't hear anything else. As the rain bombarded the roof, it splattered down the chimney and newspapers that had been laid for a fire crackled in the fireplace. Each onslaught jarred her nerves. Nearby, so close the house seemed to tremor in shock, a tree crashed with a ripping, tearing sound followed by a crash. And yes, it had made a sound because she was around to hear it.

" . . . . from the coast of New Hampshire, up through Maine and Canada . . . Coast Guard warnings . . . winds up to forty knots . . . gusts up to fifty miles an hour . . . ten-foot waves . . . visibility nearly zero . . . ."

She could hear only fragments of the marine forecast sputtering from the weather radio downstairs and she had no idea if it was afternoon or twilight. With small pauses to regroup, the wind came back and back again to batter the house with increasing fury. The waves crashed on the rocks and threatened to wash over the dock at the bottom of the hill. Lightning flashes lit up the sky, and from the distance came the scream of a siren.

The intermittent flashes of light metamorphosed the furniture from familiar contours into unrecognizable dark shapes. The partially ajar door of the closet appeared to be about to reveal the unspeakable. Sitting up, she peered around at the balcony overlooking the living room. A cloth wall hanging painted by Anne years ago stirred as if alive. Another flash of light illuminated the poster: "Just because you're paranoid . . . ."

The marine forecast was gone and the house hummed with the emptiness as if all the inhabitants had fled. Her worst dread realized. But she was no longer helpless. She could now save herself if the need arose.

But where was Anne? Lucy? Dede and Whitney?

Unhesitatingly, she got out of bed and went to the bathroom. She even flushed the toilet, her sense of being alone was that strong. Peering over the balcony railing, she saw no sign of movement. She returned to her room and began exercising. As she bent and pulled and stretched, a memory took shape. The family had been vacationing in the Caribbean, and while boating, she had lost a gold earring in fifteen feet of water. She had dived repeatedly, but each time, nearly within reach of the earring, she had been forced to the surface, gasping for air. Although she could see the jewel amid the shells and the sea fans, it kept eluding her. She never recovered it.

Now she was suddenly overwhelmed with a sense of plunging into her memory for an object far more important than a trinket. A vital fragment of information. It had been dangled before her . . . in someone's words, in someone's letter . . . but now, no matter how deeply she dived into her mind, she couldn't reach it.

* * *

Lifting her head from the wild strawberry patch, Anne Abbott became aware of the storm approaching from the northeast. Like Whitney and Dede, she had been lulled by the balmy early morning. Now a faraway rumbling warned her of a turbulence bearing down on the Island as inexorably as Birnam Wood to Dunsinane Hill. Capping her jar of berries hurriedly, she made it back to the house just before the rain struck. The phone was ringing as she slammed the front door behind her.

"Anne? It's Herb Curtis."

"Hi, Herb."

"I was out liftin' pots and I'm pretty sure I saw Whitney and Dede out ovah' on Cinder. If it weren't for somethin' happenin' to my engine, I'd a taken a look, but it was all I could do to get myself in."

Actually, Herb *had* "taken a look," but what he had seen had embarrassed him so much it had overcome his natural instinct to help someone in danger.

"Oh my God," Anne cried, "I forgot they were taking a boat out."

"You *knew* those two were takin' a boat out?"

"Well, you know how those two are. Thanks for calling, Herb."

Soaking wet from the short run to the house from the car, Lucy came into the kitchen carrying paper sacks of groceries.

"Did you ever see the like?" Hanging up her slicker and leaving her boots in the front hall, Lucy began unloading meats, vegetables, fruits, cans of soup and cartons of spaghetti. "I never saw such a storm come up so fast."

"Lucy, Herb Curtis just called. He thinks he saw Dede and Whitney out on Cinder."

"They always were crazy, those two."

"I'm going down to the dock." Frowning, she hesitated. "Maybe you ought to alert the Coast Guard. Just in case."

As Lucy went to the telephone, Anne pulled on her foul weather gear and opened the door. A blast of wind tore it from her hand and she had to use all her strength to shut it before lowering her head and starting to run.

Spruce trees on the hills behind her were leaning over as if they were a line of people leaning into the wind. She made her way, her hands gripped on the railings, to the end of the dock and stood at the top of the metal ramp that led down to the floats. Here the gale was even wilder. Waves crashed against the pilings before exploding into a boiling white foam. Lightening slashed open the curtain of rain, and she caught sight of something far out. A second flash revealed the dinghy pitching and rocking, each wave threatening to swamp it. Two orange dots, Dede's and Whitney's life jackets, were visible above the sides, and then they disappeared as the breakers blocked her view. The rip and chop threatened to capsize the tiny vessel with each surge.

Rain stinging her skin and blinding her vision, Anne searched the hills behind her and the bay in front of her for some sign of help, but she saw nothing but wildly swaying trees and a watery chaos with no sign yet of the Coast Guard.

Since it was high tide, the ramp to the floats was horizontal. She walked along the metal surface of the ramp cautiously, holding tightly onto the metal railings. Fenders slamming against the floating dock, the Abbotts' small mock lobster boat and a Boston Whaler rocked wildly. There were no other boats on the floats or out at the moorings since they were still in dry dock.

Anne let go of the ramp railing and, in between waves, ran the four or five feet across the wooden float to the violently rocking lobster boat. She climbed aboard and retrieved a life jacket from the cabin. Then she started the motor and released the lines. The cove resembled an animal writhing in its death throes. The boat climbed and fell, the windshield wipers clicked ineffectually, and the wind shrieked. There was a only a three-foot Dodger covering the cockpit and the rain pelted her back. It was nearly impossible to see more than a few yards ahead. The wheel spun out of control, the boat hit a wave broadside and sent Anne sprawling. Crawling back to the wheel, she dragged herself up and held on tightly. Each heaving wave seemed capable of swallowing the boat.

A crisscross of lightning gave her a stage-lit view of the toy dinghy only yards from her starboard side. She locked the wheel into position and ran for a life ring attached to a long line. She tied the line onto a cleat and flung the ring. Dede, who had caught sight of the lobster boat's hull rising and dipping, made a grab for the ring as it came down. And missed. Her mouth was a wide, dark oval as she screamed directions to Whitney. Hauling in the ring, Anne dashed back to give the wheel a turn into the wind and lock it again. The next moment the dinghy vanished.

Completely befuddled by the pandemonium of the storm, the disappearance of Dede and Whitney, and her own powerful, undirected rage, Anne chugged as close as she dared to where she had last seen the dinghy. She was panting with exertion and was making a low whimpering sound. She caught sight of two orange-jacketed dots pitching in the sea. They had somehow fallen out of the dingy. They were clutching each other as they slid down a wave into a trough.

Again, Anne threw the ring as hard as she could and this time Dede caught it. Whitney grabbed it as well. As Anne began towing them in, a shift in the wind tossed the boat to one side, and the same moment, Whitney let go. He no longer seemed to be trying to swim as he spun, went under, came up choking, and slid away into another trough between the waves.

"Dede," Anne shrieked, her voice immediately carried away by the wind, "Don't let go! Don't let go!"

Clinging to the ring, Dede's head swiveled frantically back and forth and then she lunged towards Whitney as Anne let out more line. Dede gulped agonized breaths of air as she rose to the top of a wave and then started to descend. The top of the wave collapsed on top of her and she nearly blacked out, but she held onto the ring. She came up, bumped against Whitney and he made a grab for her. He missed but then reached again and grabbed the line as Dede seemed to collapse against his shoulder and Anne again began to haul them in.

At that moment a pillar of ocean smashed broadside into the lobster boat. Anne lost her footing and slid across the cockpit to slam into the engine housing in the stern. She tried to clutch at the slippery fiberglass surface, managed to stand up, lost her grip and was thrown overboard into the heaving black water.

*　　*　　*

It sounded as if all the souls who had ever been lost at sea in Penobscot Bay had been ripped from their watery graves by the storm and were now swirling around the house, screaming for help, sending indecipherable messages to the loved ones left behind. The rain raked the glass like needles and the house creaked. Soot from the chimney swooped down into the room.

If she had been given one wish, it would have been to wake up in this bedroom and discover that the entire time from Nevah's death onward had been a nightmare.

No one had checked on her for some time. Although it was hard to detect movement within the house over the clamor of the gale, she still had a strong sense of being alone. She slipped off the bed and went to the window. A flash of lightning illuminated what appeared to be a boat out on the cove, and all her intimations of disaster coalesced.

She opened the door leading to the balcony and listened. Nothing. All the other bedroom doors were shut. No sign of human activity. What was going on?

Then, without warning, the outer door slammed back, and a figure, only slightly darker than the surrounding dimness, burst into the hallway and, with great effort, shut the door again. Sport sank back into the shadows. The figure went to the telephone, waited, swore and hung up. Next, it poked a switch. No light came on.

"What can I do?" Lucy wailed querulously to herself. "Can't drive, can't walk, No telephone. Anyway, would be too late."

The words pinged on Sport's nerve endings. It was as if a gate had swung open. Without thinking, she stepped out of the gloom and went to the head of the stairs. "Lucy!"

Lucy whirled and peered upwards. "Who's there?"

"It's me, Sport. What's happening?"

The scream Lucy gave could not have conveyed more shock and terror than if it had been Nevah at the top of the stairs. Lucy backed up to the door and might have bolted back into the storm if Sport hadn't snapped, "Lucy! Stop it! It's me."

Her hand on the doorknob, Lucy stared unbelievingly, "Sport?"

Holding onto the railing, Sport started shakily down the stairs. "Lucy, what's happening? Who're you calling? What's too late?"

"I never looked t' see you get better."

"What did you mean when you said you couldn't drive? Who're you trying to call?"

"When'd you start walkin'?"

"Lucy! Please, please answer me! What's going on?"

"The phone stopped workin' soon as Anne left. The road's blocked right in front with a tree. It's too far to walk – "

"Where's my mother? Who're you trying to call? I saw a boat out on the cove."

"Folks as ignorant as those two deserve what they get."

Now at the foot of the stairs, Sport leaned on the wall. She shut her eyes, waiting for her legs to stop shaking. She couldn't tell whether the shaking was from exertion or fear. The trepidation that had been building ever since she had awakened, was overwhelming her.

"Who's ignorant? Who deserves what they get?"

"When did you get better'? How did it happen?"

Sport's voice rose to a shriek. "Lucy! What the hell is going on?"

With an effort, Lucy shook off her befuddlement. "Whitney and Dede. They took a boat out. One blind and the other a cripple!"

"Dede and Whitney are out on the cove?"

"And the phone's out of order. A tree's blockin' the road in front. How'm I supposed to get the Coast Guard?"

"Where's my mother?"

"She's down at the dock."

"Oh God, oh no. Let's go, Lucy."

"Let's go? What're you aimin' t' do?"

Not answering, Sport went to the hooks on the hallway wall and began tugging down her foul weather gear. Her movements were uncoordinated, like a child's in the first stages of learning to dress. After a moment's hesitation, Lucy began helping her. She caught the door after Sport swung it open and slammed it shut. Then, holding hands, they started down the incline, Lucy in front, both of them holding onto the rope with their other hands. The path had changed into a muddy and slippery stream. Lucy kept darting glances back at Sport as if expecting her to vaporize. A big spruce had toppled over down the incline, smashing four or five more trees below it. Rain slashed at their faces, wind tore their breath away, and now Lucy was sliding down the incline, the rope burning her hands, while Sport leaned on her from behind. The closer they came to the float, the more deafening the waves became. Although the storm still raged, the tide had receded enough to expose the beach littered with oil cans, plastic bottles, lobster buoys, milk jugs, oars, wooden planks, and plastic orange and yellow lines. Sport had time to think that this was all that would remain when the world came to an end.

In a few minutes, they were standing on the float, Sport clutching at Lucy's arm. Tears streamed down Sport's face as she stared helplessly at the raging waves. Somewhere out there were a crippled girl, a blind boy and a middle-aged woman. Her dearest friends and her beloved mother. The waves shifted, revealing a terrifying tableau: an overturned dinghy, a bobbing lobster boat and tiny splashes of orange in the churning water.

*   *   *

Steve's last patient of the morning, a young man who had nearly severed his little finger chopping vegetables, was just leaving when the rain started. Steve stood for a moment at the doorway of his rented cottage and brooded on the rubbery clouds dipping low over the village. Neighboring islands were quickly fading into invisibility.

Back inside, he fixed himself a ham and brie sandwich on French bread and a glass of cranberry juice. Then he settled down into an ugly brown couch to read an old article in the Smithsonian about cycloramas.

As the tempo of the storm accelerated, patients began canceling their afternoon appointments one after another. Programmed to check on the Abbotts under any set of unusual circumstances, Steve dialed their number. Although the telephone was still animate at that point, there was no answer. Frowning, he stared unseeingly at the town harbor where boats were lunging on their moorings. Although it was time, there was no sign of the midday ferry, and he guessed service had been suspended. There were few cars in the town parking lot. Evidently the island population had hunkered down.

Shrugging on his slicker and boots, Steve went out to his Jeep. His was the only vehicle in sight and he could barely see the road through the rain pelting his small windshield. When he reached the fork he went to the left, only to discover that the bridge over the inner harbor was completely flooded. Backing up, he took the right fork and drove the long way around the island to the Point. Balsams, spruces, alders, and birch trees swayed and wheeled under the onslaught. Intermittently, he caught glimpses of the sea chaotically ripping itself to shreds on the rocks.

As he approached the neck of land that lead to the Point, he nearly hit an apple tree blocking his path. Braking sharply, he caused the wheels to spin in the mud. He switched off the engine, pulled the hood of the slicker over his head and continued on foot. As he passed the Wrights' deserted house, he caught another glimpse of the ocean, a boat bobbing on the surface. A lobsterman caught by the storm? The hazy blending of land, sea and sky made it impossible to see clearly.

Half jogging, half floundering on the muddy roads, he finally reached the Abbott house and went in without knocking. He shouted but no one answered. Jackets and boots were scattered helter-skelter in the entrance hall as if the inhabitants had evacuated in a hurry.

Steve dashed upstairs, leaving a muddy trail on the steps.

Incredulously, he stared at Sport's empty bed and scattered sheets. He whirled, half expecting her to materialize behind him. Then he sprinted through the other equally deserted rooms. Racing downstairs again, he looked out. Yes, the Rover was parked in its usual spot.

"Jesus," he said aloud, "have you all been washed out to sea?" His own words reminded him of the boat he had glimpsed out on the water. Giving himself no time to think, he ran out the front door, not bothering to close it behind him.

He could see two small figures huddled on one of the floats. He grabbed the rope and started sliding through the mud down the hill.

Shouting above the shrieking of the wind, he ran towards the figures on the dock. Both of them were on their hands and knees trying to untie the docking line on the Boston Whaler. One of them finally heard him and looked up. He recognized Lucy. Her face was distorted, her eyes wide with confusion and fear. "Doctor! Thank God!"

"Lucy! What the hell is going on? Where's Sport?"

The other figure, slowly raised her head and Steve stumbled and nearly fell. Sport was still ineffectually struggling with the line that held the Boston Whaler to the dock.

"Steve! They're all out there! Mommy and Dede and Whit!"

Dazed, Steve looked from her streaming face to the boat out in the bedlam beyond the dock. Abruptly, he pulled himself together. "Take her back to the house," he ordered Lucy. Shoving Sport aside, he took the line from her and partially unhitched it.

"I'm going with you," Sport sobbed. "I have to go with you."

"Lucy! Get her back to the house!"

But something had happened to Lucy. Transfigured from the kindly, obedient image she generally projected, she became what she was: a fifth generation native of the island, accustomed to storms, boats and emergencies. Moving with surprising speed and no hesitation, Lucy grabbed a life vest from the boat, pulled it onto Sport, and grabbing her by the arm, led her up the ramp and onto the granite pier that supported the long wooden dock. She expertly tied a line from the railing on the ramp around Sport's waist and pushed Sport down until she was seated. Sport stared, unable to react.

"Stay put!" she snapped at Sport. Then to Steve: "You'll be needing somebody with you." Before he could react, she was back down the ramp and in the Whaler with Steve, pulling on a life vest, waiting for him to get the motor running so she could let go of the docking line. The boat moved away, leaving a sobbing Sport collapsed on the dock, her arms around the railing.

The Whaler dove down each trough and climbed back up the next wave. The wind deafened them and the rain blinded them. And then, without warning, they were nearly on top of the two orange-vested figures, still clinging to the life ring. The line tying the life ring to the lobster boat seemed to have been severed.

Dede, the life ring around her chest, was floundering desperately towards them while Whitney clung to the life ring with his hands and seemed to be trying to kick. Handing the wheel to Lucy, Steve leaned far over the side and caught Dede's hand. Her face was a puckered mask of fear and exhaustion as she tried to help.

"Come *on!*" Steve yelled. "Come *on!*" With a powerful heave that detached her from Whitney, Steve dragged Dede up out of the water and sent her sprawling onto the bottom of the boat. Lucy maneuvered as close to Whitney as she dared and Steve made a grab for him. The moment he had grasped Steve's hand, Whitney was able to haul himself over the side of the Whaler.

"Anne!" Dede was screaming. "Anne's out there!"

Steve looked around wildly. He could see the lobster boat bobbing with no one at the helm, but nothing resembling a human being in the tumbling confusion. "Where? What? Is she wearing a life jacket?"

"She fell. Out there . . . . She went overboard!"

Lucy began steering towards the lobster boat. Tying another line from the Whaler to his life vest, Steve waited until they were as close to the larger vessel as the ocean allowed, and made a grab for the side. The next moment he was washed into the sea.

Lucy turned the wheel frenziedly to avoid crushing him. As soon as he surfaced, he made another grab for the stern of the lobster boat and hauled himself aboard. Then he took the line from his waist and fastened the two boats together. With Whitney pushing from below, he hauled Dede into the cockpit of the larger, more stable boat. Whitney and Lucy followed. They untied the Whaler and it was quickly tossed out of view.

With Lucy now steering the lobster boat, the three who could see scanned the heaving, reeling pandemonium for some sign of Anne. It was Dede who spotted her first. "Over there! See? Portside!"

A nearly invisible speck was riding the waves like a toy action figure. Steve again tied his life vest to a long line, and with the boat pitching wildly, went over the side again.

The bobbing speck kept evading him. It disappeared into holes and then climbed up the side of waves beyond his reach. His breath became shallow sobs and he felt himself grow weaker as each wave broke over his head.

And then finally he was able to grasp hold of an arm. With Lucy maneuvering the lobster boat as close as she dared to the exhausted Steve, Dede screamed directions at Whitney. Frantically Whitney hauled in the line and Steve grabbed the stern. Steve tried to climb up onto the stern with one arm while holding Anne with the other. He couldn't lift her, but Whitney flailed his arms about until he found Anne's arms and dragged her over the side. Steve, gasping and spitting, pulled himself the rest of the way up over the stern and fell into the boat.

Within seconds Whitney was on his knees, his fingers laced, his elbows straight, his palms pressing into Anne's sternum as he re-lived a nine-year-old nightmare.

Fourteen

Sport was alone.

It was two weeks since the funeral. The mourners had left. The refrigerator was stacked with donations of rotting casseroles and desserts. Dede and Whitney were now living in Dede's house although the wedding wasn't scheduled until the fall. Heather was making the arrangements and she wanted it to be just right, despite the circumstances.

Two days ago, Lucy had transferred her ministrations to a woman living in Rockport suffering from multiple sclerosis. On Lucy's last day in the house, she and Sport had sat on the back deck looking out over the water on one of those rare days in Maine when it was too hot to move yet the ocean water remained uncomfortably cold for swimming. Lucy had talked about moving to San Francisco to live with a cousin once she finished the Rockport job and Sport had encouraged her, while inwardly thinking how much poorer the community would be for Lucy's absence. In fact, it was hard to imagine how these Maine island communities could withstand the pressures of tourism and real estate for even another generation.

Now, on a third day of impenetrable heat, Sport sat on the same deck looking down the hill towards the cove. She, who had once treasured intervals of solitude while walking on beaches, reading, writing, sailing, now dreaded being alone. But perversely, she was glad that her father had gone back to his firm in New York. She had refused to accompany her sister on errands earlier in the day and she couldn't bear to be with Dede and Whitney.

Suddenly she thought of something.

She went up to the balcony and lowered the ladder that led to the slope-roofed attic. She climbed up slowly and unsteadily. She opened a dormer window to let some air in but it was still insufferably hot.

Neatly stacked in a corner were the Christmas gifts she had never had an opportunity to open. She stood at the open window, looking down the hill towards the cove. She recalled a late summer afternoon the year before Dede's accident, just before she and Talbot were about to leave for school. She and Talbot had rented a two-seated kayak and taken it to a river a couple of hours north of Rockland. The river had been high but slow and they didn't see anyone for several hours. The rocks that could be challenging in low water had lain below two or three feet of black velvety water. After a little while, they realized that there was no need to paddle, that if they simply lay back, the kayak would effortlessly float down the middle of the stream, only occasionally slipping into the reeds when they came to a turn in the river. She had carefully stepped over her seat to the back and lain in Talbot's arms. They had closed their eyes and felt the delicate warmth of a late summer sun on their faces, the warmth between their bodies.

"You know, Tal," she had said, "maybe we've been paddling hard as we could all this time for nothing. Maybe all we need to do is float. Like this."

"Sounds like a plan," he had said in a sleepy voice.

"Maybe we'll have a thousand afternoons like this one, floating down a river in the warm sun. Someday we'll have kids and they'll be floating in a rubber raft behind us. They'll be singing 'Row, Row Your Boat' in sweet childish voices. We'll leave the Nevah Wright nightmare behind us, along with all the troubles other people have, and just . . . . float on down the river."

Talbot had only smiled and said "hmmm . . . ." in the same sleepy voice.

Then she thought back to last Christmas Eve before her "accident," when Steve and Talbot's nephews had recreated the spirit of '76, and everyone had determined to be happy and Talbot's brother-in-law had told her that everything would be alright now.

After a while, she walked over to the gifts, undoing the ribbons and tinseled papers, folding them neatly beside her. The Abbotts might indulge themselves with boats and other toys, but they weren't wasteful. From her parents she found gold earrings in the shape of periwinkle shells; from Sarah, blue silk lounging pajamas. Dede and Whitney had given her a small seascape that, according to the gift card, Dede had painted and Whitney had somehow managed to frame with overlapping mussel shells. From the Harrington-Clarks, there were two books and from Lucy, hand knitted mittens.

She opened the biggest gift, Steve's, last. A set of wood-framed, leather-thonged snowshoes, hand-crafted by an islander.

As Sport sat and contemplated the residue of an event which seemed to have taken place in someone else's life, she heard tires swishing on the path below. From the dormer window she could see a pickup from Black's garage although she could-n't see who was driving.

Descending the attic ladder and the stairs to the lower level, she saw one of the boys who worked for Mr. Black opening the passenger door. A tiny person, that at first she thought might be a child, was slowly emerging from the cab. It was Edith's mother, Hope Lantagne. She spoke briefly to the boy and then started towards the house. Her movements were quick but her steps were tiny so that her progress towards the door was slow. The boy in the car turned off the motor and slouched down in the seat to wait.

Sport opened the door. Hope Lantagne looked almost the same as she had looked that night last fall at the Wrights' house. In fact, she was more unchanged than almost everyone else around her, Sport thought. The only difference was that her white hair had been recently "permed." She wore a new-looking lime green poly-ester pants suit that was too large for her.

"Sport? I heard about your mothah'. I'm real sorry," she said. Her words were as quick and abrupt as her movements.

Sport's gaze shifted from Hope to the boy sitting behind the wheel in the pick-up. "He don't mind waitin'. Kin I come in?"

Sport stepped aside.

As she entered, her alert blue eyes surveyed the entrance hall, the balcony, kitchen and what was visible of the living room with intense curiosity.

"Kin I set?" The intelligent eyes regarded Sport with the same curiosity she had exhibited towards the house.

"Yes. Of course." Vaguely, Sport indicated the steps leading down to the living room, but Hope chose the nearest kitchen chair.

"Would you care for coffee? Tea?"

"No thank you. I just had some. I'm stoppin' with Mary Emmons. She's my cousin. Her granddaughta's gettin' married, you prob'bly know."

She waited for a remark from Sport, but although Sport would have been happy to oblige, she didn't know what was expected of her.

"I come from Augustah' for the Emmons' wedding so I decided to see you."

"To see me?"

"I don't like bein' the cause o' distress t' you, but it ain't right for suspicion t' be attached t' the wrong people."

"Distress to me?" Realizing how she sounded, Sport made an effort to tighten her thought processes. "I'm sorry. I don't understand."

"Mebbe I'll have that tea now," Edith's mother said in a kindly voice to give Sport more time.

Moving even slower than her elderly visitor, Sport snapped the electric teakettle on. Then, choosing Earl Grey, she prepared a tray with the best porcelain teapot, cups and saucers, silver spoons, sugar and milk. She placed some of the donated cookies from the refrigerator on a plate.

When they were both seated at the kitchen table with their untouched tea, Hope Lantagne began.

"Johnny wrote t' me aftah' he read in the papah' about your mothah' drownin'." Thoughtfully, she added two teaspoons of sugar to her tea.

A spasm of pain coursed through Sport but all she said was, "Johnny Wright wrote to you? Where is he?"

"He nevah' said but it was sent from Alberta Canada. What he wrote was that her bein' dead made him free t' tell the truth."

Unexpectedly, Sport was reminded of her lost pearl earring again. The one she had been unable to reach on the ocean floor. The one she had equated with knowledge and the frustration of not being able to grasp it.

And now she knew she didn't want it any more.

"You evah' suspected you was little Eddie Wright's half-sistah'?"

Sport closed her eyes and waited for the dizziness to pass. She was often dizzy these days and wasn't sure if it was her slowly recovering brain or the news that made her feel faint.

"Like I said, I don't like bein' the cause o' distress t' anybody. You ok?" Sport opened her eyes.

"You want me t' leave?"

"No." Sport reached out and put her hand on Hope's arm, knocking over her teacup. Edith's mother stood up, looked around, found a towel on the counter and swabbed up the spilled tea.

"I'm ok. Go on."

Absent-mindedly, Hope Lantagne began cleaning up the tea things. She hobbled across the room, carrying the cups and saucers to the sink and then came back for the tray. Sport's patience for allowing Hope to calm her own nerves by engaging in mundane housekeeping was wearing thin.

"Please. Don't worry about the dishes. Sit down and explain."

Unruffled, Hope Lantagne regarded Sport for a moment, hitched her pants up slightly by the waistband, and sat back down.

"I allus suspected Johnny's heart was out o' his keepin' whenevah' your mothah' was about. I knew somethin' was goin' on, but I didn't let on t' Edith. Weren't no use. Johnny mighta' bin in love with Anne, but Anne was just markin' time. She had nothin' bettah' t' do. She was waitin' for biggah' fish."

Sport realized that Hope was talking about her mother, the mother she had loved and who was also her best friend.

"But when your mothah' became pregnant 't weren't part o' her plan. She wanted t' be rid o' the baby but Johnny wouldn't hear o' abo'tion. He knew how Edith yearned for a little one o' her own. He told Edith he was goin' t' get her a baby from an unwed mothah' but that he couldn't tell her much more about it . . . ."

Hope paused and sighed.

Sport sat very still, staring at Hope.

"Well, Edith wanted folks t' believe little Eddie were her own, so she came up t' live with me in Augustah', pretendin' she planned to have the baby near her mothah'. Your mothah' knew she'd nevah' have a chance with the summah' boys if they knew about the baby so she slid out in the middle of her summah' waitressin' job, saying she had to get back to college early. I don't think even her own folks knew about Eddie."

Sport thought back to her grandmother. She couldn't recall much about her. Anne had left her with her grandmother for a week while she and Henry went to Europe. Sport had been about five and her only memories of the event were her grandmother allowing her to lick the bowl all three times they made brownies and then hugging Sport and crying when Anne came to pick Sport up at the end of the week. That was the only time Sport ever did stay with her grandmother although in later years, on several occasions, she asked Anne to let her go back rather than leave her with her nanny.

"I suspect in the end Anne suffah'd for her sin. Watchin' her own flesh and blood callin' Edith ma. People change. I believe your mothah' came t' love Eddie very much. Wouldn't surprise me she counted on makin' it up t' him some day."

Another memory flickered in Sport's mind. She thought back to sitting in the wheelchair on the cliffside path. Steve was prattling about his telescope and heading down to the beach. Johnny, hidden by a bend in the road was saying, "I wasted a heap of my life and I want somethin' for myself afore I die . . . I'm not talkin' about you and me. I'm talkin' about murder."

Sport could have told Hope Lantagne that while Anne might have hoped to make it up to her son one day, she'd had to settle on giving the money to her son's blackmailing father.

"Reckon your mothah' went crazy when little Eddie drowned. Crazy as Edith, but less noticeable."

Sport wished that Hope would stop talking. She'd had enough but she couldn't say the words that would make Hope stop.

"Your ma was the one responsible for what happened. She was the one killed Talbot, crippled your . . . ."

Sport jumped up.

"Stop it!" Sport leaned over the imperturbable Hope Lantagne. "You don't know the first thing about my mother. She gave her life to save Dede and Whitney! And as for me, she wouldn't hurt me for all the Nevah Wrights in the world!"

"'Pears t' me she meant you no serious hahm. Fact is, I'm not sure she evah' had a plan. She just went crazy that day and ran into Dede with the boat. But once she'd done that, she couldn't seem to stop herself. And after Talbot, she couldn't let you be the only one to get off scot-free could she? I don't think she meant no serious hahm t'othahs' neithah'. Just wanted t' teach them a lesson. Folks is complicated. Hatin' and lovin' all mixed togethah.'"

With an effort, Edith's mother put her hands on the table and pushed herself to her feet. Holding onto the back of the chair, she stood in front of Sport. She raised a hand as if to stroke Sport's cheek but then apparently thought better of it.

"Once Johnny told me the truth, I had t' tell you. Can't hurt Anne now. I won't be tellin' no one else."

Sport turned her back on Hope and walked to the window. She didn't hear the door close softly as Hope left.

*   *   *

Long after Hope Lantagne had disappeared down the road in the pickup, Sport remained standing at the window, staring at the motionless grass and trees, feeling sweat ooze down her forehead and back.

Consumed with misery but not disbelief, she didn't move. It was as if, by remaining immobile, she could erase the years since five teenagers had gone scuba diving.

She thought suddenly of the misspelled note tumbling out of a picture album in the attic. Johnny had written the note to her mother. Anne, pregnant, disappearing to have a baby. Eddie, entering the world as the offspring of Edith and Johnny. Anne snagging one of the "summer boys". Henry discarding Thora for the younger, prettier Anne. Anne watching her son grow up as the adored child of Edith Wright.

And then they decided to give Eddie scuba diving equipment for his sixteenth birthday.

What passions had seethed through Anne when her son drowned and she held four teenagers responsible? What had tipped the precarious balance in her psyche to commit far more egregious sins than the ones she had committed already?

Long after Hope Lantagne had disappeared down the road in the pickup, Sport remained standing at the window, beginning the process of rewriting her life to fit new facts and new truths. She knew already that it would take years.

Fifteen

"Maine is the first part of the country to see the sun in the morning" Sport said informatively. "Bet you didn't know that."

Steve, lying on the grass at the top of the hill behind the Abbott house, watched the early morning sun paint Sport's face the color of a conch shell's inner swirls. On the horizon, the first aureate bands appeared in the sky. It was early September. The ferrymen had helped the summer residents park their Volvos and SUVs on the ferry as tightly as jigsaw puzzle pieces and then floated them away from their summer idyll. Most of them would never see the ice that clawed its way over the island in between the sparkling summer seasons. The air was quiet and limpid, as if the island itself were breathing a slow sigh of relief.

Putting his hands behind his head, Steve asked, "May I ask you a dumb question?"

"My first of the day."

"Why is Maine called 'down east'?"

Incredulous, Sport lifted herself on one elbow and stared at him until he held up both hands defensively, palms facing out, face apologetic.

"You've lived here more than a year and you don't know that?"

"Well, before I took the job I didn't give Maine a whole lot of thought. And afterwards, there were only patients to ask. You can't ask patients dumb questions. They won't trust you to snip out their gall bladders."

Sport jumped up and went back into the house. She returned in a moment holding.a small, worn paperback, and lying down beside him again, began to read.

"'Cleared away and sailing a northeasterly course out of Boston, the first landfall is the dark and jagged coast of Maine. That's where Down East begins.' Should I continue?"

Steve shrugged. "As you wish."

"Well then, 'In the great heyday of sail, windjammers took advantage of the prevailing westerlies on the run to Maine and the Maritimes. They sailed downwind with canvas bellied taut and shrouds singing. Downwind to Maine became a manner of speaking, slipping with time into the salty brevity of the term Down East. The word had a lilt and it had a sure meaning.

"'Language is a repository of history. Windjammers have vanished into the past; but Down East is still downwind from Boston.'" She looked back at the cover of the faded, almost antique-looking book. "From *Down East magazine, 1954.*"

Steve smiled. "You really love this island."

Putting the book down and shading her eyes, Sport said, "Anne used to read that to me each spring when we arrived here, the way other mothers read 'A Visit from St. Nicholas' every Christmas Eve."

She turned away and watched an osprey plunging into the cove, feet first, for sardines. Then, uprooting a stalk of meadow rue, she began dismembering the white blossoms the way she had as a teenager when intoning "he loves me, he loves me not." But this time she did it silently.

"Sport, what made you decide to live on the island for another year?"

Lightly, she said, "I couldn't tear myself away from you. Also I still have work to do on my thesis. Hell, I've hardly started. I want to try to finish it before I start job-hunting. Henry agreed to keep me in fuel oil and peanut butter until then."

"How come you won't tell anybody what it's about?"

"Hey, give away the plot, you won't buy a copy."

His forehead a washboard, Steve tried to see her averted face. "You're so flippant these past few . . . I mean . . . you know. So hard-shelled."

He waited, but Sport was silent. After a moment, he asked, "What makes you so sure you're now out of danger?"

"Oh heck, I've had my 'accident'. Only one to a customer."

"Ready to bet your life on that?"

"Hey, Schwartz, you trying to get rid of me?"

"Hey, Abbott, you holding back on me? You've been acting . . . well, of course you have a right . . . but there's something different about you."

Again Sport was silent.

After a moment, Steve said, "How did you get your father to agree? Isn't he concerned about your safety?"

"I doubt if my father is running on all cylinders these days." She sat up, clasped her knees and buried her face in her lap.

"I don't know if he ever will again." She raised her head and watched an ant hill swarming with inhabitants, reminding her of Grand Central station during rush hour. She was glad to be here and not there.

"Did you know," Steve said casually, "that Edith never had a child? I mean, never gave birth to a child?"

Sport transferred her study of nature to that of Steve's face. She was silent. "How come you're not surprised? How come you're not asking me how I know?" he asked.

"How you know? You're a doctor, aren't you?"

"Why aren't you surprised?"

Recalling what Henry had always described as the best defense, Sport said, "Aren't you violating medical ethics?"

"Well, with Nevah and Edith both dead and Johnny apparently gone from the face of the earth, I don't feel quite as constrained. So why aren't you surprised?"

"Jesus Christ! Drop it, Steve!"

Momentarily shocked, Steve stared at her. Then, wetting his lips, he started to say something, but changed his mind. Instead, he trilled, "Lil, lil, lu lu" at a white-breasted loon glimpsed down on the water, but the loon wasn't fooled into mistaking him for a mate. The light kept mutating moment by moment, each variation changing the hue of Sport's complexion. Her hand scrabbled on the ground, contacted a jasper stone and she caressed its smooth, rounded surface. With effortless grace, she reached back and flung it at a distant tree trunk. Steve's eyes followed the course of the stone and then flung one of his own. It landed short of Sport's, hitting nothing.

"How come you can do so many things better than I can?" he complained.

"You're probably better at surgery." She hesitated and then added, "Also at saving people from drowning."

He turned to watch a lobster boat, thirty feet long and broad in the beam, unself-consciously picturesque as it chugged across the landscape. A herring gull, soaring high with a struggling creature in its claws, seemed to be posing for any landscape artists that still lingered on the island.

"I'm going to miss this island," he said.

For a moment the significance of the words didn't register with Sport. She was watching the herring and its pitiful prey. "Poor little thing," she said. And then it was as if all the blood in her body had converged in her head, making it difficult to breathe.

"You're going to miss what?"

"Well, you know how it is. Treating bee stings and earaches is ok for the beginning of a career. Or maybe the end. But not the in-between part."

She waited until she thought she would be able to speak normally. Then: "Oh, you mean you'll miss it in the winter, but you'll still come back summers like the rest of us. Vacations anyway."

"Vacations. Yeah." He looked out to where the Harrington-Clark sloop, its bronze-edged portholes glittering in the sunlight, was rocking gently on its mooring.

"Your mother was one brave lady," he said, like someone skipping on hot stones, unable to alight on a safe one.

Sport rose, brushed twigs and grass off her jeans and tee shirt, and without consulting him, headed down the path to the beach. She shaded her eyes, looking out to where the sun was embroidering the dark outer islands with golden threads.

Steve jumped to his feet and followed. In a few moments they were both down at the beach. Unsure of how to regain his own conversational mooring, he said, "What idiots Dede and Whitney were to take off in a boat that day."

Sport stopped walking so abruptly he stumbled into her. He grabbed her arm to keep from falling and then quickly dropped it. For a moment she was distracted from his words by what he had done. Not the grabbing of her arm, but the swift dropping of it. Fleetingly, it occurred to her that, although they had been lying on the grass in close proximity for about an hour, he had never tried to touch her.

"No they weren't!" Her voice was sharp. "The weather was perfect when they started out. Besides it was an adventure. I mean, Dede supplying the eyes and Whitney the muscle."

"An adventure that cost your mother her life," he blurted out. He glanced at her apprehensively and was surprised at her lack of reaction.

Anne was a great one for balancing the ledger.

Saying nothing aloud, Sport scuffed along, sneakers digging into the round stones of the beach.

Unsure of what he was doing, but wanting to establish some truer form of communication beyond what had been said so far, or maybe wanting to finally understand even just one or two things about her, he said, "You admire that in people, don't you? That kind of rash idiocy."

He'd gone too far. She turned to face him.

"Bet your ass I admire that kind of idiocy. The idiocy of those who set out to explore the ocean when it was common knowledge that the earth was flat or to get shot off into space, with no guarantee of a return ticket. 'My purpose holds to sail beyond the sunset, something, something, until I die.'"

"'. . . and the baths of all the western stars . . . .'"

"What?"

"That's the 'something, something.'"

"Well I also admire that idiot who took off in a small boat in fifteen-foot swells to rescue three people he had no reason to love."

And perhaps even the idiot who gave her life for a boy and girl who were, at least in part, responsible for killing her only son.

Then you forgive me, Sport, my darling?

No, Anne, I don't think so.

As they walked on the beach silently now, their sneakers slipping on the wet stones, Sport looked out at the sea, smooth and treacherously beckoning today. As changeable and as unpredictable as human beings. She bent to scoop the cold water into her cupped palms and splashed it on her face.

"I made biscuits. Not from scratch. From a package. Come and have breakfast with me."

"Sport, I have something to tell you."

Sport picked up a periwinkle shell, the tenant still in residence, and dropped it into her pocket. Unbidden, came a memory of her excited and happy wait for Talbot the night before he was killed.

And then, something about Steve's words struck her. He hadn't said, Sport I have something to *ask* you. He'd said, Sport, I have something to *tell* you.

And he did.

The combination of apprehension and exhilaration that had shot through her when she had assumed he was about to propose marriage, was obliterated by the knowledge that he was not.

"It's about Sarah and me. We're going to get – "

"I knew that," she lied. "Why didn't Sarah tell me?"

"My fault. I asked her to let me be the one." He looked up to watch a huge "V" of geese honking their noisy way across the morning sky. Hesitantly he resumed speaking.

"Sport, there was a time . . . I mean . . . well, I was mad for you. I had this, well, I guess it was an obsession . . . You were the golden . . . well, you know. When I first met you I thought it was hopeless. But later . . . it's a wretched thing to have to admit . . . well when Talbot was gone . . . we were thrown together so much it began to feel . . . well, possible . . . ."

Sport stared out at the water, making sure she revealed nothing. She almost appeared the way she had after the accident, incapable of speech or motor ability. He looked at her beseechingly, almost as if asking for forgiveness, but when he became aware of her vacuous expression, he became alarmed. Grasping her arm, he pleaded, "Sport, are you ok?"

Roughly, she threw off his hand. She ought to have carried it off: laughed, hugged him, told him how happy she was to have him as a brother. A half-brother, she might have joked.

The growing awareness in her face reassured him. "Sport, when you had the accident, that clinched it. No way was I ever going to abandon you. I was either going to awaken you with a kiss . . . like that character, you know who I mean . . . or I was going to spend the rest of my life taking care of you. But when . . . ."

"Hello there!"

They had been so knotted together, so insulated from the rest of the world, that they both jumped. Vaguely, they peered in unlikely places – the sky, the woods, the nearest island – until they realized they had been hailed from a small sloop just rounding the jutting ledge. Sails furled, the boat was under power. At the helm, a male figure in cap, sweatshirt and shorts, shouted, "Hi, there! Can you tell me where I can find a mooring?"

Steve recovered first. Pointing at an empty mooring, he called out, "Well, you can probably hang out there for a while."

"No!" Sport's reaction was loud and sharp. "That's private. Keep going east and you'll get to the public harbor."

The yachtsman hesitated and then turned to confer with his crew, a pony-tailed woman dressed as he was. Then, motor chugging, the boat slowly turned and started towards town.

Steve regarded her quizzically. "No outsiders welcome, right, Sport?"

"You got it."

Steve bent to examine a miniscule hole in the wet sand. He found a mussel shell and began digging with it absent-mindedly.

"So, anyway, you woke yourself up without any assistance. As you always will." He began digging more vigorously. Plunging his hand into the hole, he came up with a sizable clam. "Wow! Look at that!"

Sport felt as if she were seesawing between the meaningless and the monumental, between clams and Steve's announcement. Her life was taking another turn, and she couldn't see around the bend. Taking off her sneakers, she carried them as she walked ankle deep into the surf. Steve walked parallel to her but remained on the pitted sand.

"Stupid of me, Sport, saying you've been behaving differently these days. Who wouldn't be, considering what you've gone through. I didn't mean to surprise you, telling you about Sarah and me. But it wouldn't be fair . . . not that I think it matters to you . . . but I hope . . . ."

Floundering, he stopped and then started on another tack. "Soon you'll be ready to return to, well, your own world, and you'll finish your thesis and knowing you, I'd guess you'll be up to your neck in whatever it is you like being up to your neck in. Heading for Africa to help AIDS victims, jumping off cliffs, learning to fly. Hey, you're even going to find another Talbot . . . ."

She stopped walking and turned on him. The fury in her eyes brought him to a standstill. Witheringly, she said, "There is no other Talbot."

For a moment longer they were both immobile and then Steve said quietly, "Personally, I know about sixteen."

He thought she was going to strike him. But instead of stepping back, he braced himself. Then she surprised him.

As quietly as he, she said, "That's the way it may appear to you. Because all you saw was the East Coast preppy. Whereas I . . . ."

"Whereas you," he continued softly, "are going to cherish a highly sanitized, unrealistic, inhuman, unchanging God-like image for the rest of your life. And I have no intention of pinch-hitting for Talbot Harrington-Clark for the rest of mine." As he spoke, Steve's voice shifted from the hesitant, the almost beseeching tone of a moment before to one approaching anger.

"Who the hell asked you to?"

"Right. No one."

As they stood glaring at each other, Sport thought she detected a fleeting hint of regret in Steve's expression. A suggestion that, despite his protestations, he wasn't entirely cured of his "obsession."

She was still considering this when he said, "I love Sarah."

"Why Sarah of all people?" Sport asked, immediately shamed by the hint of despair that had come into her voice.

He stared at her silently. Then he let his breath out in a long sigh and shook his head wonderingly. "Why Sarah of all people?" he repeated. "If you don't know, I can't tell you."

"Because she doesn't pose a threat to you? Because you feel safe with her? Because you don't have to prove anything to her? Because she's as comfortable as an old shoe? Because you have a weakness for sick chickens? Because . . . ."

Suddenly, Sport stopped as if she'd come upon a mirror and seen something unspeakable. Filled with self-loathing, she spun away and headed back up the hill toward the meadow where the guests had played badminton a few months ago, the night that Johnny came to say good-bye.

Following behind, Steve said in a grim voice, "Because she's warm-hearted and cares about people. Because she's loyal and smart and capable and pretty. And because she has an easy laugh. And yes, because she's vulnerable . . . ."

Sport hurried to get out of earshot. She lifted her eyes as if to watch another flight of geese but actually so that her tears wouldn't spill over. She didn't know whom the tears were for. Sarah? Her mother? Talbot? Nevah? Edith? There were so many by now.

Herself?

Abruptly she stopped walking and waited for him to catch up.

"I'm sorry. Forgive me. I didn't mean any of those things I said about Sarah. I don't know what made me say them. Well, perhaps I do. Because you . . . never mind. I love Sarah. I've always thought of myself as the tough one, but it's Sarah I've always leaned on. The morning after Nevah drowned, my big sister flew up to assure me it wasn't my fault. When Talbot was killed, she hung around until I stopped thinking about suicide. All my life, whenever anything good or bad happened to me, Sarah was the first person I called."

Switching directions, she headed down to the beach again and began jogging towards home. Steve followed and watched as she stopped at the foot of the steepest part of the bluff and began to climb. Digging fingers and toes into clefts, she tested her holds before placing her weight on them.

Steve watched from below, bracing himself directly beneath so that perhaps he could catch her if she misstepped.

"Sarah is no sick chicken," she called out, "but if she had been, it would have been my fault. Mine and Henry's."

She disappeared over the lip of the bluff.

Less gracefully, he began his own ascent. Panting, out of breath, occasionally slipping backwards, he managed to pull himself over the top. He looked around for her, but she was out of sight. However, he could just hear her singing.

> *"It's a dark road*
> *But it'd be darker*
> *If I had no one*
> *To come home to."*

THE END

The Authors

Mildred Davis is the author of thirteen mystery novels, including *They Buried a Man* (Simon & Schuster), *The Voice on the Telephone* (Random House), *Three Minutes To Midnight* (Random House), and *The Room Upstairs* (Simon & Schuster) which won the Mystery Writers of America Edgar Allan Poe Award. Her daughter, Katherine Roome, is the author of *Letter of the Law* (Random House), and co-author with her mother of *Lucifer Land* (Random House), an historical novel set in Westchester County during the Revolutionary War. Mildred Davis lives in Westchester County, New York and Katherine Roome lives in Washington County, New York.

To order additional copies of this book
or other books by the authors, contact:

HARK LLC
www.murderinmaine.com

FROM THE SAME AUTHORS

CPSIA information can be obtained
at www.ICGtesting.com
Printed in the USA
LVHW091454220519
618742LV00001B/89/P